COMATIC DREAMS

Les Lowe

ZionUnleashed

Publishing

Comatic Dreams
A ZionUnleashed Book

Published by ZionUnleashed Publishing
New York, New York

ISBN – 978-0-6152-1686-7

Library of Congress Control Number: 2008931630

Printed in the United States of America

<u>Dedications</u>

For my Mom and Dad -
without them, I would not be who I am today

For Kel-lay, Melodie, MoMo, Miss. R, and Nick –
without them, this book would not be in your hands now

CONTENTS

Chapter 1: Struggles

A mother sits with her four-year-old son, his head in her lap, her belly bulging, the Christmas tree filled with presents while the fireplace snapped and crackled into dying embers. A tear fell from her cheek, as she looked at a picture on the end table of her husband in his military uniform. Another Christmas she would have to spend alone on the base with her son. She loved her son, but this would be the third year Ben would be without a father at Christmas. She knew when she married a military man that her life would be lonely. Although then, she thought it would only be for a few years. She was unaware that the man she loved would also be married to his country.

This year was different. She was pregnant with their second child. It was different; she was emotional. The only thing that put a smile on her face was her son.

Spoiled as he had become, he would not be the only child for long.

Several months had passed bringing in an overly hot summer. Her husband had only been home a week ago, for two days for the 4th of July. She was enormous at this point. Little Ben would ask his mother why she was getting so fat. Every time she would smile and explain to him that she was pregnant and that he would soon have a baby brother or sister.

On July 13th 1984, the day of a full moon her water broke. Home alone with her son with no one to help her. The little boy quickly dialed 9-1-1. An emergency vehicle was there in less than five minutes; however, the baby was born in the ambulance on the way to the hospital. A baby boy named Alex. The two brothers would grow to be extremely close, especially moving from base to base. Until one evening, which changed their lives forever.

# # #

"You're gay?" Benjamin exclaimed.

"Yes, big brother, I am," Alex replied.

"And of all days, all days, you pick today to tell me? To tell mom and dad?"

"It's time Ben, IT IS time! I have lived with this for long enough." Alex did everything he could to refrain from shedding even a single tear, especially in front of Ben. Even though Alex could see the disappointment in Ben's face. This had to be the hardest moment of Alex's life.

# # #

"It's been nearly six years since I came out to them and Ben hasn't spoken to me since. Until now! And now he wants to go to dinner tonight and talk."

"What does he want to talk about?" asked a very attractive brunette girl with olive-colored skin and exploding, crystal-blue eyes sitting across the table from Alex at their normal Saturday morning diner.

"Maria, I have no idea! There is so much to say, but at the same time there is nothing at all. What do you say to your brother, your best friend; who basically disowned you after seventeen years?" Alex drank his coffee slowly, his face paler than normal. He started to examine the diner; his eyes traveled from table to table.

He noticed a young, cute couple that looked as though they had just spent the most wonderful night of their lives together and were finishing the night off with early morning coffee, before parting ways or heading home together. Over at another table, four younger kids that had been out partying all night were getting ready to eat their morning breakfast.

Then on to an older couple that gazed at one another across the table as if they had spent an eternity in bliss. The old man, was still holding the old woman's soft white frail hand as the waitress took their order. They were probably there waking up to their weekly Saturday routine, just as Maria and Alex had done. This was not the first time Alex had seen the old couple, but today they looked different; they looked happier than usual.

The diner was a spot for a lot of

regulars: the early morning lovebirds like the old couple, to the late nightclub kids that were still not tired from the long night of partying. Alex and Maria usually sat at breakfast reminiscing of the days when they would have gone all night long partying and ending their nights at this very diner. This was the very spot that Alex first met Maria and from that day on they have been best friends.

"Alex, don't you think you're overreacting? After all, it is your brother, how bad could it be?"

"See that's the point, why now? Don't get me wrong Maria I love the guy, but it really hurts too much to think about him dissing me again? I can't take it, not now!"

"You mean since the accident?"

"That's when it started, that's when he wanted to talk. It's like since then that he has wanted to be a part of my life, but he wants to overlook the fact that I am gay… still! How do I tell him about my life with Jimmy?"

"Hello my beautifuls! Did I hear my name? How are you this lovely morning?" asked Jimmy, Alex's boyfriend. A tall, slender dark-haired guy with emerald green eyes had sat down putting his arm around Alex and gave him a kiss. "What's wrong? You guys look like you just got done partying with drugged-up kiddies and now could use some major sleep?" Quickly, his happiness drained at the two who had apparently been in deep conversation and were still holding eye contact with one another.

"His brother called," Maria said in a very quiet voice; still not breaking eye contact with Alex.

"MARIA... Stay out!"

"He wants to have dinner with him tonight."

"MARIA..."

"Alex, are you OK? Is it that big of a deal to have dinner with him? If you want, I'd gladly go with you," Jimmy said forcing a smile on his face, hoping to comfort Alex in his time of need; knowing that it would not faze Alex. In fact, thinking about it, it would probably only make matters more difficult.

"My Jimmy, my beautiful Jimmy, maybe I should take you with me. Maybe then Ben will be forced to realize that I am not straight and that I never will be. Maybe then he will accept me for me," Alex answered as he raised his eyebrows and gave him an evil grin. That smile, the one Jimmy and Maria knew all to well as being the smile of sarcasm and mischievousness which Alex tended to turn to instead of showing his true feelings. At least the comment had spun Alex out of the depression to which he was falling victim. This in an odd way made Jimmy happy. At least he was not sounding extremely depressed.

"MMM... you know those eyes turn me on. It's what caught my eye across this very diner all those years ago. Has it really been six years??" Maria said while she counted the years on her fingers; looking puzzled or amazed that so many years had gone by.

"It has been can you believe it?" Alex

replied with the same puzzled look.

"And I can't believe you two have been together for almost two years now. WOW!"

Jimmy and Alex had been living together for almost a year now. Until about two months ago, their relationship had been perfect. It was at this same time that Alex started leaving the house earlier than Jimmy to go to the diner. Jimmy liked it though because it would give Maria and Alex time to get through a cup of coffee and the unnecessary gossip that he was not interested in. That was when the accident happened, the accident that had brought Alex's brother back into his life and now seemed to be ripping the two apart.

After breakfast, the three paid their bills leaving the normal gracious-sized tip for the routine waitress. As they walked out of the diner, Alex passed an old friend who kept him apart from Maria and Jimmy for several minutes. When he met up with them outside, Jimmy and Maria had decided to go shopping. Alex decided not to, but would go to the gym instead. He had to release his tension before his dinner with Ben.

Alex arrived at the gym shortly after 2 PM with all intentions of working out as long as he could. As soon as he changed into his gym clothes the adrenaline kicked in, but the motivation died. After what seemed like hours, he slowly walked out of the locker room and onto the track. After warming up and walking a few laps, he picked up his pace and started a steady jog and then into a furious run.

Throughout his run, the only thing that

kept going through his mind was the problems that the accident had caused. *Why in the world does Ben want to come back into my life?* He then started to think about them growing up. About the day he came out to his family.

# # #

"Dude, are you ready to see your brother tonight?"

"It's been so many years and I have been really shitty to him."

"He's gay, what do you expect?"

"Is that really a reason to disown him though?"

"It is when it's disgusting and morally wrong!"

"DUDE! He's still my brother; no matter what I think. I want to take the time to get to know him. His life. His friends."

"OK. I don't know what's getting into you, but it just sounds crazy."

"Look damn it, after what's happened I feel that I should at least attempt to understand what's going on with my little brother."

# # #

The more Alex sweat, the faster he ran, the more he thought. He thought about growing up; about moving from place to place, about the first time he knew he was gay.

Alex's dad was in the military and so they moved around a lot. The only thing that Benjamin and Alex's mother, Joanna Casey, ever wanted a military base to be, was a birthplace for her children. As soon as Alex was born, they moved off the base and into suburban America. Joanna wanted her kids to grow up in public schools and not as military brats.

The kids stayed in any given school four years at the most. Starting out in North Carolina, then to Virginia, then to New Mexico, then to California and once their father, Frank, retired from the military they ended up in Ohio. While Alex ran, he thought of his time in New Mexico.

# # #

I wonder if we had never lived in New Mexico would I have turned out the same. I was between the ages of eight and twelve when we lived there. My best friend and I did everything together. It's weird to think about because we would even shower together, but yet we would talk about the girls. We got caught once by my brother, naked in our makeshift tent in my bedroom. We had just started to fool around and wonder if it would have gone farther, had we not been intruded upon. Benjamin never mentioned the situation after that. It was like it never happened and yet it stands out in my mind like it happened yesterday. Benjamin is five years older than me, how could he not remember?

Then we moved to California. I was fourteen when I had my first sexual encounter with another guy. It would be two more years until I came to terms with it myself and another year after that, I told my family.

About a year after living in California my dad came home and said we were moving again. This time it would be different. He was retiring. Since both my parents had family in Ohio that was the last move we would ever have to make. However, my parents left the choice up to Benjamin and me. After I had thought about what I had done the year before, I was ready to move. I thought it was the place and the people; if only that were the truth. And so it was, we were moving to Ohio.

After we moved to Ohio things got better. I had a girlfriend. Ben had a girlfriend. Mom seemed happier. Dad stopped drinking so much and was no longer a violent man; the stress in the military was that great I guess. Now, could it be possible that the military was making me feel the way I was about other guys? Of course not; after about a year my relationship with Samantha had ended. Surprisingly, we both were looking for someone different. I had met a guy and she had met a girl.

After a year of pretending Samantha and I were still dating, it was time to tell my family the truth. I had no intentions of it happening on my parents' anniversary. My brother had caught Samantha and his girlfriend kissing. He came to my room where Matt and I were, to tell me that Samantha and Tracy were cheating on him and I with one another. This was no surprise; it was our secret from the outside world. Well I didn't know about Tracy, but I did know that she knew Matt and I were together and that Sam had only been posing as my girlfriend. Ben came to me furious and so I told him the truth.

Ben was so angry with me, but there was

no way he would be able to keep this quiet. There was no way I would let him tell mom and dad that I was gay. It was their anniversary. It was the day I ruined for everyone. I can remember the pain, the upset, the anger, and I can remember the words.

That was the day that Samantha and I moved in together. After all we were best friends.

# # #

"OWWW… Jesus Christ, watch where you are running!" squealed a young woman while sliding across the floor slamming into a wall.

"Oh my god, I'm so sorry. I was lost in thought," Alex said as he extended his hand out to the young women he had just knocked onto the floor.

"That hurt. I feel like I just ran into a brick wall and not had someone pummel me over," the girl said as she took his hand and stood up, straightening her gym clothes.

"I'm so sorry. I can't believe I ran you over. My mind has just been racing. I don't even know how long I've been running," said Alex hunching over with his hands on his knees trying to catch his breath.

"Well, if I am going to get run over and not even be on the track you might as well start by telling me who hit me," the girl said while smiling.

With a small chuckle he replied, "I'm Alex, but you can just call me 'Brick Wall'."

"Well Brick, my name is Athena and I guess you can call me Athy."

"Or, just call you Goddess, since I

should not be worthy to speak your name after thrusting you to the ground." Alex blushed slightly after realizing how sexual his comment had sounded.

"You are a very funny boy, Brick," Athena said and then began to laugh. "Well Brick you had better get going; you are probably going to be late for whatever you were running so fast to get to."

"It's already five! Oh Shit! Athy it was great to meet you and maybe I'll run into you again sometime."

"Oh do not worry about that; I will see you around soon."

And as soon as Alex turned around to say goodbye, the girl was gone. Confused and pursing his lips, he shrugged his shoulders thinking that she had nerve to call him fast and then basically vanish into thin air. He headed to the locker room and then home.

Alex got home at about 5:30. Walking in he found Maria and Jimmy surrounded by bags from their shopping excursion. They both looked like they'd had a great time shopping. Alex was pale and soaking wet from the sweat. Alex gave Jimmy a quick kiss and then one to Maria and started toward the bedroom.

"Sweetie, are you all right?" Maria asked in a very concerning manner.

"Maria, I'm just running so late. Ben will be here soon to pick me up. I need to be ready for when he gets here."

"You can see him just like that if you'd want. Who cares what you look like? He's an asshole anyway, for neglecting you for the last six years."

"Jimmy, he's still my brother."

"Baby I know and you should go. You just shouldn't try to dress to the nines to impress him."

"Jimmy not now! I need to shower."

Alex left the room slamming the bedroom door accidentally and slightly, but on purpose. He wasn't upset with Jimmy, just frustrated and not looking forward to an evening with Ben.

# # #

"Maria, I really hope things go well with him and his brother tonight. I can't do this much longer."

"Jimmy, things will get better. You think this is bad? You should have seen him when we first met. It was when it first happened. Right after he told them he was gay and he moved out. Even though he seemed to be able to keep his composure in front of everyone else, around Sam and I he was a fucking mess. Then again, I think if that crazy shit wasn't going on in his life we wouldn't have been the friends that we are today."

"Where is Sam anyway? I haven't heard from her in weeks."

"Oh her and her girlfriend are on some crazy cruise. They should be back next weekend. Just in time for Pride Weekend. Then again who knows she may not come home from school again this summer."

"Her girlfriend? What happened to her boyfriend?"

"Oh he's around somewhere. I'm sure."

Their conversation was interrupted by a

knock at the door. Maria let Ben in to wait for Alex to finish getting ready. The conversation was bland and awkward. The others could feel the discomfort that Ben felt. Ben focused what little bit he had to say on Maria. Through his nervousness, he could feel a strong attraction to her. Ben tried to make conversation with Jimmy, but everything he said just came out wrong.

After an agonizing twenty minutes of waiting, Alex was ready to leave. Ben had said nothing to Alex, just a nod when Alex had asked if he was ready to go. Ben said his goodbyes to Maria and Jimmy and followed Alex out the door. Outside, Alex thanked Ben for offering to drive, but decided that they should drive separately.

Chapter 2: Ravines

The mood was very awkward and uneasy for both Benjamin and Alex. After Ben had put their name in for a table, the only conversation the two had was as if they were causal acquaintances with the normal 'how are you?' 'Good, how are you?' There were long periods of uneasy, uncomfortable spouts of silence in the middle of the conversation.

At the table the silence continued with them only speaking when the waitress came to the table. Once the waitress had taken their orders and brought the drinks the conversation began to flow a little smoother.

"Alex, we can't sit here in silence all night."

"You're right Ben, you're the one that stopped talking to me so you…"

"Damn it! Alex, can we just not. I'm here. I'm trying. I messed up. Can I try?"

"That's exactly what I'm telling you. I'm here to hear what you have to say. So speak."

"Can we do it without the anger?"

"Benjamin! What do you expect? It's been six years since you spoke to me! You don't think I should be mad? Or upset? Or whatever else I feel?"

"You're right, you have all rights to be as pissed off as you want to be, but can you at least let me try?"

"What…"

"Without the drama. Without the anger. I know it will be hard, but at least try, OK?"

"I'm listening."

"Remember when we were younger?"

# # #

When Alex was born Ben was five. Ben had promised his father, General Frank Casey, to take care of the family, especially now that he was a big brother; just in case anything were to happen to him while defending his country. From that day forward Ben looked out for Alex. No matter what happened, Ben was there.

In 1989 on Alex's fifth birthday, Ben and Alex had been playing in their tree house in the woods behind their house in Virginia. The tree house was built in an old tree that grew about four feet high and then twisted to extend almost straight out over a ravine. There were railings that came up off the sides of the tree to prevent anyone from falling off the side into the ravine. They played in the tree house almost every day. It was their escape from their lives; their ever changing lives, from their father, from the world.

Joanna called for her baby boy to come down for his birthday party and as any excited boy would do, he ran toward the door of the tree house. He tripped on a plank of wood that had started to come loose, breaking as he started to fall leaving a hole in the floor. Ben yanked on the back of Alex's shirt forcing him to fall backwards, instead of out the door. Had Ben not reacted so fast, Alex would have fallen into the deep ravine, into the roaring river swollen from the series of thunderstorms over the last few nights. Alex landed on the floor twisting his wrist with a loud snapping sound. He had broken it.

Ben carried Alex down the slanted tree safely to the ground, trying to keep his balance with only one hand. Joanna ran to the base of the tree as soon as she saw Ben carrying Alex. Once the boys reached the bottom she could see the tears in Alex's eyes. Ben tried to explain what had happened. She angrily started to scold Ben as she carried Alex to the house. She calmed down when little Alex stopped his crying long enough to tell his mother that she would have had to fish him from the bottom of the ravine, had it not been for Benji.

General Casey heard this version of the story and after drinking his usual nightly six-pack of the worst and cheapest beer, he started yelling at Ben.

"That's your brother, you worthless brat. How could you shove him to the ground?"

"Dad, I didn't do it on purpose. If I didn't pull him back, he would have fallen down the ravine."

"Boy don't you talk back to me that way." Frank said as he backhanded Ben across the face.

"Daddy, don't hit Benji please. He was helping me," Alex cried out as the tears started to run down his face even harder. Alex noticed that even after being hit Ben had not shed a tear.

"Joanna shut that boy up; he's sounding like a little fucking sissy boy. And take him to the hospital already," said Frank as he pointed toward the door, not taking his eyes off of Ben. "Benjamin can stay here with me." His eyes started to turn as red as his face from the alcohol and the anger.

"I think Ben should come with us to the hospital."

"NO! The boy stays! And if you know what's best for you…" Frank said and took a deep breath "you'll get the hell out of my face."

"Frank! You're son needs to go to the hospital and your anger isn't going to help either of the boys. It's only going to upset them both. Alex needs his big brother with him."

"Jo don't argue with me in front of the kids." Frank raised his hand toward Joanna.

"You hit me and it's your body they will find at the bottom of that ravine," Joanna said. Her voice never raised, it remained as polite as ever despite the fury she was feeling. She grabbed Ben with her free hand and went to the hospital.

That wasn't the first time their father had been abusive and it wouldn't be the last.

Although Frank would never hit Joanna in front of them, the boys could hear the arguments in the middle of the night and could see the marks in the morning. As the boys grew older and with every new town they moved to, they became each other's best friends. And as they grew older, their father drank less and less and therefore became less and less abusive both physically and mentally.

# # #

"The chicken alfredo with linguini," the waitress interrupted what had obviously been a deep conversation, "and the vegetable lasagna. Enjoy boys and can I get you refills?"

"That'd be great thanks Amy," replied Alex. "Now that we've rehashed our great bonding moments, what now?"

"At least you're smiling some. So, tell me about you? Who were the two at your apartment?"

"Well, Jimmy is my partner. We've been together for two years and have been living together for the last year."

"And the hot girl?"

"Ben, she would never go for you. She despises everything you are."

"What the hell do you mean by that?"

"She… Maria was one of the first people I met after mom and dad threw me out of the house and you stopped talking to me. She got the brunt of my anger, of my hurt and of my pain. Well her and Sam."

"And how is the lovely little freak Sam doing?"

"Oh my god Benjamin, I thought this was supposed to be a nice conversation," Alex said as he rolled his eyes and tilted his head toward the ceiling.

"Sorry, there is still a part of me that is upset about how she lied about who she was and how she manipulated you."

"See that's the problem; you think someone did this to me. And besides, there were two liars in that 'cover up'. I was born this way. Don't you remember when we lived in New Mexico? You caught me and Eric. We were playing with each other."

"Yeah and Eric was older than you. He took advantage of you. Plus, you were kids, kids do that."

"Did you?" Alex said with a pause, but started talking again before Ben could answer. "If anyone took advantage of anyone, I took advantage of him. It was my idea. I did the same thing with Scott. Used the same situation with him that I used with Eric and he was older than Eric."

"You did?"

"Yes, I did. I've been into guys for as long as I can possibly remember."

"So, if that's true, then everything we learned at church when we were younger is wrong. I was wrong. Mom and Dad were wrong."

# # #

The Casey family had been the perfect Christian family looking in from the outside. They had attended church every Sunday. Some Sundays when General Casey was deployed, Joanna would let the boys skip church, but she still attended faithfully. During service, General Casey would always make sure his donations were of a charitable size; always trying to outdo anyone else. General Casey must have never learnt the seven deadly sins. Although, General Casey knew he broke all of the deadly sins, it was his pride and gluttony that would later haunt him and his family.

In the last few years, General Casey had started drinking again. The life of retirement had become boring and depressing. The only happiness the General found was in cracking open a cold can of beer. Both kids had moved out of the house, one not of his own free will, and Joanna was spending more time with her friends and had gotten a part-time job to keep her busy. Frank refused to get a job. After spending thirty years in the military, he felt like most jobs were beneath him. Being a rent-a-cop at the local Wal-Mart didn't much thrill him.

Joanna on the other hand, loved working with animals and so she loved her part-time job in the local pet store. She had grown tired of Frank's drinking and needed an escape. She was tired of it the first time he was drinking. This time seemed worse for her. Even though he wasn't abusive this time, at least physically, she couldn't take the depression. As long as he was going to drink, she would have nothing to do with it. Joanna felt that at this point in her life, divorce wouldn't be worth the time and effort. She had her life anyway. She had a job, her friends and a warm body to fall asleep with and to satisfy her sexual desires when needed.

Joanna was ecstatic when she heard that her husband started hanging out with a new friend named Wes. She never knew anything about Wes nor did she ever meet him, but her husband wasn't moping around the house and wasn't bothering her as much. General Frank started staying out later, especially on the weekends and driving home after having one too many at the bar. The drinking and then driving was the only thing that General Frank and Joanna had to fight about.

On the afternoon of Friday April 13th, a surprisingly and unusually warm day for this time of year, General Frank and Joanna had gone to an annual BBQ at some friends' house. The friends that were hosting the party were not serving alcohol, which made Joanna happy, and for once Frank didn't really seem to mind. Frank enjoyed spending time at the Griffins with all their friends. After a wonderful evening with their friends, at about one AM, they got into their car and started for home.

Joanna was enjoying the conversation with her husband. It was the first time in years that she was extremely happy. She reached over and held her husband's hand. Frank had smiled at his wife's touch. He too had been enjoying the evening and the time with his wife in the car. It was the first time in years that he had felt really happy. They decided to take an extended drive because they had been enjoying their conversation so much.

The roads began to weave and wind. Frank

knew the roads and was therefore, paying attention to his wife. By the time Frank realized that the car coming around the bend was on his side of the road, it was too late. The other car had collided with the Casey's car head-on; pushing the car through the guardrail, over the side of the ravine and plummeting to the water below. The car was so compacted from hitting the side of the ravine that the only way to identify the bodies was through dental records and the license plate number. An underage drunk driver, who had stolen the car after drinking at a friend's house because he didn't want to go home to his abusive father, had taken their lives.

At the funeral, Ben and Alex were on opposite sides and never spoke. When family members approached them, the two never spoke of one another or even made eye contact. Alex felt uncomfortable at the funeral. He stood over the coffins of two people that had raised him for seventeen years; but he had no idea who they were for the last six years, more so his father than his mother.

Alex spent more time at his mother's coffin wishing he could see her face one last time; to be able to hug her, to kiss her, to thank her for the last year, to apologize. Over the last year Alex and Joanna had been meeting weekly for dinner. The dinners could not replace the previous six years. Alex felt guilty that he had cancelled dinner with her that week because Jimmy had surprised him with dinner plans. He felt that he had never got the chance to say goodbye to his mother. Even though he knew deep inside that when a person's time comes to pass, no-one has time to say goodbye, it didn't stop him from feeling that way.

Ben had watched Alex as he wept over his mother's coffin. He wanted to go to Alex, but did not know what to say to him. He watched as his aunts, uncles, and their only living grandmother spent time with Alex at the coffin. He just could not get up the courage to go over and speak to him. After Alex left the coffin, he went to the back of the room without looking at Ben as he walked past. He couldn't; it would only have made him cry harder. Ben then took his time at the coffins. He too spent more time over his mother's coffin. He had been so angry with her until the police showed up at his door. She had not called him that day to wish him a 'Happy Birthday'. He also spent more time there because for him, she was the glue that kept the family together all those years. He knew this time he was going to have to be that glue.

Alex watched his brother standing at his parents' coffins. He noticed that Ben had not shed a single tear. At least what he could tell from where he was standing. His emptiness and hurt started to turn into anger and fury. He left the funeral without a trace. There were no goodbyes or tears left for him there.

After two months had passed Ben had got Alex's number from a relative. He found the courage to call Alex. Surprisingly, Alex accepted his call and agreed to meet for dinner.

# # #

"You were having dinner with mom for a year?" Ben asked, pulling his head back and raising his eyebrows in surprise.

"Yeah. She had been dealing with a lot, especially with 'the General' drinking again. She apologized for everything that had happened. She couldn't believe that she allowed the military and Christian life to imbue her." Alex paused as a tear came to his eye. "She apologized Ben; she apologized for everything stopping her from talking to her son, for letting the bullshit affect her love."

"Alex…" Ben said with a tear welling up in his eye. It was the first time in Alex's life that he had seen Ben shed a tear for something other than physical pain and even that was rare.

"Can I get you guys anything else?" said the waitress, pausing to notice the watery eyes of the two guests that sat before her. "Are you guys OK?"

"I think for the first time in our lives we will be OK," Ben answered her.

Alex couldn't bring himself to look either of them in the face; let alone speak. The waitress left the check telling them to take as much time as they needed and excused herself to let the brothers be alone.

"Alex, are you OK?"

"Ben just like you said, I think for the first time 'we will be OK.'"

"Do you mean it?"

"The true question is," Alex paused wiping the tears from his eyes, "do you mean it?"

"This is what I'm offering," Ben said as he took a deep breath, a hard swallow and then a big drink of his water. "I want to be a part of your life. I want to get to know who you are, your boyfriend, Jim right… his name… is Jim or is it Jimmy? I want to get to know your friends, especially Maria." Ben paused briefly to notice a tiny smile appear on Alex's face. "I even want to get to know, understand or whatever you want to call it, Samantha, as odd as that may sound."

"You're pushing your luck there now aren't you?" Alex could barely finish the sentence without laughing. "You can barely... wait, you can't even begin to wrap your mind around me being gay and you want to try to understand Sam? You're right, that is a riot."

"OK. OK. OK. Maybe one step at a time I guess. But you have to understand that I have started to realize that you and I needed to talk. That we needed to…"

"Wait you have been thinking this for a while now? You mean like before the accident?"

"Yeah, I didn't know you had been seeing mom every week for dinner for the last year of her life, just as I'm sure you didn't know that mom had been getting on my case about making amends with you."

"MOM? Mom was talking to you about me?"

"Not directly exactly, I guess. I guess if I had paid attention, I would have known you guys had been talking. Wow! Now things make a lot of sense. Mom had been talking about her and religion. She was talking about how horrible it would be if we never knew who you were before it was too late. It's almost like she knew something horrible was going to happen."

"Well if so, it would be mom that would know. How did she always know creepy shit like that anyway?"

"Mother's intuition I guess. I dunno. But anyway she started talking about how wrong we were for not talking to you and especially since you live, ya know, like ten minutes away."

"Wait, you mean to tell me that you never once bothered to ask mom why she hadn't talked to me?"

"Actually, no I didn't."

"Such a meat head. Such a typical man, not even think or put two and two together. Dumbass. And I'm the freak of the family!"

"Ya know what, it's shit like that that's going to keep your sorry ass in exile," Ben joked with Alex trying not to break into laughter.

The two boys sat and talked and laughed for a few hours. It wasn't until the restaurant was closing that they decided that it was time to go. By the time they were leaving it felt like the years apart were slowly closing in on one another. Alex didn't know if he could ever forgive his brother for not speaking to him for six years, but the effort was there.

Ben knew that one tragedy was enough in his life; that not speaking to his brother again was ridiculous. Ben couldn't and wouldn't want to face another horrible thing without his brother being there. They both knew that life was too short.

As they walked to their cars, Ben assured Alex that everything they had talked about was nothing but the truth. Alex had his doubts, but something told him that he could trust his big brother like he was able to do when they were kids. Before parting ways, Ben walked to Alex and gave him a long and strong hug. The hug was sincere enough to bring a tear to Alex's eye once again. Ben asked Alex if they could hang out the following weekend. Ben even requested that they go to a gay bar, but only if Alex could get Maria to be his date. Shock came over Alex and he happily accepted. They both got into their cars and went their separate ways out of the parking lot.

# # #

"Are you kidding me? It's past midnight! You've seriously been with your brother this long?" asked Jimmy.

"I know. It's hard to believe, but after what seemed like an eternity of awkward silence we just started talking; it just felt normal," Alex said with a huge smile just holding Jimmy in his arms.

"And just like that, you two are OK?"

"Well, we aren't totally OK, but get this he even asked to go out with us this weekend," Alex paused, "to a gay bar!"

"Get the fuck out? But if it is going to make you happy like this, I am game. UM. Wait! What's the catch?"

"Maria has to be his date!" Alex said,

as he started to slowly take off his clothes and then Jimmy's.

"Fat chance on that happening, but like I said, if it will leave you like this, he can have Maria."

Chapter 3: O Maria

The next morning Alex got up early, took a shower and had breakfast ready and on the table when Jimmy walked into the dinning room. Jimmy was getting a cup of coffee when he heard knocking on the door. Before anyone could answer, it opened. Without turning around Jimmy had already started saying hello to Maria. There could only be one person coming over this early in the morning, and of course only one person who smelled as beautiful as she did.

Alex had called Maria an hour earlier asking her to come over for breakfast. She was very eager to hear how things had gone with Ben the previous night. In fact, she hadn't slept much that night waiting to find out. When he called she was already awake, lying in bed. As soon as she heard his voice on the phone, she was half way to the shower before he could even ask her to come over.

The three sat at the dinning table

discussing the previous night for over an hour before Alex had even thought about uttering the stipulation to the following weekend. Maria, who had graduated top of her class and had an extremely gifted mind, didn't always catch on to things that were not spelled out in front of her. Over the next half hour Alex started dropping hints about how wonderful and cute a couple Ben and Maria would make. It wasn't until Alex confirmed with her that she would be his date that she realized what she had just agreed to.

Maria spent the next twenty minutes arguing with Alex about how much a bad idea it would be for her to be Ben's date. Maria had always had a negative attitude towards Ben. She had spent the last six years wiping the tears from Alex's face on his parents' death anniversary when he would think of how his family abandoned him. While she was happy for Alex that they had spoken, she wasn't too thrilled about having to be his friend. Let alone his date. She had placed all the blame on Ben, especially since his parents were no longer around to blame.

Later, in the middle of watching a movie Alex received a phone call from Ben. Ben had asked if the four of them could have dinner on Wednesday evening. Jimmy was uncomfortable with the situation, but agreed to go. He in his own strange and unusual way thought it would be fun or interesting to go. Maria on the other hand, took getting through the rest of the movie to persuade. She settled with Alex buying her dinner this evening and on

Wednesday and a free car wash for the rest of summer. After agreeing, Alex realized that the summer didn't start till the end of the week and that meant that the car-washing season for him would be a long one.

# # #

Ben had woken up that morning to a very disgruntled roommate. Ben and Richmond had been roommates from freshman year of college, fraternity brothers, and then moved in together after graduation. Richmond was a masculine guy, your typical jock, with blond hair and blue eyes. He grew up in a very strict Catholic family. Being gay was one of the worst sins one could undergo.

"So, how was your evening with your faggoty little brother?" Richmond asked, flicking his wrist while standing on his toes twirling as a ballerina would.

"Dude, come off it! He's my brother. He's been through a lot and honestly, I'm to blame for some of that."

"He deserved it. You shouldn't be talking to him now. Homosexuality is wrong. The Church says so. The government says so. God even says so, he plagued them with AIDS after all."

"That really explains why the majority of the world it affects is heterosexuals right?"

"It affects the people of the population it needs to affect and here in the United States it's the disgusting perverted fags. Sure your brother isn't one of them? The diseased?"

"Rich!" Ben paused he couldn't bring

himself to say another word. Part of him believed much of what Richmond had said, but it was Alex; he couldn't believe it. Ben didn't know who to be more furious with, his brother for being a homosexual, his 'best friend' for spouting such hatred and ignorance, or his own religious beliefs that agreed with him.

"Dude you keep hanging out with him and something bad is going to happen to you as well. The heavens have their ways of cleaning up the garbage. You can mark my words on that!"

"So, now I'm garbage for owning up to a promise made to my dead mother?"

"No! It has nothing to do with your mother. She was an awesome woman. Nothing should have ever happened to her."

"She had been having dinner with Alex for over a year. Are you saying that God is the one who took her life because she accepted her dick-loving son into her life?"

"She was having dinner with him? Then it's very much a possibility. Like I said, the heavens have their ways."

"Dude, you're sick," Ben replied, but couldn't talk about it anymore. Instead, he decided to change the subject. "There is one benefit for hanging out with him. There's this hot chick that he's friends with."

"Seriously, since when do you like fat chicks?"

"She ain't fat. She's smokin' hot."

"Really, so why don't you call her up and ask her out then?"

"Ya know what, I think I'll do just that

right now."

Ben picked up the phone and called Alex to invite him and Jimmy to dinner on Wednesday and to make sure that he invited Maria to come along with them. It would be easier for him so that he didn't feel like it was a double date, and wouldn't feel like the third wheel.

As soon as he hung up the phone Richmond started, "Dude, you're a pussy. An' now you're doublin' with the homos and the fag hag. Definitely have to tell me how gaareat that one turns out." The look on his face was as if he had just bitten into the sourest lemon sucking all the juice to the peel. He turned and walked out of the room shaking his head, before Ben could answer, making sounds of a cat choking on his own fur balls.

Ben acted like he didn't care what his roommate had just said; but he cared. He cared deeply. Parts of him were excited to see Maria, others were wary. His emotions were on a roller coaster of confusion leaving his stomach twisting into tiny knots and making him very queasy.

# # #

Over the next two days all Alex could think about was having dinner with his brother, his best friend and his boyfriend. It was like being in a dream. He had never imagined that his brother would be back in his life. He was so happy that Jimmy would catch him singing and dancing around the house. Jimmy was astonished to have the guy that he had fallen in love with back in his life. For the last two months, he felt like he had been dating a complete and total stranger. At times when he would catch Alex dancing or singing or both, he would just be as quiet as possible so he could watch him. He would sit and watch Alex until he was spotted.

Maria spent those two evenings at their place trying to understand as much as she could about Ben. Alex and Jimmy felt it seemed as if she were a bit more anxious about the dinner than she led on to believe. When they would call her out on it, she would tell them that she was doing it for Alex's piece of mind. All three knew she at least had a physical attraction for him. Had she not known anything personal about Ben, she would have made a pass at him the second he crossed her path. She just couldn't get past the disgust she felt every time she thought about his past. Alex was making it much easier for her though.

Alex told Maria and Jimmy all the wonderful things about Ben from when they were kids. He told them about the tree house and about how he almost fell into the ravine. The tree house had more good stories than bad. There was one time that Alex had climbed into the tree house to hide from his father, knowing that his grades would be coming in the mail that day. As he approached the door he could hear voices coming from inside. He slowly walked toward the door and peeked inside; Ben was inside with a girl and they were both naked, just touching one another. Ben heard the creek of loosening floor and hollered out at Alex causing him to lose his balance and to almost fall again, laughing all the way back down the tree.

The more stories Alex told of Ben, the more Jimmy and Maria seemed to like him. These were the stories that Alex bottled up inside of him the day he left home. They were easy to keep buried inside when you're filled with pain and anger. Somehow, Alex couldn't think of anything negative that Ben had done growing up. Ben, to him, was the perfect brother. It was hard for him to conceptualize that his own brother had disowned him.

# # #

That Wednesday when Alex got home from work he was surprised to find Maria already inside waiting for him. She was wearing a beautiful baby blue dress that matched her eyes perfectly and made her skin tone look much darker than usual. Her beauty even took Alex's breath away; it left him speechless.

"What's wrong with you?"

"Um…" Alex replied trying to connect words together to make a cohesive sentence. "You look amazing! And you say you're not interested in my brother."

"I'm doing this for you, my love. There is nothing that will stop me from making everything work out for you. Not even if he turns out to be the biggest asshole in the world," she said with a stern look on her face, but she could not control her cheeks from turning a beautiful rose color. Even through her makeup.

Jimmy had the same reaction when he walked in the door and basically the same conversation. Sometimes Maria felt that she was stuck in a Twilight Zone or was listening to a recorded message when she spoke to either of them. Their reactions were exactly the same on most situations and, more times than not, had the same responses.

Before Jimmy and Alex could finish getting ready, there was a knock at the door leaving Maria to answer it.

"WOW!" Ben said as his mouth dropped open.

"Typically when someone answers the door you say hello."

"I'm sorry, it's just that, that, um... that..."

"Hello Benjamin, how are you this evening?" Maria asked. She couldn't take his stuttering any longer, although she loved every moment of it.

The four of them decided on where to go to dinner and this time they all went in the same car. Alex felt comfortable enough to spend what little bit of time they had in the car without there being any awkward silences. The ride had indeed been a very pleasant one. There was not a moment of silence in the car all the way to dinner.

Ben told Alex that he wanted to get to know his friends including Jimmy, and so he spent all of dinner asking both of them about their lives. He of course started with Maria.

Maria was of Mediterranean descent. Her family moved to the United States during World War II. Her grandmother was Jewish and her grandfather had been in the military. When the war broke out her grandfather used his military connections to escape the country. It was very dangerous for her grandfather, but he wouldn't let anything happen to his wife and unborn child. Most of her grandmother's family had been seized by the Nazi's and been taken off to concentration camps before her grandparents could flee to the States. By the time the war was over, her grandparents had denounced their home countries and became US citizens; Maria's father was born and the boughs of her grandmother's family tree had been destroyed.

Maria's father met her mother in 1973 while stationed in Greece, during the Vietnam War. Her mother was barely eighteen and ten years younger than her father. After dating for two years, the war ended and her father was sent back to the states. He married her mother and brought her back with him. Later that year, Maria's brother was born. Eight years after that, in 1983, Maria was born.

Maria was raised Jewish. Her mother was Jewish and her father was part Jewish. It was always an upsetting time when she used to go to her grandmother's house. Holidays for her were the worst. Her grandmother would tell very vivid stories of the holocaust. When Maria was old enough to make her own decisions, she stopped attending church and while she recognized her religion she was a non-practicing Jew.

Ben was interested in Maria's story and wanted to meet her grandmother, but that would be impossible. Her grandparents had both passed away two years previously. To not further upset her, Ben turned to Jimmy and asked him about his upbringing.

On his father's side, both grandparents were American-Indian. On his mother's side, his grandfather was Egyptian and his grandmother was of Irish descent. His family's religious beliefs were harder to describe to Ben. His family being American-Indian kept the very spiritual beliefs of the Indians. They believed in the spirit being one with nature. The closest thing he could use to describe his religion to Ben was being a sect of Wiccan belief. Ben struggled with this concept because everything he knew about Wicca was that it was witchcraft and that they believed in the devil. This was the one time of the evening that everyone at the table got very angry with Ben.

Ben could not understand how his brother could get mixed up with people like Jimmy. The more they tried to explain to him, the more confused he became. The only thing that calmed him down was when they explained that Jimmy and Alex were more atheists or agnostic than anything else.

Ben was calmer, but now upset that his brother had denounced his faith.

"Ben, I haven't denounced my faith."

"Really, what do you call it then? You just said you were atheists."

"No Ben, that isn't what I'm saying. I believe in something. I just don't know what. That makes me agnostic."

"Um… Unless I'm wrong it's the same thing. You're not Christian."

"Now wait a minute here," Maria interrupted, slamming her hand down on the table causing nearby tables to look over.

"You were just OK with me being a non-practicing Jew and that sure the hell isn't Christian."

"Yeah, but that's cause… cause… you still believe in God," Ben said finding it hard to articulate his words.

"WE BELIEVE IN GOD or something!" snapped Jimmy. "We just don't have an exact religion. We know there is something more out there, whether it be God or Zeus or Shiva or the Rat King of Sewage for all I care. We just want to know that we are doing what we need to do in this life and respect others. We haven't just denounced all of our beliefs, but have more of a collective one."

Ben stopped arguing with them about religion. He knew it would be a hot topic. It was a dangerous topic at home, living with Richmond. And once again, Ben changed the topic to avoid upsetting anyone else.

The evening sailed by much smoother after changing topics; all four of them were having a good time. There were the occasional looks between Ben and Maria that Ben thought might have been moments of a more romantic connection. There were times when Ben wanted to show more affection toward her, but was afraid to do so.

On the drive back to Alex and Jimmy's, Maria closed her eyes and allowed her head to dangle, jerking herself awake every so often. While she was pretending to doze in and out of consciousness, she let her hand drift over and onto Ben's. As a natural response, Ben flipped his hand over and clasped his around hers. Maria let her head lean against the glass with the smallest smile on her face.

At the house everyone said their goodbyes and noticing that the only extra car in the driveway was his; Ben offered Maria a ride home. She kindly declined, but told him that he could walk her home since she only lived two houses down. Maria and Ben said goodnight to Alex and Jimmy and walked toward the sidewalk.

The walk to Maria's was in utter silence. The sky was very dark and clear. All the stars in the heavens could be seen. There was a romantic chilly breeze in the air. Neither of them knew what to say to the other, nor did they dare to fish for the right words. The silence was a comfortable silence. Ben put his arm around her shoulders to keep her warm.

He asked her if they could get together on Friday night before they went on Saturday. She said yes to his offer and like a perfect gentleman he reached over and gave her a goodnight kiss at her doorstep. He turned and walked away, only looking back when he reached the sidewalk to make sure she got inside OK. Once she was inside, he balled his hands into fists, bit his lip and punched the air above him in excitement.

# # #

"You're going out with him on Friday?" asked Alex in total shock. His mouth still hanging open with his eyebrows scrunched together.

"I sure am. Isn't it gr…"

"UM… whatever happened to," Alex paused after cutting her off and with his overly dramatic imitation of her gestures and voice, he continued, "'there's no way I can like him because of the way he treated you. I'm only doing this for you'?"

Maria couldn't stop laughing at his impression of her. After regaining composure she only had one thing to say to him, "That doesn't look or sound like me at all and just for that, I'm going to go and have as much fun as possible with him. We'll see you at the diner on Saturday morning," and she walked out the door before letting him respond. She knew the thought of them spending the entire night together would eat him up from the inside.

# # #

On Friday evening, Ben and Richmond had another argument about Ben seeing Maria. Ben couldn't understand why Richmond was having such a hard time with him spending time with Maria. Richmond could not find it in his belief to allow Ben to walk such a narrow path into danger. Ben explained that Alex and Jimmy wouldn't be there; that this was a real date with Maria, just the two of them. For Richmond it was still too close to the fire, that Ben could be burnt. He left the house after an hour of arguing feeling his nostrils flaring, his ears burning and his teeth clenched. He was already late picking up Maria, which only made his temper rise. He just drove thinking to himself 'how could Rich feel that way?' And he continued to drive around her block until he felt calm enough to see her.

She was not upset that he was late and

could understand. Her feelings grew stronger for him as she listened to what he had just gone through with his roommate. She couldn't believe that he still showed up; that he was actually making an effort. It meant more to her that he was there, than him being late.

They had a wonderful dinner together. The moments of silence were comfortable ones and the moments of conversations were even better. After dinner, as cliché as a first date could be, they went to a movie. Some romantic comedy where the two stars fell in love through every disaster imaginable. Ben let her snuggle up to him laying her head on his shoulder throughout the movie. Afterwards, they decided to keep the date going by walking along the boardwalk of the river. The night was perfect. There was not a cloud in the sky. There was a cool breeze that felt good brushing against them on the hot and sticky evening. They sat on some rocks that took some jumping to get to, out in the river and began pointing out constellations. Before they knew it, the sun was coming up. There was a beautiful crimson line that formed from where day met night. They watched as the morning oranges and yellows slowly pushed the night skyline over them. It was time to head to the diner.

Alex wasn't surprised to see Ben walking in the door with Maria. Jimmy on the other hand, was completely shocked. The two took their seats across from Alex and Jimmy and just smiled at them without saying a word.

"It's nice to see that you're wearing the same outfit that you had on last night,"

Alex said as he took a drink of his coffee.
"It doesn't look too wrinkled. And I hope you
plan on getting some kind of sleep before
this evening."

　　"But O'course we will Alwix," Maria said
in a childish voice, "and it'll be in
separate houses don't you worry your little
heart to death now. However, Ben may need to
crash at your place."

Chapter 4: Heaven or Hell

    Ben explained what had happened between him and his roommate the previous evening. Alex thought his brother had been close-minded, but was appalled that he had chosen to live with such an asshole. He refused to allow Ben to go home that morning. He fixed up the guest room and the two said their goodnights, at this point, good mornings.

    Around three in the afternoon, about seven hours after going to sleep, Ben met up with Alex and Jimmy in the kitchen. Jimmy had started making brunch when he arrived. The three of them sat and talked for several hours.

    Maria who had entered without knocking interrupted their conversation. She was wearing a hot-pink spaghetti-strapped blouse that had an angular cut down her right thigh, a pair of blue jeans, and high heel shoes that had a slightly chunky heel. She was ready for an all night dancing extravaganza.

As she had done for the last few times, she took everyone's breath away and left them all speechless. It had been a few years since Alex had seen Maria put this much effort into the way she looked.

Maria had arrived before any of them had gotten ready. She rushed each one of them to the shower and picked out outfits for each of them. Earlier that afternoon, she had gone shopping for an outfit for Ben. Ben came out of the bathroom wearing a brown button-up shirt, blue jeans, and brown dress shoes. Taking one look at him Maria made him go back to remove the undershirt and roll the sleeves up. Alex was wearing a tight t-shirt with a tight pair of jeans with a boot cut leg. And Jimmy was in a dark blue short-sleeved button up shirt with khakis.

It was nearly ten before everyone was ready to go and Maria was hungry. They decided to go to dinner before heading to the dance club. Dinner was pleasant and time seemed to pass by quickly. On the way to the car the conversation became more eerie than anything else.

"Oh my God, look at the moon it's huge," Jimmy said as he stopped in the middle of the parking lot pointing at the moon.

"Well we all know what happens when there's a full moon," Alex said and in his best vampire voice, "all da freaks zay come out at night."

"Oh really, well you know you were born on a full moon and on a Friday the 13th, so I guess you get a double whammy right?" asked Ben.

"Right exactly, but then again, I guess you're just as much a freak since you were born on a Friday the 13th as well," replied Alex.

"Wait, Ben, you were born on a Friday the 13th as well?" asked Maria. "Guys, this is way too spooky. I was born on May 13th which happened to be on a Friday."

"Well, at least we know I'm not as much of a freak as you all are. I was born December 18th and as far as I know, it wasn't a full moon," said Jimmy. "So, I don't know what I'm doing here with all you Friday the 13th freaks, especially on a full moon night."

"Well then, I shouldn't mention that my 23rd birthday this year is not only on a Friday, but it's also a full moon," said Alex.

"WOW!" said the other three in sync.

After that, the group sat in the car in silence all the way to the club. Alex drove slower than he normally would have. The other three watched out the window at the huge white glowing moon, the random sparkling stars and the thin gray-colored clouds that stretched across the sky. It reminded Ben of a classic creepy horror movie that he watched when he was a kid. His excitement and fear of going to the club quickly took over him.

They turned down a deserted road that led past what appeared to be an abandoned warehouse. The road was only paved to the back of the warehouse and then it became a dirt and gravel track with large ruts from where cars had driven up and down the hill. It opened up into a larger parking area that had been cut out of the middle of the woods. When they got out of the car Ben could hear a stream running close by, but couldn't see it.

As they walked up the road toward the warehouse the only thing that Ben could think about was the location of the bar. He had driven past this very spot wondering why they hadn't demolished the run-down place. Now he understood. He thought about why a gay bar would need to be hidden from the world and unlabeled.

"This is Electric Earth?" asked Ben.

"Yep, 'tis E^2. As we call it. Nervous?" asked Alex.

"A little, but right now though I'm sorta expecting Leather Face or Michael Myers to come after me," replied Ben.

"Yeah, the outside could use a little work, but then again, it keeps the gay bashers away. They have no clue this place really exists," said Jimmy.

"Well except the occasional bottle being thrown from a car in the front of the building or the lesbian cat fights in the middle of the road, it's a pretty safe place," said Maria.

"It's cool. Just a little out of a horror movie set up. We aren't gonna get locked inside and eaten by a bunch of vampires are we?"

"Now wouldn't that just be the ultimate end to your soon to be misery of attending a gay bar!" said Alex.

Inside the bar Ben couldn't stop looking around. The walls were waterproofed cinder blocks in most places and curved sheets of metal in others. There were two floors. The lower floor consisted of three bars, one large one in the front that reminded him of an island with people on all four sides waiting for their drinks. The second one was on the right side on a raised platform with bar seating and this point in the evening there was no one there, not even a bar tender. The third one was smaller at the back of the club, on the left edge of the dance floor. There were two dance floors, one large in the back of the club with a large walking area between the large bar and the dance floor, and the second dance floor was raised as high the second bar, but on the opposite side of the club. The second dance floor appeared to be more of a performance floor.

The upstairs was a bit more interesting. It was a voyeurs dream. The walkways were huge catwalks hanging above the first floor. Not only could you see downstairs from both sides; the floors were grated so you could look through to the bottom floor. There were small lounges off to the sides that had one-way mirrors in them looking back out over the catwalks, and TV screens showing the dance floor down below. There were two bars on either end of the upstairs floor. They had solid floors and standing areas before the catwalks. Drinks were not allowed onto the catwalks to prevent spillages through the floor to the people below.

The entire club was full of black lights and beams of different colors danced with the people on the dance floor. There were occasional strobe lights from the catwalks above reflecting onto the dance floors below. There was a constant billow of mist that gave the club an eerie, but erotic setting.

Once Ben had taken a look around, he was overwhelmed at the size and the interior of the club. His emotions continued to sway most of the evening between being comfortable, uncomfortable, excited and frightened. The club was like no other club he had ever been to or imagined. After a few drinks, Maria had him out on the dance floor. She had unbuttoned a couple of his top buttons so he didn't look too uptight.

Ben didn't realize how many people had arrived in just an hour of being there. It was shocking to him that there was this many gay people in the community or that many that would go out. He assumed being surrounded by a couple of colleges made a huge difference. At one point he had looked up and saw the catwalks above him filled with people. They danced to a few songs and decided it was time for some fresh air.

Maria tugged on his shirt pulling him out of the line at the small bar in the back. He followed her through a door next to the bar, onto a small patio with two sets of stairs. Ben's eyes grew larger. He couldn't imagine that this place could get any larger.

"Well, do you wanna go up or down?" asked Maria.

"Are you kidding me, how big is this place anyway?" Ben asked.

"Well big brother, it is one of the best dance clubs in the area. People drive in from the larger cities just to come here."

"Seriously?" asked Ben, "You're fucking with me right? What kind of dream state did I wake up into?"

"The twilight zone, big brother or well, more like the homo zone. You should come on a party night," replied Alex. "So, I think the lady's question was do you wanna go upstairs to Heaven or downstairs to Hell?"

"What the fuck are you talking about?" Ben asked.

"There are yet two more bars Benjamin my friend. There's one called Heaven and it's up on the rooftop and one called Hell down below. Ya left Earth when you walked through that door," Jimmy told Ben as he pointed to the door behind them.

"I left planet Earth as soon as I walked through the front door of the entire club."

Ben thought his awe was tapped when he was inside, but this just went beyond his imagination. They took him first to Hell where they were playing disco music on a cozy wooden deck painted in yellows and reds that was mostly covered with people. Below that were picnic tables that sat over gravel. There was an L-shaped bar on the deck and a couple port-o-pots in the gravel pit. Ben couldn't take the disco music and asked to go to Heaven. As they passed the doors to the main club, someone was coming out. He could hear the disco music from below, the dance music coming from the opened door, and music he couldn't quite make out from above.

The music from down below started to fade out as they approached Heaven. Ben couldn't make out the music that was coming from Heaven because there were no words being sung. It was popular music from many eras and genres, but the words had been removed. It was peaceful and relaxing. Everything in this area was blue and white or painted blue and white, including the wood and metal. The brightness of the full moon made the blue and white shimmer. Ben felt like he could have been floating on a cloud in Heaven.

He was quickly pulled back to reality when he noticed two guys, wearing only tight bikini bottoms and angel wings, making out. The two guys were very attractive with their perfect bodies covered in glitter and Ben couldn't stop watching them. Even though he had been with his brother and Jimmy a lot in the last week, the thought of why the two weren't with women instead wouldn't leave his mind.

They had a few drinks in Heaven and returned to Earth to dance. Ben and Maria left the boys to go to a vacant lounge on the second floor. Jimmy and Alex happened to be dancing erotically right in front of the camera that was viewing in the lounge that Maria and Ben had chosen. Ben was very happy being there with Maria, but very disgusted at some of the things he had seen over the course of the evening. Now sitting there watching his little brother on the monitor gave him chills and an ache in his stomach.

When the club was about to close, it would turn the lights on and you'd finally see how ugly or cute the person you were randomly dancing with was. More times than not, they were cuter in the dark than when the lights came on. The group decided to leave the club before the, what Alex called, the ugly lights came on.

As on any other night out dancing, they would go for breakfast at their normal diner before going home. Ben was worn out, more mental than physical, but worn out nonetheless. He was ready for a nice hot shower and his own bed, but against his better judgment he was ready for breakfast as well. Since he was still trying to impress Maria he didn't want to be the death of the party.

As they approached the diner they realized that they were not the only ones with the same idea. The typically vacant parking lot was full, forcing them to park down the street along the storefronts. The night air was eerie and chilly under the full moon's bright light. There was a small alleyway that separated the diner from the shopping plaza. The alley even seemed more alive this morning with the silvery light shimmering off all the metal. Maria got a chill making the hair stand up on the back of her neck as they walked past the dancing glitter of the alley. Ben noticed her discomfort and put his arm around her as they continued to walk toward the diner.

They didn't spend much time at the diner. It was getting close to four in the morning and everyone was tired. They paid their bill and started toward the car. As they approached the alley a man with a gun jumped out wearing a ski mask and started yelling while waving a gun at them.

"Get down on your knees, you dirty faggots," yelled the man.

"He said get on your knees. Just like you're going to suck dick; you should all know how that is done. Get down NOW!, said another man as he walked up from behind them also wearing a ski mask.

As Benjamin turned to tell his brother to do as they said, a third man walked out from the alley. He was carrying a long pipe. Before the others could tell him to look out, the guy struck Ben in the back of the head. Ben could feel the blood running down his neck as he fell to his knees and then around his face as he fell face first to the ground. The others dropped to their knees. Maria started to scream as a fourth man came from between the cars and placed duct tape over her mouth. Then he placed tape over Alex and Jimmy's mouths.

Ben tried to raise his head. He could feel the gravel scraping his face as he was dragged into the alley. Blood blurring his vision, he could see the others being forced into the alleyway. One of the guys took out a knife and cut Ben's shirt off of him and slammed him against a large pipe running up the building. Ben could feel cold handcuffs clasping his wrists behind the pipe. No matter how hard he tried, he could not speak. He faded in and out of consciousness but struggled to stay awake; hoping to identify the masked men that were in front of him.

After the man had handcuffed Ben to the pipe, he walked over and grabbed Maria and slammed her against the wall. Her limp body fell to the ground at Ben's side. The man with the pipe walked toward Alex. The man with the duct tape was now holding Jimmy down.

"Is that your boyfriend, faggot?" asked the man holding Jimmy. Jimmy couldn't speak because of the tape across his mouth and wouldn't move out of fear. "I asked you a question, cock sucker."

Jimmy still would not move. The man with the gun walked over to Jimmy. He ripped the tape off his face and stuck the gun into his mouth. "I think the man asked you a question. I think you had better answer him."

Jimmy nodded his head yes. "Good boy," the man said as he removed the gun from his mouth, "now tape his mouth shut again and hold him while he watches his lover die." Jimmy's face turned red as he fought off the tears. The man taped his mouth shut again.

The masked assassin raised the pipe and brought it down across Alex's face. Alex could feel the blood running down his face. He could no longer see out of his left eye. The masked man raised the pipe high above his head again and this time brought it down across Alex's stomach. The man holding Alex could no longer hold him. Alex fell to his hands and knees. He struggled to pull his body up as he sat back on his ankles. Barely able to hold himself up, he rested his butt on his feet and tilted his head backwards looking at the full moon behind him.

The pipe was then given to the man that had just been holding Alex. He took a swing and Alex attempted to catch the pipe, but with only one eye, he misjudged where the pipe was coming from. Jimmy and Ben could hear the cracking of Alex's wrist and forearm as the pipe hit him. His body fell face first into the pavement.

"Get up, faggot. GET UP!" screamed the gunman as he kicked him.

Alex lay there motionless. Jimmy started to struggle. The man holding him pulled him to his feet, dragged him to the wall and slammed his forehead into the wall. Jimmy fell to the ground. Weakened and barely able to move, he looked over at Ben and Maria, and then over to Alex. Ben's eyes met Jimmy's and he too looked over to Alex, but still could not utter a word.

"I will not tell you again, faggot, get up!" the gunman said as he pointed the gun down at Alex's head.

"Dude, OK, this has gone far enough and gone on long enough; let's get the fuck out of here before someone comes," said the man with the pipe.

"We will go when I say we can go, until then, do as you're told," said the gunman.

Maria had awoken and was pulling herself up. She managed to pull the tape from her mouth. "Leave him alone," she screamed.

Startled by Maria's scream, the gunman pulled the trigger. He shot Alex in the back of the head. The man froze and then began to shake. The other assassins started shouting, "Oh man, dude, it wasn't supposed to go this far. Fuck, dude, we have to get out of here." The man with the pipe grabbed the gunman and the four men ran down the alley and disappeared. Maria regained enough strength to get up and go to her purse. She got her cell phone and called 911.

The four were taken to the hospital. Maria and Jimmy were examined and both released with minor concussion. Ben was held for a few hours longer in the ER while they put stitches in the back of his head and waited for a bed to be available, so that he could be admitted for further observation. They wanted to see if he would regain the movement over his legs; he had been paralyzed from the waist down. The doctors explained that in most cases like this the paralysis was temporary and he would hopefully regain movement on his own, but if he hadn't regained movement in the next few days surgery may be needed.

Once in his room, Maria and Jimmy had joined him to wait on news about Alex. Ben was still feeling a bit fuzzy and had no idea that Alex had been shot. Maria explained to Ben what had happened and that Alex was in surgery.

"You mean he's still alive after all that?" asked Ben.

"Well he was still breathing when the paramedics got there, but alive we don't know," Maria answered as her eyes swelled and tears began to fall down her cheeks.

None of them could talk about what had happened any more, nor could they sleep or eat. They sat in silence for the rest of the morning. Ben would occasionally turn on the TV and flip through the stations; stopping on the news programs every so often in the hope they would mention the incident. Hoping they would say they had caught the son of a bitches who had done this to his brother, to all of them, but nothing. The thought that the story wasn't even mentioned angered him.

At about noon the doctor came into the room. "Alex is in ICU now, but the outcome doesn't look good," said the doctor, "you can take turns visiting him, but I'd start making final plans. I'm sorry there's nothing more that can be done at this time."

Maria went to ICU first. Alex was lying in the bed with a tube coming out of his mouth and he was connected to several machines. His left eye was patched over. There was an IV in his right hand. A nurse came in and Maria inquired about Alex's eye. The nurse informed her that the eye, although the last thing they should be worrying about, was removed and sewn shut. Maria couldn't stand any more. She collapsed into the chair next to his bed, put her head on his lap and began to cry.

Jimmy came in to get her. The two hugged and cried in the hallway. Maria returned to Ben's room and Jimmy stayed with Alex. He crawled into the bed being careful not to pull out any of the tubes that were attached to Alex. He lay there with his head on Alex's shoulder. Occasionally, he would kiss him on the cheek and whisper, "I love you, please wake up," into his ear. He had trouble getting out of the bed when he noticed Ben had arrived to see Alex.

A single tear came to Ben's eye when he watched Jimmy get out of Alex's bed. He couldn't remember the last time he witnessed that much love between two people. Jimmy walked out of the room, looked at Ben and said, "This is what happens when there is too much hate in the world."

It wasn't meant to hurt Ben intentionally, but the words that came out of Jimmy's mouth hurt Ben more than the pipe that had been smacked into the back of his head. Ben felt more shame over the events of the past six years on hearing those words that the tears started to pour down his face.

Ben dried his eyes and had the nurse push him into Alex's room. He sat there just telling Alex over and over how sorry he was and how weak he had been. "All these years little brother, you called me the strong one because I never shed a tear, but look at you. Just look. You live this hard lifestyle; a lifestyle that has very well left you for dead. It angers me little brother, it angers me. Why couldn't you just be straight? Why did you choose to be gay? But you were strong enough to do it. You stood boldly and didn't take shit from anyone. I'm the weak one. I was afraid to let you in, to be a part of my life. I don't think I would have been able to live without my family. You did it. You did it for six years. You said you'd never seen me cry. That's because I'm a coward. Real men don't cry and that's bullshit. You were never afraid to show your emotions. Alex, I'm so sorry."

The lump in his throat had overtaken him. Ben couldn't talk anymore. He couldn't hold it in anymore. The tears flowed down his cheeks. The back of his head started to burn with pain. It was hard to look at his brother in this state. Finally, he called the nurse to take him back to his room.

Maria stayed in Ben's room with him and Jimmy stayed in Alex's room. Maria climbed into the bed with Ben and they lay there not saying a word to each other. They both knew what the other was thinking, *'what would happen to them if Alex died?'*

Doctors would come in and check on Ben every other hour to try and get him to wiggle his toes or walk. When the doctors weren't around, Maria would hold his feet and one at time push his legs toward him in a bicycle movement. After the second day in the hospital while Maria was performing this exercise on him, Ben regained control over his legs. Not realizing he had even regained control, he almost kicked Maria to the ground. The movement came and went sporadically. Maria or the nurses could be walking him down the hall and his legs would just collapse, as though he had noodles for legs. By the end of the second day, the periods of no movement were less frequent and didn't last as long.

Jimmy would come up to check on Ben occasionally or vise versa. The only sleep Jimmy could manage to get was when he was curled up in the bed with Alex. It was the same for Maria and Ben, the only sleep they could get was when they were sharing a bed. Ben was kept overnight for a third night just to make sure he would be all right.

The next morning the doctors cleared Ben

to go home. He was to report back to the hospital three times a week for the next three months for physical therapy. Maria was happy to be taking Ben home. She left to go home, shower and get fresh clothes for everyone. It was the first time in three days that she had even thought about taking a shower.

When she arrived back at the hospital, Ben was ready to go. He changed into the clothes she had brought him. As he was signing the release forms, Jimmy came into the room. His eyes were bloodshot and glassy, his cheeks were flushed, and he couldn't speak as he was panting; almost hyperventilating. Maria took his hand and led him to a chair. Both Ben and Maria tried to get him to calm down, tried to get him to tell them what was going on. Finally, he caught his breath long enough to speak.

"Gone! Never coming home! Dead! Damn it, God why? He's dead!" Jimmy said as he placed his face into his hands and cried.

Chapter 5: Rest in Peace

Over the next few days Ben did not speak
to either Jimmy or Maria. He even found it
difficult to speak to Richmond, especially
since he wasn't ready to deal with his
nonsense or his 'I told you so' attitude. His
brother was dead and that was the last thing
he wanted to hear.

On the fourth day Richmond started
playing Christian music so loud that Ben
couldn't take it any longer. Ben had been
locked in his room and now he was forced to
deal with the world. As soon as he walked out
of the door, Richmond started into Ben about
how God punishes all of the most evil
sinners. This tragedy was not a tragedy at
all; merely an act of God's fullest mercy
commanded by his soldiers that walked this
Earth. Ben sadly began to believe the words
that were coming out of Richmond's mouth. His
nerves couldn't take it any longer so he had
to leave the house. He started walking, to

where; he had no idea.

Ben started believing that what had happened wasn't by accident at all. Granted he knew that the group was targeted for homosexuality, but he couldn't understand how they knew which one of them to target. He was the first one that was hit and then never touched. Maria had been thrown against the wall, but not severely injured. It was Jimmy and Alex that endured most of the pain. *'Why didn't they just keep attacking me?'* ran through his head over and over as he walked. Maybe it was an act of God's will and that just maybe, the attack had a purpose.

The thoughts only angered him more as he walked aimlessly through the city streets. The thought that he was starting to accept his brother as gay was infuriating him. He had let his guard down, he had let his religion down, and he had let himself down. Most confusing for him was that by not letting those walls down, he would have been letting his mother down.

As soon as the thoughts of letting his mother down entered his head, he began to think of her death. He wondered if God had punished her for letting Alex back into her life. He stopped, clenched his teeth together, closed his eyes tightly and took a deep breath through his nose exhaling very long and forcefully. His anger turned to his mother, for if it was a punishment by God, then his father was an innocent bystander that didn't deserve to die. A car blew the horn and swerved from hitting him; he had stopped in the middle of traffic.

Now feeling alone in this world, alone with no one to turn to, all because of what he felt were silly choices. This was daunting to him. He had Richmond, his high and mighty, Christian warrior roommate that did no wrong. Or he had Maria, the beautiful homo loving, everything is wonderful about sin, but who had deep feelings. Neither of them he wanted to deal with right now; they were his extreme opposites. At one point, Ben wondered if he had been as over the top as Richmond prior to this whole disaster. He wondered if the women in his life, his mother and now Maria, had misguided him off the beaten path. It was time for him to get back on the right path.

However, before he knew it he was standing in front of Maria's house. He had no idea how he had gotten there or if he had even known how to get to her house without driving. He hadn't been walking along main roads, but rather through side alleys, parking lots, small wooded areas, and other abandoned places. He looked at her house as he scratched his head just above his right ear and then started shaking his head in confusion. He had thought he was walking east, when her house was in the west.

"Ben, is that you?" said a woman's voice from behind, startling him.

"Um… um… yeah," Ben replied as he turned around to see Maria standing before him.

"Where have you been?" Maria asked as she walked over to hug him, "We have been trying to get hold of you for days."

"I've been thinking," he said as he stepped out of the way avoiding her hug.

"Is everything all right? Why are you pulling away? What the hell is wrong with you?"

"I'm thinking that everything that is you, that is my brother; is tainted in evil."

"Oh Jesus, you've been talking to Richmond too much."

"This has nothing to do with Richmond. It has everything to do with my beliefs."

"You really believe that don't you? Then why did you come here? Why… are you standing in front… of my… house?"

"Honestly, I couldn't tell you. I don't really know how I got here."

"Where's your car?"

"At my house. I walked."

"You walked! You're telling me you walked all the way from your place to mine? And you think I'm 'tainted in evil'? What kind of sick perverted game are you trying to play with me, Benjamin?"

"Maria, I'm not playing games with you. I'm really confused on how I feel and what's going on right now."

"Well then come inside and let's talk. We'll try to figure this out. We need to figure something out by tomorrow."

"What's tomorrow?"

"Uh… That would be your brother's funeral."

"Oh…"

"Oh, Oh is all you can say. WOW, you do need to figure stuff out.

Maria shuffled Ben into the house. The two sat and talked about everything that Ben had been thinking. Maria did an excellent job at not getting angry with him for the words that were coming out of his mouth. She couldn't believe he was using religion to justify the horrible acts that he witnessed. Nor could she believe he was using it to justify his parents' death. By the end of their conversation, Ben was crying and in her arms. He was completely confused. And somewhere during the conversations he realized he was in love with her.

Their conversation carried well on into the evening. At about nine o'clock Maria decided to make something to eat, considering neither had eaten since he had gotten there shortly before one in the afternoon. The conversation over their late dinner had been a lot more uplifting. So uplifting that it was even romantic. There were candles lit on the table, wine and soft music playing in the background. This was the Ben that Maria remembered.

After dinner, she had offered him a ride home or the couch to sleep on. He took her up on the couch because he wasn't ready to leave her or deal with Richmond. They talked until after midnight when she realized how late it had got. Maria went to get the blankets and pillow for Ben to sleep on the couch while Ben went to the bathroom. When he opened the bathroom door she was standing there waiting for him. She kissed him and led him to the bedroom. That night they made love for the first time.

The next morning they were both up, showered and ready for the day by nine, well sort of ready for the day. Maria drove Ben to his place to get ready for the funeral. She was not going to let him mess this up. When they got to his place, Richmond was not home. Both of them were relieved at this.

Once inside, Ben changed quickly and met Maria back in the living room. They went towards Maria's, picked up Jimmy and the three of them had enough time to stop for breakfast. During breakfast no one spoke. Jimmy was upset with Ben for not returning any of his phone calls and for abandoning him to make all the funeral arrangements. Ben still didn't know how he felt about Jimmy. He was struggling between his beliefs he shared with his roommate, the love he felt for Maria, and the beliefs she had imposed on him.

After breakfast they went to the funeral home. They each took their seats in the front row, with Maria sitting between the guys. The coffin sat in the front of the room about twenty feet from their seats. They sat there in silence, staring at the coffin.

The beautiful mahogany coffin had not yet been opened for viewing with its white lace flowing out from the inside. It was surrounded by flower arrangements. The main one made of nothing but white roses was centered behind the coffin, spanning almost the entire width. Two smaller ones made of red, orange and purple roses wrapped around the far end corners. There were two more made of white, purple and pink hyacinths that wrapped around the front corners.

It was so quiet that you could hear the petals of the roses sliding back and forth on the casket as the wind blew them from an open window. Occasionally the door in the back of the room would open and close as people entered and took their seats. The growing crowd that had started to fill the room behind them eventually drowned the petals sweet soft movements out.

The funeral director raised the casket lid for the showing. Alex lay on a cream-colored silk coffin liner with a deep red pillow under his head. His arms were laid to his side while his hands were clasped together, holding what oddly looked like an olive branch and a very old copper-colored coin.

Ben allowed Jimmy and Maria to take their moments with Alex before he did. When he was finished, he returned to the others finding them with the same confused look.

"Jimmy, what is with the olive branch and coin?"

"Ben I have no clue. I've never seen either one before today. Do either of you know what's on the coin? I tried to get a good look without literally taking it from his fingers."

"Honestly," Maria said pausing to bite her lip, "it sorta looks like a woman with extremely thick locks of hair. Almost like snakes."

"You mean like Medusa?" asked Ben trying hard to fight back the inappropriate laughter.

"Yeah, smart ass!" Maria responded, now biting her lip to keep from laughing. "Like Medusa!"

"I don't know why you're both sniggering. I don't see anything funny about any of this. That's my partner, your best friend and your brother for cryin' out loud," although as soon as the words hit his lips he also couldn't resist a smile.

The service began with the priest reading a passage from the bible, Genesis 8:8-12 about Noah releasing a dove into the skies to search for dry land. After several attempts the Dove returned with an olive leaf and after another seven days, Noah released the dove, which did not return to him. The priest read another passage about the resurrection of Christ, 1 Corinthians 15:20-23. The words that came from the priest's mouth in Psalm 55 panged the hearts of many.

"Give ear to my prayer, O God,
And do not hide yourself from my supplication
Attend to me, and hear me:
I am restless in my complaint, and moan noisily,
Because of the voice of the enemy,
Because of the oppression of the wicked:
For they bring down trouble upon me,
And in wrath they hate me.
My heart is severely pained within me,
And the terrors of death have fallen upon me,
Fearfulness and trembling have come upon me,
And horror has overwhelmed me,
So, I said, 'Oh, that I had wings like a dove
I would fly away and be at rest.'"

Ben heard the word dove and for the first time looked up toward the priest. After hearing the word for the sixth or seventh time, he couldn't understand why hearing dove had bothered him. Ben could no longer concentrate on the service. Everything that was spoken sounded as though it was being spoken in a foreign language. Until from the back of the room, he heard the door open.

Ben turned to see who had walked in so late. A woman wearing a light gray, almost green colored dress robe was walking through the door. There was a bright light coming in from behind her, making her look like a beautiful goddess with no face. She appeared to be seven and a half feet tall. Ben wondered how she had got through the door without ducking.

Maria turned to see what had distracted Ben. She quickly got Jimmy's attention. The three of them just stared at the oddly shaped woman in the back of the room. The priest's voice became very loud and boisterous, bringing the attention of the entire congregation back to him as he closed with Psalm 17.

After the priest had concluded, Ben, Maria, and Jimmy turned around to the back of the room, but the woman was gone. Being as tall as she was she would have been easily spotted in the crowd. The door hadn't been opened or it hadn't closed, she had just disappeared.

Everyone made their last prayer and stood quietly moving toward the door. Outside there were cars passing by at the end of the parking lot, but it was as though they were not making a sound. The birds were flying and the wind was blowing with an eerie silence. Everyone at the funeral proceeded to their cars to form the procession. Even the magnetic funeral flags being stuck to the cars were making contact lacking the snapping noise as the magnet connected with cars. Ben wiggled his fingers in his ears a few times, but there was still nothing; no sound. He couldn't find his voice to talk. He was barely able to find the strength to walk to the limo behind the black hearse. The absolute silence was keeping him frozen.

The cars followed the police escorted hearse to the cemetery. Ben couldn't believe he was on his way there again, especially twice in one year. The limo turned into the driveway behind the hearse and through the oversized, gothic-style, wrought iron gates attached to the stone wall surrounding the graveyard. Ben looked out of the window, up at the gargoyles protecting the cemetery. He felt as though their eyes were piercing his, as the limo passed them. He felt the same about every statue as they drove past them on the winding road to Alex's plot. To his amazement, he thought that an angel statue turned its head to follow him and another stood up to bow its head to him. Ben thought he was going crazy, because no one else had seen anything.

Everyone gathered around the gravesite to pay their last respects. Ben stood at the head of the grave to give his eulogy.

"I thank everyone for coming out here today. Unfortunately, this is the second time this year I stand in this very cemetery. The first time, Alex and I buried our parents, and this time I bury him, my younger brother.

It's hard for me to believe that this year he
would have been twenty-three. It seems like
it was only yesterday he was turning five.
Granted, I haven't been in his life for the
last six years and I have no way to make that
up to him now. I can't stand here and pretend
that I agree with his way of life or even
begin to understand it; but I can say I loved
my brother. When Alex turned five I promised
him that I would always protect him, I would
always be there for him, and this is the
second time I have broken this promise to
him. I should have been able to save him.

"Alex was born on July 13, 1984 during a
full moon. It just so happens, he was brought
into this world and taken from us by the
moon's glorious light. Because he was not
only born on a full moon, but also a Friday
the 13th, Alex never believed in superstitions
or bad luck. In fact, he always felt that
those days were lucky days for him. I too was
born on a Friday the 13th and a full moon.
However, I just thought it was plain old
creepy. But these are the things we will all
remember about Alex. It's his quirkiness that
always made him the life of the party." Ben
paused as his throat became sore, he tried to
swallow but it was difficult. He fought back
the tears, but he had to wipe a single tear
from his right eye.

Ben continued, his voice was a little
shaky and cracked as he tried to speak.
"Sorry! I promised not to cry and I urge all
of you to do the same. Not cry that is. For
if Alex were standing here right now, he
would be furious that we were sitting here

weeping over him and not having a party to celebrate his life. Laughing about the good times and snubbing at the bad times. Alex had an extremely strong soul. He knew how to love and he knew how to laugh and he knew how to kick you if you were down; if you deserved it, but still showing you love at the same time. He was the most wonderful person I knew. I can't believe I abandoned him and I can't believe he's gone."

Ben leaned his head forward and squinted over the crowd toward a tree in the distance. Under the tree stood what appeared to be a woman. It was the same woman from the funeral home that had appeared and disappeared with no trace.

"Ben! Benjamin, is everything OK?" Maria asked as she stood up and walked over to him.

"That woman. Do you see her? It's the woman from the funeral home," he whispered to Maria. She too was squinting, looking toward the tree.

"Ben, I don't see anyone. If it is her, ignore her. She'll find us if she wants to talk. Anyway, right now I think you're too upset," Maria said placing her arm around him and kissing him on the cheek.

"I'm sorry everyone. I have nothing more to say. Thank you all for coming and I now turn the podium over to this wonderful woman, Maria." Ben kissed her softly on the lips, walked over and knelt by the coffin, and whispered, "I will miss you baby brother. I love you and I hope from wherever you are, looking down on us, you know this now. I hope you forgive me."

Maria gave her eulogy. She turned things over to Jimmy and he then turned things over to the priest. The priest offered for anyone else to say a few words. A couple of people got up and said great things about Alex. Each person brought either tears or laughter to everyone listening. At the end, everyone took turns to place a rose on the casket and then it was lowered into the ground. Jimmy, Maria and Ben each took a handful of dirt and with one last prayer, tossed the dirt into the grave.

Chapter 6: Man in the Moon

Following the funeral, Ben spent several days at Maria's. During that time Maria and Ben grew closer, but the relationship with Jimmy was stagnant. Whenever Jimmy came around Ben would find something to do in the other room. He would offer to make dinner, do work on the computer, or just sit in silence. Jimmy would try to make conversation with Ben, but Ben only gave him one-word answers. Jimmy knew that Ben and Alex had to be brothers, they both pouted in the same way.

Each night after Jimmy left, Maria would try to talk to Ben about his actions toward Jimmy. Ben couldn't articulate what he wanted to say to her. It wasn't that he neither liked nor disliked Jimmy; it was just that he couldn't understand. Seeing Jimmy was a reminder for him letting his brother die. And in some respects, he felt guilty wishing it had been Jimmy that had been killed that night and not Alex.

Eventually, there was a break through with Ben two nights before the 4th of July. Whatever Maria had said to him changed his attitude toward Jimmy. He was ready to understand his feelings and he was ready to try and build a relationship with Jimmy. The next morning he went to work and since he only had a half-day of work, he went to Maria's right after. He made his father's famous lasagna and took it to Jimmy before Maria got home from work.

Answering the door in utter surprise, Jimmy let Ben inside. The two of them sat talking while eating for a couple hours, before Maria ventured over. She was shocked to see the two of them having dinner and conversing with more than two words in each sentence. They all continued to talk for several more hours before Maria was ready to leave. She couldn't believe that she was the one wanting to leave before Benjamin. On the way out the door, Ben asked Jimmy to join them for the 4th of July festivities the next day. Maria was astounded.

The next day, the three of them set out for an early afternoon movie. Afterward they had a picnic in the park. Ben and Jimmy played Frisbee, while Maria read a book. They played volleyball for a while with some other groups of people there. The day quickly turned to night and before they knew it, the fireworks had started.

Maria lay with her head in Ben's lap and Jimmy with his head in hers. Ben had been dealing with Jimmy well, but watching him lying there with his head in Maria's lap made him uncomfortable. He couldn't tell Jimmy to sit up or to lie somewhere else without offending Maria; especially now that he and Jimmy had just started getting along. Ben just laid his head back and watched the fireworks ignoring his feelings.

Afterwards, they went to get dinner. They had a hard time deciding where to go. Normally they would have just gone to the Diner, but since Alex's death none of them could bear going there. They decided to just eat at the closest sit-down restaurant. At dinner Jimmy brought up Alex's birthday and that it was coming up the next weekend.

"Here's what I think we should do," Jimmy said as he slouched into his seat when he saw the looks on their faces. He felt like a deer caught in the headlights. He couldn't speak.

"You think we should do something?" Ben replied.

"Of course we should," said Jimmy. "We should celebrate his life and party it up like he were still with us."

"You've got to be kidding me!"

"No Ben, I'm not kidding you. You said it yourself at the funeral, 'Alex would not want us sitting around here weeping for him.' We should do exactly that. We should honor celebrating his birthday the way he would want us to."

"So, what do you propose we do then?" asked Maria.

"We do what he would have wanted us to do."

"You mean, go to E^2 and then to the Diner

afterward?"

"Exactly Maria, that's exactly what we do. Alex wouldn't want us to sit around and pout and he for sure wouldn't want us to sit around and forget him either." Jimmy had accidentally raised his right eyebrow, cocked his head slightly, and looked at Ben as the words flowed from his mouth.

"I'm sorry; do you really believe I am trying to forget my brother?" Ben said slightly raising his voice.

"What? No, why would you think I was thinking that? That's insane, Benjamin!"

"You clearly gave me a look when you said that."

"Boys, it wasn't meant like that. And anyway, that's off topic. I think it's a great idea. Can't say I'll be in party mode, but I know it's what Alex would want us to do," replied Maria.

"So, Ben, are you in?"

"I guess so, but aren't you nervous about going there after what happened?"

"Look Ben, tragedies happen all the time and if we let them haunt us for the rest of our lives, then we'd never come out of our homes. We'd be hermits."

"I guess you're right Jimmy, but there is a time frame for some things I think. And right now my gut is telling me that it's too early to be going back to where it all happened."

"Ben, everything will be fine," said Maria giving him a kiss on the cheek. "After all, what's the worst thing that could happen?"

Ben stayed at his place Thursday night and then at Maria's for the weekend. On Monday he was back at his place. Richmond gave him a hard time for spending so much time with Maria, but it didn't really seem to faze him as much. Every now and again, he would get caught up in the emotions that Richmond was throwing off. However, every time he went to that angry place he thought of Maria, it grounded him.

Friday the 13th came upon Ben faster than he could have thought. He wanted to cancel on Maria and Jimmy more than either of them could ever know. After work, he went home to change and get clothes for the weekend. He knew he would end up staying at Maria's the entire weekend. On his way out, Richmond was coming in.

"Dude, where are you going?" asked Richmond.

"Out!" Ben replied, fighting back smart-ass comments knowing it would only provoke Richmond more.

"You're going out with that whore and her fairy friend aren't you?"

"UGH… give it a rest Richmond. She is not a whore. She's my… my… my girlfriend. And you're lucky I don't lay your sorry ass out cold for speaking about her like that."

"Ooooh, big man gonna protect his girlyfriend. Are you going to protect the fagot too?"

"Jesus Richmond! He's my brother's partner. Was my brother's partner. Think you could tone down the God Warrior a little bit?"

"Uh No. The bible says it's wrong and therefore, God says it's wrong. And you're only asking for trouble if you continue to hang around them. You do realize this, right?"

"And you wonder why I haven't been spending time around here! Honestly, was I this much of an asshole before I started talking to my brother again? Cause dude, you're off the charts on the asshole meter."

"Actually my friend, I think you were worse than me. I don't know how they corrupted your mind. I don't know why or how you let them corrupt you."

"I guess that's what happens when you have people in your life that you care about. You can see both sides of the fence."

"And you really want to be a part of that side of the fence? That side of darkness?"

"I really don't know what I want, but I have to believe there is some kind of common ground somewhere. There can't be this much hate in the world. But at the same time, there has to be some kind of rhyme or reason to all the sin."

"You still have the good guy in you somewhere. I hope that guy doesn't get lost in some whore's pussy just cause you're getting some action."

"Oh my God, Richmond. You're such a fucking pig." Ben pushed Richmond aside and walked out the door. He couldn't take listening to him anymore.

"Don't use God's name in vane," Richmond yelled after him. "You'll be back soon.

You'll be back when you realize how wrong it is to stay on that side. Graze in the grass that should be forbidden."

Ben could barely hear what Richmond was sputtering on about. As he got into the car, he was shaking his head. His drive to Maria's was a difficult one. He let the words that Richmond had been saying get to him. Several times he almost turned around to go back home. Once he even pulled into a parking lot to make a U-turn.

Stunning as usual, Maria was ready to go out before everyone else.

"You know, for being a girl, you're always done way too fast for us," Ben said with a smile, giving her a hug and kiss.

Maria during her lunch break that day had gone to the store and bought Ben a new outfit for the evening. By the time he was finished putting on the new outfit Jimmy was there, ready to go. They went to a fancy dinner at Perséphonê, Alex's favorite restaurant. It was one of the best meals that Ben had ever had. He couldn't believe he had never been there before.

After dinner, they headed to the club. They turned into the poorly-lit drive and down the hill to the dark parking lot. Parking next to an old, run-down, what looked to have once been a dark midnight blue, but now a white-washed blue van with huge rust holes throughout it's sides.

"Eww, have you ever seen such a disgusting vehicle here before?" asked Maria.

"Um, no. That would be a huge negative. Who would drive that piece of crap here anyway? Look if some guy wanted to hook up and brought me out to this I'd freak out on him or laugh my ass off and say 'hell no'."

"Well let's just go inside and have a good time or at least try to have a good time," Ben said as he hurried them out of the darkened parking area. He felt the hairs on the back of his neck standing up as though all the warmth had been sucked out of the air. As he shivered off the feeling, he looked up to the sky. There he saw as big a face as could be looking down on them. It was the man in the moon, full and large, Ben felt like he could shake his hand from Heaven the rooftop bar.

Inside, there was a masquerade themed party going on. Everyone was wearing masks. Ben felt even more out of place than the last time. Not only was he straight, but now he didn't have a mask either. He and Maria spent the evening in Heaven bar talking under the stars. Jimmy spent most of the evening with them, but occasionally would go to dance for a couple of songs. At about quarter to two in the morning they all were ready to leave.

As they walked through the inside of Electric Earth, Ben noticed a woman on the other side of the dance floor. She was very tall and beautiful. He stopped, causing Maria and Jimmy to run into him. The woman looked at him held her hand up making a stop sign and then started shaking her head no. When Maria asked him why he stopped he just responded with a 'sorry' and kept moving. After the last time he had seen the woman in the cemetery, and no one else had he wasn't about to look foolish again.

Outside the front doors an old friend had stopped Jimmy to ask how things had been going. Maria stood in Ben's arms, off to the side.

"This whole night has been weird. I feel like something's wrong or out of place," Ben said to Maria.

"I think it's just being here and it being the Masquerade and all. It's just your nerves getting to you."

"I don't think so, but you're probably right."

"All right, sorry about that, you guys ready?" Jimmy asked.

Maria and Ben replied together, "Um… yeah."

"So, is it just me or was anyone else just not feeling like being at the bar tonight? I mean it's weird. I had fun and all, but it's just…" said Jimmy as he paused.

"Jimmy? Jimmy, wanna finish your sentence there bud?" Ben asked.

"Just lost track of thought. Better yet, I don't know how to say what I wanted to say. Just a weird night that's all."

"I know the feeling."

They started down the dark, dirt road. The huge moon seemed to fade from view under the trees. As they approached the parking area, it was even darker and quieter than earlier. The only thing they could hear were the frogs croaking in the creek behind the lot.

"Did you guys just hear that?" Maria asked as she pulled Ben's arm tighter around her shoulder.

"Hear what?" Ben and Jimmy both asked.

"It sounded like someone walking in the brush over there. There was no-one in front of us!"

"Maybe its two boys getting it on in the dirty old truck parked next to us," Jimmy started laughing.

"That's not funny at all Jimmy. What if it's not? What if it's…"

"What if it's your worst nightmare coming true?" said a man as he walked out from around the van wearing a dark blue mask and a jester's hat.

"Nice mask, mumsy helps the wittle boy pick it out for him?" Jimmy said in a baby voice.

"Oh, so we have a comedian faggot out here," said the jester, looking to the hidden side of the van.

"And what, you weren't out here just sucking some guy's dick? Or were you just plain ole fucking?"

"Jimmy! What the hell are you doing? Shut up and just get in the damn car!" Ben yelled at Jimmy as threw him the keys.

Jimmy walked over to the passenger's side door. When he put the key in, the driver's side door of the van flew open, pinning Jimmy between the two vehicles. The driver got out of the van wearing all black with a black-feathered bird mask. The eyes were beaded orange and the beak was yellow coming down over the mouth. The man just snickered.

"So, we meet again!" said the driver.

"You've got to be kidding me," said Jimmy.

"Kidding you I'm not and this time we're prepared to do whatever we want," said the driver.

Maria turned around to run back up the hill, but instead turned to find a gun pointed at her forehead. She closed her eyes tight as a tear fell down her cheeks, clenched her teeth tight and swallowed hard. This man was also wearing all black with a green frog mask.

The unseen man walked out from the side of the van. He was carrying a lead pipe wearing all black the same as the other guys. His mask was all white with a tiny golden halo hovering over his head.

"This is the messenger and he will deliver you from your sins you filthy swine," said the jester. "Bring the pinned piggy over here."

The birdman grabbed Jimmy by the back of the shirt and forced him to the back of the van. The jester opened the back doors, took out duct tape, and then taped Jimmy's mouth by wrapping the tape all the way around his head several times.

"So, you like to take it up the ass faggot? We have a surprise for you then," said the jester as he pulled Jimmy's pants down.

"What the hell are you guys doing? All I have to do is…" Ben stopped talking as the frogman placed the gun against Maria's forehead.

"Turn around missy and watch the

entertainment," said the frogman.

The jester walked over and taped Maria's mouth shut in the same manner as Jimmy's and then taped her hands together. He then taped Ben's hands leaving his mouth untouched.

"This is the game. You talk and she dies. It's pretty simple. Got it? Cause I love it." said the jester. Ben just nodded his head yes. They were both brought over closer to the van.

The angel had taken the pipe and started to sodomize Jimmy with it. Maria and Ben both clenched their eyes shut.

"No, no, that isn't the game. Open your eyes and watch or he'll put a bullet in her head," said the birdman.

They watched as the angel continued to shove the pipe deeper and faster into Jimmy. The tears rolled down his face and they could hear him screaming, even through the tape.

The wind blew, the trees seemed to move and the moonlight came billowing through lighting up the parking area. The angel let go of the pipe and picked up a second pipe from the back of the van. Jimmy started to move, squealing even louder.

"Shut him up, shut him up now!" said the angel as he walked toward Ben and Maria. The birdman pushed the pipe deeper into Jimmy causing him to pass out from the pain.

"Rich…" Ben couldn't finish his word; the angel turned to him as he heard Ben speak and smashed the pipe into his skull. Ben lost his vision and couldn't speak. As he fell to the ground he could feel the blood running down his face. He felt the pipe strike the back of his head again and then being dragged through the dirt until he lost consciousness.

"Goddamn it!" yelled the angel, "let's get out of here."

"Dude that's why you weren't supposed to speak!" said the jester.

The driver threw Jimmy to the ground behind their car, leaving the pipe inside him. The frogman smacked Maria in the back of the head, catching her as she fell, and threw her on top of Jimmy. The four men got into the van, sped up the hill and out of sight.

Minutes had gone by before someone came down to the parking area. Two younger guys and a female thought upon spotting them that there was some sick game being played. That was until they saw all the blood. After calling 911, the girl discovered Ben's body lying in the shrubs in front of the car when she went to throw up.

The two boys moved Maria off of Jimmy. As they moved her she started to gain consciousness. Then they removed the pipe and fixed Jimmy's pants before anyone else came into the parking area.

"Where did they go?" asked Maria.

"No idea. We just saw this dirty old van flying up the hill. They almost hit Cassie."

"Who's Cassie? And where's Ben?" asked Jimmy as he was coming to and he tried to pull himself into a seated position, but he hurt too bad to sit up.

"She's our friend and I don't see another guy here."

"Guys, he's up here with me. Sorry, I would have said something sooner, but I've been a bit busy trying to retain my dinner."

"Cassie is he all right?"

"Robert he isn't moving. I think he may be dead." She threw up again.

"Jason can you go help Cassie and check on that guy?" asked Robert.

Jason went to the front of the car. He knelt down and felt Ben's neck for a pulse.

"He's got a pulse, but it's very faint and he's very bloody."

Before anyone could respond to him the red and white lights of the paramedics brightened the darkness. Shortly followed by the red and blue lights of the police vehicles. The paramedics came over to Maria and Jimmy and they both pointed over to where Ben was lying. Ben was examined, braced on a stretcher and put into the ambulance. When they came to Maria she shook her head no and pointed to Jimmy. Jimmy started to cry from embarrassment. He explained what had happened and they took him away in an ambulance.

There were only two EMS vehicles and Maria had to wait for another one to arrive. She argued with the police and the EMT's to allow her to drive over to the hospital, but with her head wound they wouldn't allow her. She refused to talk to the police about what had happened until she knew what was going on with Jimmy and Ben. Finally, another paramedic showed up and took her to the hospital.

At the hospital, Maria was the first to be discharged. After she got her update on Ben and Jimmy she agreed to sit down with the police to give a statement. She told them about what had happened and she told them that she believed it was the same guys that had attacked them previously. Since the guys were wearing masks both times and that there were four men this time instead of five, the police didn't believe her. She explained to them what they had said, but no matter what she told them; they weren't going to dismiss that it was possible it was just a coincidence. They chalked it up to being in the wrong place at the wrong time.

"I know who it was though and it would make sense that they would do it to us twice. It makes sense. It all makes sense now. God does it make sense." Maria continued to babble to herself about it making sense before the police finally stopped her.

"What do you mean you know who it was? They were wearing masks."

"I'm telling you I know who it was because Ben recognized the voice. That's why they left. I get it. And an angel that little…"

"Miss, can you please tell us the conversation you're having with yourself there, so that it makes sense to us and so that we could possibly help you out in this matter!"

"Of course I can, it was Richmond. It was Ben's roommate Richmond. He talked about being God's angel, doing his work for him or whatever it is he told Ben. His mask tonight was an angel mask and then Ben recognized his voice. That's what got Ben hit."

"Can you be sure of this?"

"I could possibly pick out his voice,

but Ben is the one that would be able to do that better then I could."

"We could go question him, but unless you are sure we wouldn't want to put anyone through any unnecessary discomfort."

"You're kidding me right? Let me shove a pipe up your ass till you pass out and see if we can talk about unnecessary discomfort."

"There is no need to get hostile. We understand you have been through a lot this evening."

"This evening doesn't even begin to tell you what 'WE' have been through in the last month and half. And to think that monster was here the entire time. In the same house with Ben."

"Ma'am, really we need you to calm down. We'll get a statement from your friends when they are available to talk and if they collaborate what you're saying, then we'll question this Richmond."

"Excuse me, Mr. Miller is able to see people now," said a nurse to them.

"Great, now go talk to Jimmy and do it quickly so that I can go in and talk to him," said Maria and before the cop could open his mouth, "yes, before me because I don't want you to come back and say that I told him what to tell you… you… guys."

The police interviewed Jimmy and received the same story that Maria had given. The last thing that Jimmy had heard was Ben yelling Richmond's name before he couldn't take the pain any longer. Maria was then allowed to see Jimmy. He was a little sore, which was to be expected, but was doing well.

"Is there anything else you two can add before we leave?" asked the policemen.

"Yeah you could say that you're going to do something about that son of a bitch Richmond. He's killed one of us, sodomized another and who knows how Ben's doing."

"Until Ben can tell us he'll be able to identify the voice, we will not intrude on this man's life. Especially since it sounds like you already have a personal vendetta against him. I think it may be your wishful thinking that heard what you heard."

"I'm sorry; you're not the one that just had a pipe shoved up your ass. I heard the same thing she did, now do something about it!"

"I think you should really go do something about this. And I think you should go do it now before my father hears about this." A soft, stern female voice came from the doorway surprising them all. It came from a short bleach-blond, blue-eyed girl. She had an over- night bag over her shoulder and was pulling a suitcase.

"Excuse me Miss and who are you?"

"The name's Samantha, but you can call me Sam, or Ms. O'Leary," she paused when she saw their eyes about to pop out of their heads, "yes boys, that O'Leary, or you can just call me the guy who signs your paychecks' daughter."

"Get out. Sam is that you?" said Maria.

"It's me in the flesh."

"Oh my god I've missed you. Where the hell have you been?"

"My dad finally got a hold of me the

other day and he told me what was going on. I was trying to surprise you, but when the taxi was going past the club I saw the paramedics leaving. It took me forever to find out what was going on. I just had the cabbie drop me off here."

"It's been crazy around here."

"I'm sorry, why are you two still standing there? Shouldn't you be off interviewing your prime suspect?"

"Yes, I think we do have somewhere to be." As the police officers turned to walk out of the room a nurse followed by a doctor walked into the room.

"Ms. Logarakis can we have a moment with you please?"

"Call me Maria and whatever you have to say, you can say it to my friends. I have a feeling I'm going to need them right now."

"Well, there is good news and there is bad news. The good news is that Ben is alive and stable. The bad news is he's in a coma. With the seriousness of the trauma he could wake up in a couple hours, or it could be weeks, or it could be never. Right now it's just too hard to tell."

"May I see him now at least?"

Maria went to Ben's room and sat down beside him. She took his hand in hers, kissed his sleeping lips.

"Ben, if you can hear me I hope things are OK. God I hope you can hear me," she began to cry; "we've been through so much in our short time together. You've made everything OK for me. This has been the hardest time in my life and it seems like it was nothing until I had you by my side. You can't leave me now. You can't. Damn it Ben." Maria jumped, "Jesus Christ, don't sneak up on people like that!"

"Sorry my dear, I did not mean to startle you. My name is Nurse Zorbas, but you may call me Athy for short."

"Do I know you from somewhere?"

"I'm sure you've seen me around my dear. I've seen you around. Anyway, keep talking to him. That's what keeps the living from dying when they are in a coma. My dear though, there should be no tears. He's only in a coma after all. Only in a coma."

Chapter 7: Beyond Zion

Ben awoke, jumping quickly to his feet in the brush in front of the car. He touched his lip and realized it was no longer bleeding and neither were his head or his forehead. In fact, there was no pain at all. He felt healthy, alive and very well.

He looked around, barely able to make out his car in front of him due to the thick fog that surrounded him. Yelling for Maria and then for Jimmy, there was no response. The sounds of the frogs were no longer there, the moon was gone, and he could not tell if he was still in the parking lot or not. The last thing he remembered was getting hit in the head with the pipe, but even that didn't feel real now.

Turning the key in the ignition, the car would not start. Ben figured that the club would allow him to use the phone to call for a tow truck. As he started to walk toward the club he realized the hill he had to climb to get to the club was missing. He knelt down where he thought the hill should be to touch the ground; it was smooth and there was no gravel. The cold from the ground made him shiver at the touch. He thought it felt like marble.

"What kind of club are we in now guys? And how did you get my car in here?" There was no response and his voice did not echo.

After taking a deep breath, he walked back to the car to get a flashlight from his trunk. The trunk would not open. Ben slammed his fist against the trunk screaming as loud as he could, "Is anyone out there? ANYONE!" Still there was no response and no echo. He jumped on top of the trunk and sat there with his head in hands.

Awhile had gone by when an owl flew in front of him, screeching. The owl's talons brushed his hair as it flew overhead. He looked to see if he could see where the bird had flown to, but saw nothing but fog. Straining as hard as he could a light appeared in the distant. He pondered wondering if it was a mirage. Illusion or not, he was determined to find out what it was or something about where he had awoken.

As he walked further and further, the light didn't seem to be getting any larger. At one point he stopped, clicked his heels three times and said "there's no place like home, damn that doesn't work. Ahh, that's right, I don't have the stupid ruby slippers." He continued to walk.

Tired from walking, he finally stopped. "I give up, the light is not there. It's an illusion." He turned around to find himself staring at a door that read *Marygolde's Tea Room*. Marygolde's was a quaint little cottage topped with a thatched roof and a tin, crooked pipe chimney that had smoke billowing from it. The scent of sweet mint and barley quickly filled the air. He scratched his head in confusion for the building had not been there when he had just walked past. It looked like something out of a fairytale.

Ben jumped as he felt a hand press against his shoulder. He was too scared to turn around. The figure began to walk around him and Ben closed his eyes tightly. He felt someone standing in front; he could feel their eyes peering at him. Slowly he opened his eyes to find a familiar face standing before him.

"You're that woman, the woman from the funeral home, from the cemetery, and from the club. Not quite as tall, in fact pretty short considering, but you are her, aren't you?"

"That I am my child, that I am," said a beautiful olive skin-toned woman. She had straight black hair curled around her face, light copper eyes and was wearing a flowing pale green robe that hid her figure. Her face was chiseled and wise, but she looked to Ben to be no older than twenty-three to twenty-five. He couldn't believe she was calling him child.

"In no disrespect, but I believe we are the same age at most, so please do not address me as 'my child'. It's kinda creepy."

"Do not be fooled by my appearances. I may look to be twenty-four, but I am nearly three thousand years old."

"Ok nice prank, but whatever, I'll play the game."

"Game, there is none to play."

"Then answer me some questions. Who are you? Where am I? Why is this building here now when I have walked so far and saw nothing?"

"My name is Athena, you are in Guarroutk, and you have not walked anywhere for your car is directly behind you."

"What? You're mad. You're insane, my car is…" Ben said smashing his knee into the front fender of the car as he turned around, "ow damn it, what the hell? How is this possible?"

Athena laughed, "You are cute. It is going to be an interesting time with you, is it not?"

"Woman you're… insane. Wait, are you telling me that you're Athena? As in, the goddess of wisdom, Athena?"

"That would be I, in the living flesh."

"You're not only insane, but you're a funny woman too. And anyway what is this place Gr-reeeek."

"Silly boy, it is not Greek it is pronounced gore-rock and, kindly, roll your tongue at the end of gore."

"Ok, so what is this place Guarroutk anyway? Is it heaven or hell?" Ben shivered, "Well, wait, it's too chilly for hell, or is it some crazy nightclub? Funny ya know, until a few weeks ago a nightclub would have never have been a suggestion. Aha, Maria put you up to this, didn't she?" He put his finger to his head and remembered that he had been bleeding "Oh and how did all the cuts and stuff disappear? There's no blood. No blood anywhere."

"You babble, has anyone ever told you that? A city was destroyed for that reason alone you know?"

"Babble wasn't destroyed."

"Was it not?" Athena asked as she pulled her head back grabbing her bosom as though he had just said something unspeakable.

"No, God was furious with them so everyone was made to speak different languages, halting the building of the staircase to heaven."

"You think that was not destroyed? Creatively destroyed, but destroyed all the same."

Ben stared at her blankly with his mouth slightly open and yet amused by her.

"Shall we go inside then Benjamin? Not best we stand out here all night. Who knows what foul beasts you could run into out here!"

"I've been walking around in a mist or fog or whatever this crap is and there are beasts that could hurt me out here?" Ben asked in a trembling, panicked voice.

"There are beasts in your very mind that could hurt you Benjamin. And yet, you do walk around with yourself everyday, do you not? So why tremble at the thoughts of another beast that could be lurking out here?"

Again Ben just stared at Athena as she turned to open the door. Soft music played by a cello and some other weird stringed instrument that Ben could not decipher, sounding slightly like a harp, came peacefully floating past his ears. A very loud chatter broke the peaceful music almost as soon as it had started. Ben followed Athena into the cottage. Quickly stopping, he gazed at the enormous interior of Marygolde's.

There were hundreds of tables with one large bar to the side. Each table was made of a different material; ranging from wood, iron, stone, even plastic, to any variation of types of material. There was different lighting for each table that matched its table's style and no matter how eccentric or the size of the fixture, it seemed to provide light for only that table.

There were booths along the two walls that were void of the bar, also all in different styles. There was nothing along the wall with the door. In fact, if it wasn't for the tiny wall slightly larger than the door it supported, the large room looked almost triangular. Ben thought to himself how weird it was considering the building looked round on the outside, but there was nothing round about this room. Except for numerous tables scattered here and there, of course.

There was a tiny hallway off the side of the bar. The only place it could lead was to the bathrooms, if they even had those in this weird place, or possibly storage. As they approached the bar he noticed that there was an open trap door that led to the basement. Obviously, that meant that the hallway could not have led to a storage room, it had to be restrooms Ben thought.

The woman standing behind the bar was not a very attractive woman. She was neither a slender nor overweight woman with mousy-brown hair and dark brown eyes. She wore what appeared to be dirty rags sewn together to make a dress. In some places, the rags looked to be coming apart at the seams.

"'Allo Alltheena 'n allo little one. Ma nam'tis Marygolde, whatcha reckon yins be havin?" Marygolde said with a ruggedly, harsh tone in her voice. She sounded like she was trying to cover up whatever accent she had with a very poor attempt.

"It is lovely and always a pleasure to see you Marygolde. This is Benjamin. He will be with us for several days. So, if I am not around take care of him please." Marygolde did not respond only nodded her head, never breaking eye contact with Athena.

"Make sure Wes does not get a hold of him. He has already caused enough problems for the boy. That is beside the point right this very second. I will have whatever the house special is tonight. In fact, make it two. The boy will have one as well."

"Tis very well me dear. That'd be two houze specials then will it, comin' right up." This time Marygolde spoke with an almost Irish accent. "Two O'Clum-a-Roy's a here ye go!"

"Clum-a-Roy's, what are those?"

"Me deary it's called O'Clum-a-Roy's and that'd be a bit o'Irish Crème, a bit o'battery gooziness, lots o'spices, and of course a bit o'Roy's blood.

"She's kidding right? And do I even want to ask what battery gooziness is?"

"No and no, just drink it." Athena walked toward a table in the far back corner. The stone table had a dark green cloth with light green olive leaves and different types of owls embroidered on it. The area in which they sat was lit by a black wrought-iron chandelier filled with burning candles. Ben looked above to see the chandelier was suspended in mid air. The thatched roof was nowhere in sight. Just black nothingness filled the space above the light fixtures. Every now and then Ben would see a tiny yellow pinhole streak across the nothingness, like a shooting star.

"So, you never answered my question. What is this place?"

"This place is Guarroutk. It is neither heaven nor hell. It is not purgatory. There is no way to quantify Guarroutk. It is nowhere and it is everywhere. It is where the two come together."

"Give it to me ole mighty one have I crossed into the Twilight Zone or is it Star Trek with worm holes and all? I know it's like the Q?" Ben snapped his fingers while opening his eyes wide as if a light bulb had just gone off above his head.

"Do not be silly foolish boy. It is possible those concepts came from this place, a place like this," Athena shrugged, "it is not the places you suggest however.

"Now take your glass. We shall take a toast," Athena said taking her glass into her hand and holding it up in the air. Ben followed suit. "We will toast to…" Athena paused looking Ben in the eyes, "Ah yes boy, there you go that is good thinking, we will toast to Alexander and the wonderful life he lived. The caring soul that was he, the ever helpful soul that was he, the he that was he, and may he live on in triumph."

"What?" Ben said slamming his glass back down on the table spilling a little of it, "are you serious? We are going to toast to the gay boy sputtering lies about himself as he died for what he is; pathetic if you ask me."

"To die in vain I think not. To ask you I think not. Alex is a wonderful person…"

"Wait is Alex here?" Ben asked cutting through her words.

"I said nothing of the sort. Now pick up your glass and toast your brother's life as you should."

They picked up their glasses toasted, "to Alexander," and took a drink. To Ben's surprise the drink was like no other drink he had ever drank before. In fact he loved it. It was sweet and fruity, yet not too sweet that it tasted like pure sugar. Smooth, thick and creamy, but still completely liquid. The after taste was of cinnamon with a hint of mint. The coldness of the drink was the perfect temperature, but with the tiniest burp he could taste hot chocolate.

"Is the food here this crazy? Not that it's not good because it's very good, just weird."

"You will have to try for yourself another time. It is getting late. You will be needing your sleep, long day ahead of you tomorrow. You can finish your drink then I will tell you where you will be sleeping."

Ben looked around the room at all the empty tables and remembered there being loud chatter taking over the peaceful music.

"Where are all the people? I know I heard people talking when we came in," Ben said not touching his drink but looking from table to table hoping to see one person.

"They are all sitting here. Each table filled and slowly becoming empty as the hours wear on. If you do not finish your drink soon to get some sleep, you will be very tired tomorrow."

"What do you mean, they are all sitting here?" To please her he took a drink. She did not respond.

The cold, the sweetness, the tastes, the chocolate, and the warmth of the drink made Ben smile like a little boy. "Wait, what do you mean you'll tell me where to go to sleep? You're not going to show me? I walked forever before I found this place."

"In time, you will see everything. As for right now, the only thing you can see is what your mind wants you to see. You will understand as time goes by. If you do not begin to see, you will never wake up."

"Uhh…"

She stopped him before he could speak, "Drink your drink and stop asking questions. That is enough questions for the night."

Ben did not want to upset Athena and drank his drink. He couldn't stop looking at the empty tables; trying to see anyone or anything. He'd look at the door in the distance, but saw nothing. There wasn't even anyone at the bar, it was empty. Marygolde didn't seem to be there either. It seemed they were the only two in the place.

"Good now that you are done you can sleep. I am sure the drink will help your restless mind from wondering." She stood up and started walking toward the bar. Ben followed her. She stopped as a man stood up from nowhere in front of her.

"Well good evening Athena!" said a man wearing all black with black hair and black eyes. His skin was pale and older looking than Athena's, about forty. Although, Ben already knew that looks meant nothing here seeing as though Athena was over three thousand years old. "And who do you have here? The boy looks familiar."

"Good evening Wes. The boy is none of your concern. He is here and he is here under my protection. You have done enough damage to the poor boy's family."

"I have done no such thing with his family… yet!"

"What? Excuse me! What the hell are you two talking about? My family. Athena, tell me what is going on here?" exclaimed Ben.

"Look here Wes, you will tend to your matters and I will tend to mine," Athena said carefully and calmly so as to not to raise her voice while ignoring Ben's request.

"The boy and his family, mainly his father, are my matters if you remember correctly my dear Athena. They are my matters."

"They were your matters. You will stop raising questions for the boy. He is not ready for these answers. You are making it more difficult for myself and for the boy."

"Hello, I'm still standing here! Can someone please tell me what the hell is going on? Please!"

"I'll tell your father you said hello then," Wes said lowering his head, raising his eyebrows while giving Ben a very devilish smirk.

"My father? What do you mean?"

"Damn it Wes. Goodbye!" Athena raised her arm with the robe's sleeve dangling to the floor blocking Ben's view of Wes. "Goodbye Wes." Her voice slightly raised on this final goodbye. As she lowered her arm the man had disappeared back into the nothingness in which he had appeared. Although Ben could still hear the man talking, he could neither see nor understand what the man was saying.

"Athena!" Ben had yelled at her while he grabbed the dangling material from her arm, slightly pulling her backward. Athena paused, then turned on the spot. Her face twisted with anger. Ben did not know what to say. He realized he had crossed the line with her and now regretted pulling on her arm.

"I'm so sorry. I did not mean to…"

"Benjamin, I have not the time to mess with childish games of Wes Plag and I have not the time to be bothered with the foolish question that I am not going to answer for you at this very moment. You will take yourself to bed and you will bother me no more this evening. Is that understood?"

Ben could not speak. She had not raised her voice with him; it had remained the same charming voice in which she had spoken to him all night. Yet the words sliced through him, each word paralyzing him.

"Is that understood?" she repeated. Her facial expressions and tone remained peaceful.

Ben finally found the words in which to speak, but as he spoke them they did not sound familiar to him as if someone else was speaking. "But excuse me m-maam, but where am I to sleep this evening?"

"Yes, I guess you should know that now, should you not. Go down this corridor and up the tiny steps at the back. Room number thirteen shall be yours."

"Thirteen, you're friggen kidding me aren't you? This time Ben's voice sounded closer to that of his own.

With a great sigh Athena replied, "In the morning Benjamin, you can come down and order your own breakfast. I will meet you at my table."

"Your table? There are hundreds of tables in here. How am I going to know your table?" Ben squinted and scanned the deserted room that he knew wasn't really deserted.

"It is the same one in which we just sat. It will be in the same spot tomorrow. It is where we just came from. It will not be hard for you, Benjamin. I do believe you to be the boy with a bit of wit in you," she said with a slight smile turning from him. And then she just disappeared. Ben blinked half a dozen times and then rubbed his eyes. He could not believe she just vanished.

He was tempted to run back to where the man had appeared to search for him, ask him about his father, but he did not. He knew for some odd reason that Athena would know and had she, she would not be happy with him. He turned and walked toward the hallway in which he thought led to the restrooms. Shockingly enough, there were two restrooms in the hallway. He paused and looked at the doors. There was nothing labeling them as 'men' and 'women', there were no words, no colors and no pictures of the genders. There was in its place a picture of a toilet. There was nothing distinguishing them as to who was to use what bathroom. After looking at the doors puzzled for several moments, he pushed one of the doors open and entered.

The room was much larger than it had appeared on the outside, but it did not shock him. There were several stalls and no urinals. Ben figured he had walked into the wrong one and quickly walked out and into the other room. However, when he walked into the second, the room looked identical to the room he had previously stood in.

He was becoming extremely tired that at this point that he did not care if he was in the wrong room. He entered one of the stalls. At the sink he heard two people talking. The sink next to his came on and then went off. "Hello, is anyone there?" enquired Ben. There was no response. He quickly dried his hands and left.

Ben climbed the stairs that seemed to

get narrower and narrower as he climbed. At the top he slowly walked down the hall looking at the door numbers. One hundred and twenty one was the first door on his right, two the one to his left, sixty-nine the next on the right and across from it 3000. The room numbers continued to be in random order. He had given up trying to figure out how far down the hall he would have to walk to reach number thirteen. Room thirteen ended up being the thirteenth room on the left side of the hallway.

Not knowing what to expect, Ben pushed the door open. It was quit small. There was barely enough room for the tiny bed. There was a lamp hanging above the bed. When Ben looked up he saw exactly what he thought he would see; the ominous black abyss above him. When he walked in and shut the door he noticed the tiny door that led to what he thought would be a bathroom. It was just a small stand-in shower. There was nowhere to go to the bathroom. For that he knew he would have to go back downstairs.

He lay in the bed extremely comfortable. Looking up into the nothingness above him he felt a strong chill come over him. The darkness freaked him out. He could hear noises from the hallway or coming from out of the darkness or even from the bar below, he could not tell, but each time he closed his eyes the noises were completely silenced. Finally, the tiredness took over his mind and he fell asleep.

Ben heard his brother's voice yelling for him, pleading for his help. Ben ran searching for him, he ran out into the woods. Around each tree he saw a tiny glimpse of Alex and raced onward. He had reached a lake. Looking over he could see Alex kneeling on the water's edge. "Alex, I'm here. I'm coming." As Ben tried to move, he found he couldn't. His feet had sunk into the ground. The ground slowly moved around his shins working it's way to his knees.

"Alex, look out behind you," Ben screamed as a creature walked up from behind. Alex did not hear Ben, nor did he hear the creature walking up behind him. The beast paused behind Alex to look at the slowly sinking Ben, who had now reached over his waist, and then he released an ear-piercing scream. The more Ben struggled, the faster the ground ate him. When the ground had engulfed his body to his neck, the beast raised his long sharp nails and brought them swiftly across Alex's neck. His headless body stood on its knees. Ben screamed as the ground swallowed the rest of him.

Ben jerked awake; sitting up straight he realized he was still in his tiny bed at Marygolde's. Heavily panting, grabbing his chest he took a sigh of relief tilted his head back and opened his eyes. Above him he saw an outlined figure in the nothingness. It started to fall fast, getting closer and closer to him. It was the creature from his dream. As the creature's claws sank into his sides, Ben awoke again finding that he had still been dreaming.

He pulled his legs over the edge of the bed as he sat up. He placed his elbows on his

knees and his head in his hands. The sweat
was glistening on his skin. After a few
moments he laid back down. Looking up he
noticed the darkness moving slowly down the
walls. Slowly it fell over the light and then
it crept over him. It eventually hugged him;
it felt like a warm blanket. Shockingly, he
finally felt safe inside the nothingness. The
next time he would awake it would be morning.

Chapter 8: *True Beginnings*

Ben awoke feeling extremely refreshed. To his surprise, there was a fresh set of clothes laid out for him on the tiny nightstand beside the bed. He showered, changed and headed to the restrooms downstairs. As he walked into what he had expected to be the large tearoom, he noticed that it had considerably shrunk. Instead of there being hundreds of tables, there were merely a few dozen.

Sitting down at the bar he noticed that there was a large, burly man standing behind the counter. He looked around at the empty room, but he didn't see Marygolde anywhere. As the man turned and started to approach him, he thought the guy looked somewhat familiar. The guy was very tall and husky with a short beard and mustache and a kind of shaggy brown hair. He was wearing a ratted apron over his dark clothes.

"What can I getcha?" said the barkeep

with a very deep voice.

"I'm supposed to talk to Marygolde. Is she around?"

"Well I be Marygolde boy. Now what can I getcha?"

Ben's eyes grew and as he stared at the burly man before him, he noticed the resemblance in the face, especially the eyes.

"Um… Um… I… I guess I'll… um… have the breakfast special and coffee if that's possible."

"For you dear, of course it's possible," said Marygolde.

Ben just looked at the barkeeper oddly as the words coming out of his mouth sounded like the words of Marygolde, but not in her voice or her stature. The barkeeper disappeared into the back for several minutes and returned with a plate and a cup of coffee.

"Here you go boy. Now take this straight to Athena's table and don't stop for anything. She will be with you shortly."

Ben took the plate of eggs and sausage and his cup of coffee and headed toward where Athena's table had sat the night before. He surprisingly, found the table quickly and sat down. The food was delicious, probably the best breakfast he had ever had. About half way through his breakfast, Athena appeared and sat down with almost no noise.

"Good morning, Benjamin," Athena said in her typical pleasant voice.

"Good morning, Athena," he replied wiping his mouth clean of egg yolks.

"How was your sleep last night? Well I

suppose?"

"I had this bizarre dream, but after that it was the best night's sleep I've had in a long time."

"Great! Now as soon as you finish your food we will be off. There is a long day ahead of us today."

"What are we doing? Am I going to get to see more of what's outside of this place?"

"If, and only if, your mind will allow you. And right now I say no, but you will see what I want you to see."

"What do you mean? What are we doing today?"

"In order to open your mind and for you to understand your life, we must first start at the beginning."

"The beginning?"

"Eat now and I will show you later."

After that statement, Ben did not say another word. He ate his breakfast as fast as he could with a bit of excitement, as he was looking forward to whatever journey Athena had planned for him. After he finished, Athena led the way outside into the fog that Ben could remember from the previous night.

"Athena, is it always dark and foggy here?"

"My dear boy for it is your mind that is clouded. You are still inside Marygolde's. Ah ah ah…" she lifted her finger and waved it before him, "before you speak. I told you that your mind would see what it wants to see. You cannot see what is beyond that door because you are not ready to see it. Therefore, you will only see fog and will remain inside Marygolde's."

"This whole place is crazy and it's starting to irritate me."

"And that Benjamin is why you will never see beyond those doors. Your mind is closed and your thoughts narrow."

"Wait, so you are telling me I'm shallow?"

"I am telling you that you do not think beyond what you already know or feel. You do not take into consideration others beliefs. That is unless they happen to believe in what you believe. Now shall we get started?"

Ben nodded his head yes. He saw no point in arguing with her at this time. Athena reached out her hand and Ben took hold of it. She walked several steps and said, "Close your eyes Benjamin, this may sting." He did as she had asked and briefly he felt a thousand needles piercing his body, though he didn't make a sound.

"There you go Benjamin; you can open your eyes now."

Ben felt for the ground with his toes, but they just dangled there. Slowly he opened his eyes and saw nothing but darkness. He went to talk and realized he could not breathe; he began grasping for his throat. Finally, he was able to squeeze out a tiny whisper, "Athena, where are you?"

Athena took his hands down from around his throat.

"Benjamin. Calm down. Relax. You are fine."

As soon as he felt her hands he stopped panicking and realized that he was indeed fine. Opening his eyes as wide as he could open them he still could not see anything but the darkness around him, nor could he feel ground beneath him. He felt suspended in the air as if he were levitating. After he got used to it for several moments, he began to enjoy it.

"Athena, am I supposed to be seeing anything?" he asked as he let go of her hand as he felt for anything in front of him or at his sides.

Athena took his hand back into hers and pointed it out in front of them.

"There you will see it in a few seconds. Ah, there you go."

Ben looked as hard as he could, but he couldn't see anything in the darkness. Athena knew from his long hesitation and the tightened grip of her hand that he did not see what she was pointing out to him.

"Benjamin, clear your mind and concentrate. Look in front of you and feel toward where my hand is pointed, there will be a light. It is slowly growing larger and larger."

"That tiny little pin hole of light?"

"That would be the light I am referring."

Ben watched the tiny light grow and grow. When the light finally got to the size of a quarter he had to ask Athena what it was and where they were.

"You are in nothingness. What you are experiencing is the first light of what you will come to know as the universe. That light, that tiny light, is the first sun. It will be the governing sun of the first civilization. A civilization that you will get to see once it forms right below your feet. Before you say a word, I will explain as needed. For the rest of today you will get to experience life in a whole new way. Just relax and observe."

The light grew until it had reached basketball size and stopped. Ben could finally see Athena floating beside him. All he could see around him was the vast dark nothingness; it reminded him of the nothingness that swallowed him up before sleeping. Suddenly he, like on the previous night, felt warm and comfortable. He felt his feet slowly being lifted up from dangling into a normal stance.

The ground below him started to form into dirt and then vegetation. Flashes of light crisscrossed back and forth around his knees and then across his face. He could barely make out the images, but every now and again he thought he saw animals and people. Buildings sprung to life before him with bridges quickly forming to connect them to one another. As the buildings went up, the vegetation disappeared.

With a slight hesitation and soft tone Ben asked Athena, "I'm sorry, but might I ask a stupid question? How fast is time moving before us?"

"Benjamin it is a wise question that you ask of me. The answer, for as fast as time seems to be moving, merely five years have gone by since you saw that tiny pin-hole of light."

"What? You have to be kidding me. Look at this place. It's far more advanced then anything on Earth." Ben paused briefly to take another look around the harshness of darkened metal. "Which means we aren't looking at Earth, are we?"

"Very good Benjamin, very good. I think Guarroutk will be very proud of you."

"For noticing that this couldn't be Earth?" Ben interrupted before she could continue speaking.

"No, for allowing your mind to be open to the possibility that this is not Earth."

"Any plain moron could tell you this wasn't Earth."

"Yes, but you believe it. There is a difference between realization, an understanding and a belief."

"Well, I've always wondered if there were other beings out there or here or whatever, anyway, that we humans couldn't be the only ones. That would somewhat be selfish now wouldn't it?"

"Very good, Benjamin."

Ben did not respond to her, but instead stopped to notice that the flashes of light had finally started to slow down. There were buildings made of all metal and glass all around him. No longer were there trees or grass, in fact there were no signs of any living plant. The flashes of light slowed as well and Ben could see that they were people, ugly beings with darkened skin and wearing what appeared to be metal clothing. The flashes around his knees had disappeared all together.

"Athena, what's going on?"

"Ah, we are catching up to real time."

"Real time?"

"It has been over a million years Benjamin. Benjamin?"

"Yes?"

"You can close your mouth now!" Ben's mouth had dropped and his eyes grew to the size of silver dollars at the thought of the civilization that old and still existing.

"Sorry."

"It is OK, Benjamin. Time rushed a little faster once the buildings were set into motion. Nothing has changed since."

"Are you kidding? How is that possible?"

"Well see Benjamin..." Athena's words were cut short by a tall slender creature grabbing her by the arm and turning her toward him.

"What the hell do you think you are doing here? Thing!" the man snarled into Athena's face, "and what business do you have bringing that boy here?"

"He has lessons to learn..."

"I care not of the boy's needs. I only care for why you, *thing, have come to bother us." The creature's* eyes glared red into Athena's never breaking eye contact.

"The boy is none of your concern and neither am I. I will be here for a short time only and then we will be leaving," Athena replied in her wisping voice so as to avoid showing her temper.

"The boy is welcome here. It is you, *thing,* that's not welcome here. None of your kind are welcome here. None of you have been welcome here since the beginning. Your kind disgusts everything. The boy is one of us and has been brought here against his wishes, so like I said, he is welcome, but you need to be leaving. NOW!"

"I'm sorry, but can I ask a question here?" Ben interjected causing both Athena and the creature to break eye contact and stare directly into his. The feeling made Ben quiver. A large lump in his throat began to strangle his vocal cords.

"I'm waiting boy. Please do speak, but I caution you, do not defend this thing you are traveling with. They cannot be trusted," the creature responded after several seconds of awkward silence.

"Well, you told me not to defend her…"

"But? Choose your words wisely, boy."

"Why does everyone insist on calling me boy?" Ben's voice deepened, he could feel his face turn red and his ears began to burn. Before either of them could answer he continued, "Anyway, that's not really the point, so why do you have such a grudge against her?"

"She, you call IT a she? This *thing*, which you're with, is not a creature to be worthy of being called a she. It is nothing, a figment of an imagination that has created it. Since you are with it, I will go as far to guess from your home planet it was imagined. Best that be where you stay, but since you are here, again I say; you are welcome. It is not," he snarled into Athena's face with such distaste.

Ben looked from the creature to Athena and then back at the creature before he responded. As he went to speak, Athena cut him off.

"I understand not why you have such a cruel hatred for me. I have done nothing to you."

"You lying, crazy fool. You are a part of what the boy would call him. I know you are, I can feel him pulsating through your ghostly veins. You and he both disgust me."

"I know only of the creator of your planet and of this Universe, but I know not why you are angry with me."

"Stupid bitch, do not play games with me. I will not ask you again, before I force you into the nothingness in which you were created. And thing, when that happens, you will cease to walk forever."

For the first time Ben saw fear and anger in Athena's eyes. She drew in a deep breath and turned her whole body toward him.

"I will return in one hour to get you. Learn what you can from this being. Later this evening, we will discuss it," and with that Athena turned back to the creature, "take care of him please, for now you are his guardian within this realm and there will be great consequences if he is harmed here. However, I think you already know this."

Before the creature could answer her, she turned and like sand in the wind she blew away down to nothing.

"Disgusting things they are. Do you see what I mean by they are nothing? She just blew away," said the creature cringing as he watched the last bit of her departing them. "And I thought neither of you were of my concern, typical. Hungry?"

"Uh… I guess so?"

"You only guess?"

"Yeah, a little hungry."

"Good I'm starving, follow me."

The creature walked down several blocks before stopping to enter into a tiny building, what appeared to be café. Along the walk Ben noticed that there were no signs of grass, trees, or any living creature besides the alien beings. Inside the café, it looked a lot like an Earth café, there were beings sitting around having conversations. Ben noticed that there were no plates of food, no utensils, no napkins, not even placemats. There were just metal shaped glasses sitting on the metal tables. They took a seat in a booth.

"So, you're Benjamin, I'm…" the creature stopped for a second and stared at him, "let me just give an Earthling's name to call me by, call me Brandon."

"OK, well nice to meet you Brandon. What kind of food do they have here? I only see these tin cups."

"Food, my people haven't eaten food for several millennia now."

"What? How do you stay nourished? Grow? Evolve?"

With a hearty laugh Brandon responded, "We have had that down to the science long, long before your puny planet was even thought about."

"So, what does that mean exactly?"

"Here I'll show you,, Brandon said as he turned to a woman standing behind the counter, "bring us four capsules and two waters please."

"What? Capsules? You mean like pills?"

As Brandon went to answer him the woman from the counter placed two cases down on the table. One in front of Brandon and one in front of Ben, along with the two tin cups of water.

"Odd boy you are, why is he here anyway?" asked the woman.

"He was left here by one of those *things,* and since I spotted them I'm stuck being his watcher."

"Glad it wasn't me and come to think of it, I've been lucky. In my 200 years I've never had to watch one before. What's it like?"

"This is my first time and all I've been able to do is ask him his name."

"You both do realize I'm sitting right here, right?" Benjamin interjected feeling as though he was being talked to like a pet animal.

"Sorry boy, I mean Ben," Brandon responded and dismissed the waitress. Then he over heard her talking to another table, *"Do you see those clothes he's wearing, how odd."*

"Why are my clothes odd? You don't think it's odd to wear metal for clothing?"

Again Brandon laughed as if the words coming from Ben's mouth were spoken by a child. Ben was waiting for Brandon to pinch his cheeks and tell him how cute he was just like grandma used to do.

"Why are you laughing at me?"

"Not laughing at you, but we do not have

material like what you are wearing here on our planet. We only have the highest engineered materials," he held out his arm toward Ben, "here now feel. I am sure you will find it like no other metal you have ever felt before."

Ben reached out for the sleeve. The sleeve was softer than the cotton shirt that he was wearing. The shiny luminescent metal wasn't hard, which explained why there wasn't a clanking noise coming from everyone as they walked.

"How is that possible?"

"We are far more advanced than any other in this universe."

"How do you know that?"

"My dear Ben, we have seen everything that is out there. There is nothing out there to our fancying. It's all rubbish. This life here is the best and isn't smothered in disgusting beings like that *thing* you had with you."

"I don't get it?"

"I don't think you are meant to. The things here are too advanced for you to understand. Now, take the capsules, most people swallow the purple one and then the green one."

"Is it sort of like eating the main dish and then a desert?"

"Something like that. The green ones have more of a sweetened, I think that's what your people call it, taste to them."

Ben took the first pill and swallowed it with some water. To his surprise it tasted like nothing. He then picked up the second pill and went to put it in his mouth.

"I wouldn't do that just yet if I were you," Brandon said with a tiny grin on his face. "You haven't given the first one enough time to expand. If you take that one now, you'll only give yourself a stomach ache."

Ben set the pill back down into the tin that it was brought to him in. He took a deep breath and looked around at the tables. There was a younger looking couple holding each other's hands across the table and feeding each other their pills. And then on to an older couple that just sat and stared into one another's eyes in utter silence, holding their tins of water in front of them. And then to several tables with lonely souls sitting there glancing over at him and Brandon, as he caught their eye watching they would quickly look away.

"If you know of my people and as you say all the peoples of the universe, why are these people staring at me?"

"Because, and don't be foolish Ben, they've never seen one of your kind here before. There have been stories and we *know* of you, that doesn't mean we get one of you here everyday, now does it? You believe there were, what do you call them? Cavemen, yeah that's it cavemen, but because you don't see them everyday doesn't mean they don't exist right?"

"Well, they don't, but I guess you're right!"

"They don't do they? That *thing* has more to show you than I thought," and then in a hushed voice almost talking to himself

Brandon uttered, "pathetic excuses for beings they are."

"What did you just say?"

"Nothing, I said nothing, that *thing* will just have to show you. I mustn't break the laws of this whole stupid charade."

"I understand you don't like '*the thing*', but *she* does have a name and it's Athena."

"Very well, since it bothers you so much to call a disgusting foul thing by its name, I will do the same with great disgust though," said Brandon squishing whatever nose he had on his face up and pushing his tongue in and out of his mouth as though he had just tasted sourness for the first time.

"Fine, I don't really care, just as long as you stop calling her *thing*. What is it about, *Athena* that disgusts you so much?"

"They think they are superior beings over us. They govern here no more. We have sought ways of destroying them as they have sought out ways of destroying us, but it seems victory is never won on either side. Other than for them, we have never fought a day in our history. Our people are highly intelligent beings. We have never been warriors. I think that is why we have decided to stay on our planet and not bother others. If we do not bother them, then they will not seek us out. Other planetoidians have developed ways of getting off of their planets and have sought out other beings."

"We do that on Earth."

"I know you do, but Earth will not succeed if they cannot control their own population first. The answers they seek are not in space. They are within each person. No other space voyaging being is going to accept Earthlings until they can have trust over themselves."

"So, how did you guys manage to never have a war?"

"We are a peaceful race. We came into existence knowing everything we needed to know. We flourished from there. Ever since then, our people have lived in harmony with one another and avoided others in space. We have even developed a device that will allow us to disguise our planet as nothing more than a giant planet of smoldering rock uninhabitable by any such creature."

"Wait, how do you know you were brought into existence knowing everything you needed to know?"

"I think that be best answered by your Athena," a foul look came over his face as he said her name. "She would know best of all. After all she is a fragment of the creator."

"The creator? You mean like God?"

"To you it's God, to others its Athena, to other beings it's their form of this 'God' of yours. Now should be a good time to take your next pill."

Ben could see the disgust in Brandon's face as he said each name.

He picked up the pill and swallowed it, again no taste. Although, this time he felt the pill traveling down his throat and hitting his stomach, it was like an explosion.

"Ugh... what was that?" Ben asked as he

gripped toward his stomach.

Brandon laughed and then said, "Ben my dear boy, that is the best meal you will probably ever have. The opening of the two capsules has filled your stomach with whichever nutrients your body needs and then waste will be sweated out through your tiny pores."

"So, you don't go to the bathroom?"

"Of course we go to the bathroom, but it's only to flush out the water. With the type of food, or capsules, that we have here there is no need to waste our time with, uh, what do you call it?"

"Number two, pooping, shitting, dumping."

"Yes, that's it, any of those will suffice."

"Really, no one does?"

"Only if we attempt to eat actual food, which is rare and usually smuggled in from other planets. We have nothing organic here everything is synthesized or created. We control everything here."

"Really, do you have animals here? You know like cats, dogs, snakes, whatever?"

Laughing again Brandon responded, "You amuse me Ben. Yes, we have pets. They eat as we eat and they live longer as do we and we never have to clean up after them. It's pretty simple, cleaner and healthier. We have no diseases. Anything the creator has thrown at us we have fought back and won against it. The only enemy we have ever known was the creator. It is odd that we were created, given all this knowledge and then abandoned only to have the same creator try to eliminate us. It is heartbreaking."

"I'm sorry; I have no idea what to say."

Before Brandon could answer, the door to the café had opened and there stood an Earthling woman dressed in the same metal garment that Brandon was wearing. Everyone in the entire place stopped and looked at her. She walked over to their table and it was only when she was standing right before them that Ben realized it was Athena.

"Oh dreadful *thing,* you are back, already?"

"Brandon!" snapped Ben.

"Sorry, force of habit, oh dreadful Athena, is it that time already? The boy and I were having so much fun together. A real keeper you have here."

"Thank you and yes that will be all. You have told him more than he needs to know."

"But I thought that is what I was here to do."

"You have done your job well. You are greatly appreciated. Thank you for your help."

Athena took Ben's arm and before he could say goodbye to Brandon he realized he was no longer in the café, but instead standing in front of Marygolde's. This time instead of fog, Ben could see a street with grass lining it. There was a stone cobble footstone path leading to Marygolde's. The tearoom still looked exactly the same. Ben wished he could have stayed longer, but he oddly felt happy about seeing Marygolde's. It was like coming home after a long vacation.

All he wanted to do was crawl up into his bed and sleep.

Chapter 9: The Many Faces of Marygolde

Ben noticed how different things looked as he followed Athena into Marygolde's. Once inside, Ben started to feel dizzy. Everywhere he glanced, the objects appeared fuzzy. The hundreds of tables around him were filled with images of people sitting at them. It was as though he was watching a snowy television channel blurring in and out of focus. He felt drunk. He clasped his hand onto Athena's shoulder for support and instantly he felt the cold metal materializing back into her pale, putty-green robes. She braced him as they walked and helped him into his seat.

Pulling his hands around his head and shaking, he opened his eyes. It felt like walls had been pulled up all around them. He could not see beyond the light that lit her table.

Water started to drip across his arm. He realized that Marygolde had just brought them drinks and the cup was sweating. He took the glass from her and without asking what it was took a drink. There was nothing special about this drink. It tasted like ice cold Iced Tea, however it didn't matter, as it was refreshing.

Athena sat across from him, placed her elbows on the table and then rested her chin onto her hands. It was the most *human* she had ever looked. In fact, she looked as giddy as schoolgirl excited to be talking to the boy she liked.

"What are you all smiles for?" Ben asked her after noticing her staring at him.

"You saw it, you actually saw it."

"Saw what? Why are you acting weird?"

"You saw through the fog outside."

"Yes, I saw some things. So you're all giddy over me not seeing fog? What do you see out there anyway?"

"Well, I never see the fog for starters. I see Guarroutk as it truly looks."

"Then how do you know if I see the fog or not?"

"Benjamin, I know. If I did not know you, I would not be here talking to you."

"All right, are we going to discuss that place I was in?"

"Actually, no we are not going to discuss anything at this point. What you are going to do is go upstairs and get some sleep. A long day ahead lies before you."

"You are not being serious?"

Athena did not respond to him, she stood and floated out of site. Ben finished his drink and stood up. As soon as he walked out from the table's light the blurry figures reappeared. There were not as many this time, although they were still there. The noise sounded more like whispers instead of static; he still could not make out their conversations and it still made him a little dizzy.

Upstairs he sat in his tiny bed staring into the darkness above his bed wondering what dreams would come to him this evening. He leaned his head back against the wall, pulled his feet up onto the bed and closed his eyes. A red hand extended down from the darkness wrapping its fingers around Ben's neck. Throwing his hands against the one crushing his larynx, Ben opened his eyes. Straining into the darkness he could only see two beady, red eyes staring back him. The hand started to slowly pull Ben up the wall toward the darkness.

His head entered the darkness, his eyes still fixed on the eyes staring at him. He was unable to scream. He could feel his feet dragging across the bed. Once his feet left the bed he could feel the wall, he began kicking at it hoping someone would come to his rescue. He knew the darkness had swallowed him when the last bit of warmth from the room turned cold.

The smooth walls of the room were gone. As he was being pulled up the wall in the darkness with the rough walls tugging at his shirt, he knew he was no longer at Marygolde's. Above him came a tiny light growing larger as the light below him disintegrated. The head of the creature with the red eyes pulling him up the wall by the throat remained darkened by what Ben could now make out was a hood.

"That is far enough. Let the boy go," thundered a voice from somewhere above. The hand released from around Ben's throat. He started falling downward.

"Brandon?" screamed Ben.

He heard no response as he fell further. Scratching at the rooted dirt wall on his way down, he could feel his nails catching and ripping from his flesh along the way. Eventually he felt thick warm liquid covering his hands, which he expected could only be blood. Instead of grabbing for anything to slow his fall, he pushed off the wall as hard as he could. He started falling backward faster and now head first. The growing light from below disappeared under his eyelids. He fell as light as a feather; he fell peacefully into the bed just as though he had lain down to sleep.

Eyes springing open when his head hit the pillow, he looked down at his fingers, there was no blood, no pain, but there was dirt under his nails and down his fingers. Taking a deep breath in and exhaling heavily, he closed his eyes and opened them looking into the darkness. It began to move toward him as it had done the night before. This time Ben welcomed the darkness as it wrapped him into a warm cocoon.

An alarm went off waking him up. He rolled out of bed, showered, dressed and headed downstairs. Sitting at the bar he saw a shorter woman with blond hair and blue eyes. A very delicate fair-skinned woman wearing beautiful pink silk robes.

"Good morning Marygolde how are you?" Ben asked the woman.

"Well good morning dear. And what will you be having this morning? Did you sleep well?"

"You seem to always know what's best, so, please be my guest at choosing what to have. Sleeping, it's funny you ask about that. I wake up completely rejuvenated, but I have a crazy dream and then imagine that the darkness of the ceiling is… well… eating me."

"Ah, terrible beasts that lay in your mind they do. Your time here will be spent most wisely by listening and observing everything the beautiful Athena has to tell you. Those nasty dreams my son, as you learn to understand, will dissolve and inhibit your mind no longer. One breakfast coming up."

"Marygolde…" he said, she stopped and turned back to him.

"Yes, my son?" she answered noticing his sudden loss of words, "was there something you wanted to ask of me?"

"No, no, I guess there isn't really. It can wait till you're done. I don't want to keep you."

She nodded her head and turned swiftly into the kitchen. After several minutes, she returned with several plates in her hands setting them down on the counter. As she placed each plate on the counter it levitated off the bar and disappeared into thin air. The last plate she sat down was in front of Ben.

"There you go son. I'm sure you'll enjoy

it."

He did not take his eye off the bar; he didn't even look at what she had brought him, just picked up his fork and blindly stuck it into the plate. Taking her fingers and placing them on his chin pulling it toward her, she looked him in the eye.

"My son is there something wrong with you this morning? You look more alive, awake and alert than I have seen you since you've been here, but yet you are distant."

"It's just this place! It, it, it's just weird. And no-one seems to be answering the craziest questions."

"What kind of questions would you like to have answered?"

"Well, like this place for starters. There are tables everywhere; I can hear talking, but the place looks empty. Although sometimes, especially last night and now, I can see something at those tables. And now you just set plates down on the bar and they magically disappeared. What is that all about?"

"There are people everywhere in here. There are people who picked up those plates. The more you open your mind, the more you will see. Are you understanding that much?" Ben nodded and she continued, "After all, the fog cleared for you somewhat yesterday, did it not?"

"There, that is another question. How do you know that?"

"This is my domain and I know where everyone is inside it; where they are sitting, what time period they are in, who can see the fog and who can see everything. I know when you are having problems sleeping. For I am the one who sent the blackness down to protect you."

"Wait, you? So do you know my dreams as well?" Ben paused shocked at what he had just heard and asked, "Wait, did you just say time periods?"

Marygolde laughed and began to wipe down the countertop. Ben started eating his food as he kept an eye on her. She then began to speak to thin air. Ben knew she had to be talking to someone else. She grabbed some bottles from the bar and a couple of glasses. As she made the drinks, Ben concentrated hard on trying to see the person or people standing at the bar.

Ben thought to himself, *All I have to do is open my mind. Believe in believing and understand. I'll be able to see everything as long as I keep an open mind to my surroundings.*

After concentrating on the spot for several seconds, which seemed to be minutes, a tiny flicker of light and an image of two men appeared before him. He glanced over to Marygolde and realized that her image had changed as well. Standing there instead of the fair-skinned woman was a heavier-set man standing in a plaid flannel shirt and greasy blue-jean overalls. He recognized the man as Walt Henderson the bartender from Doones Bar in Zion. One of the men standing beside him was familiar too.

"Dad? Dad is that you?"

The other figure looked over at Ben and

he realized it was the man from his first night in Guarroutk.

"Oh boy, you don't belong here. Marygolde snap him out of whatever he's doing. He cannot be here," said the man with a deep scratchy hiss to his voice.

When Ben looked toward Marygolde she was her fair-skinned self again. Then when he looked back toward the figure of his father, he was gone.

"What the hell was that all about Marygolde?"

"Well, Athena will be proud of you, but you really are coming along much faster than you should. You are not ready for some things. Tah tah, before you speak," she held a finger to his lips before he could speak. She continued in a low whisper, "I will answer several of your questions, but you mustn't let on that I told you. Is that clear?" Ben nodded his head and she proceeded, "You have not had a single dream in the last two evening…"

"What? What do you mean, I haven't been dreaming?" Ben interrupted her.

"Shhh… and please do not interrupt me again. They are the demons of your mind. They are the things that are keeping you tied to this world. When you have beaten your inner demons Benjamin, you will wake up from this place."

"So, I'm dreaming?"

"The easy answer is yes, but the real answer is no. You are in a real place, but your physical body is in a coma back on Earth. *Tsk, tsk,* do not interrupt me. That was your father sitting there, but he was not here. He was on Earth at a bar in a town that you know well. I'm sure you noticed Mr. Henderson, the bartender from that bar, and I shared a body for several moments so that Wes could report anything he needed to report back here to me. You were almost seen by your father and that would have been dangerous."

"But my father is dead!"

"And that brings me back to me knowing what time period people are in. Wes is with your father right now. It is the night before the accident."

"But then I could warn him?"

"Your father made his own decisions. Warning him would have proved useless. He was given the ultimatum, he chose his path. The unfortunate factor is your mother. She is the innocent one here."

"Wait, so you know how all this comes about and you don't… didn't stop it? It was my mother's fault they are dead. She is the one who was accepting of Alex and she caused my father's death for her stupidity."

"Ah, and the mind closes again. It was not your mother's fault, as I just said; it was she that was the innocent bystander in this mess. It was your father who had to choose and it was your father who broke a deadly sin. Wes was doing his job."

"Wes killed my father?"

"No, Wes is not an evil man, but he is not exactly a good man either. As I said, he was doing his job. It is his job to clean up the life-threatening acts of people who have drowned themselves into any of the seven deadly sins."

"What was it that my father did to deserve death?"

"Benjamin that I cannot tell you. That is between Wes and your father."

"And so you can just spy in on him through Walt whenever you want."

"Diners, bars and places like that are where people tend to congregate or socialize. It's a great place for people to get to know one another. Look around you Benjamin. Each of these tables is somewhere in the universe, filled with people talking to someone guiding them on their paths."

"Are you saying that you guys are angels?"

"I would not go that far. Although, some of them, *yes.*"

"They are grounded to Guarroutk through your Tearoom and that is why it appears different all the time? Is that why you look different all the time as well?"

"There you go Benjamin. The mind is opening again. You have listened to what I have said and you have learned from it. You have not denied what I have told you."

"Yes, but this place may or may not be real and if it's just a dream; then by all means of course it could be real, but if it is real, I mean real, real, then I don't know if I would or could believe."

Marygolde sighed and hung her head down.

"You truly are a foolish boy, sometimes. For every step forward you take two steps back. You should have been a politician you teeter-totter on things too much. Now, you know why you are here."

"I'm sorry, but listen to yourself. Some things can be seen by all and some things can only be seen by a select few and it all determines on whether or not you have an open mind to believe in things that aren't real. Next you'll be telling me that if I believe in leprechauns then they too exist right?"

"Well now that was a mouthful wasn't it? And Benjamin, my dear Benjamin leprechauns are only a myth."

"So is Athena. She is Greek Mythology, but yet she exists."

"Ah boy, see that is the point. What is the difference between Greek Mythology and Christianity?"

"One's real and one's MYTH just for clarification."

"For clarification that is where you are wrong."

"Excuse me?"

"The Greeks, Romans, Egyptians and the Asians believed in a multiplicity of Gods and Goddesses, polytheist, to rule over their lives and to be worshiped for everything they needed. Unfortunately as cute as they are, leprechauns were never worshiped as gods."

"Yes, but it was mythology."

"To them it was a way of life. It was their religion. Many religions today still have multiple Gods."

"And those religions would be wrong."

"Are you so sure about that?"

"Yes, there is only one God and one God only."

"Did you not learn anything yesterday?"

Ben just looked at her as if she asked him the question in a foreign language.

"Do not look at me like that boy. Yes, I'm referring to you spending time with Brandon."

"How do you know his name? He said that wasn't even his real name."

"Do you not remember the girl he ordered the pills from?"

"That was you?"

"Yes, and I hope you realize the risks it took for me to share a body with someone there. They are a smart race and I almost got busted checking in on you."

"If it was such a risk, why did you do it?"

"To make sure you were safe from harms way. If you die in this realm, your body dies on Earth. You must protect your body here in order to return. Take in everything you learn. You will take the knowledge back with you. You will remember this place. So, with that, what did you learn yesterday?"

"Well, their civilization has been almost exactly the same since the beginning of their time. They need no real nourishment; they live on pills for crying out loud."

"Yes, but more efficient do you not think?"

"But what's the point in doing that if that's all you ever have in life?"

"Efficiency is the master goal in every race. What about the people?"

"They acted just as we do here. They still love one another, young or old. It was weird to see an older couple and a younger couple acting just like humans do on Earth."

"What does that tell you about civilization?"

"We all have the same basic needs?"

"No matter what your beliefs are?"

"I guess."

The two just stared at one another as Ben continued to eat. He didn't remember anything on the plate or even if he liked it. He figured if he didn't like it, he would have known. The thought of what he and Marygolde had just discussed swirled in his head. He remembered the words that Brandon had said, "_That thing is a part of him, a part of the creator._" It just played over and over in his head.

"Marygolde, can I ask you another question?"

"She is a part of the creator you know." She answered him before he could even ask the question.

"You know it's really creepy that you do that, but that's beside the point. What do you or Brandon, whatever, mean by that?"

"Benjamin I know almost everything and besides I just told you I was there with you at that diner. How do you think Athena knew to go back and get you early?"

"You told her?"

"Yes, and he was starting to tell you more than you needed to know. You need to learn things on your own and in time, you will. For even I have told you too much as it is. Athena will surely be pissed at me for talking so much."

"Really! Why?"

"There are far too many things for you to learn at this point Benjamin. I am not your guide and things will be explained to you when they need to be. I have overstepped my boundaries as it is. Your guide was chosen by you and what you needed."

"I chose Athena?"

"In essence you did. You are seeking knowledge. Athena is the *Goddess of Wisdom* and she will guide you toward the wisdom you seek. However, you still have to obtain the knowledge on your own. If you were seeking true love, then possibly the *Goddess of Love*, Venus, may have been your guide. If you were Beethoven you may have had Apollo as your guide."

"So, only the Greek Myths are guides?"

"No, you have a connection to the Greek Myths somehow. It could very well have been Shiva, Ra, Nüwa, Fu Xi, Loki, Gog, and so on. You could also have been left with others like Wes Plag if you indulged yourself in the deadly sins. Or you could be forsaken with others like Zipacna who are purely evil."

"Did you mention anything that was really in English?"

Marygolde let out a tiny laugh as she tried to keep her composure. "That my dear, funny boy may be why you are with Athena. You do know who she is right?"

"Sure as you said before, she is the Goddess of Wisdom the daughter of Zeus born from his head or thoughts."

"Very good anything else you know about her."

"She and Zeus share the Thunderbolt and

the Aegis…"

"And that would be?" Marygolde interrupted him.

"Her shield bearing the head of Medusa…" he stopped talking as the words came out of his mouth, his jaw dropped frozen as if he had seen into the eyes of the reptilian woman before him.

"And what else? You are doing great."

Ben spoke slowly in a much softer voice, "represented by an owl and olive branch. She was also a virgin Goddess, if I remember correctly."

"What is wrong my dear?"

"My brother's funeral. He, he was holding a coin and an olive branch. Are you saying Athena was there?"

"My boy you are piecing things together very well. You keep remembering everything you can about your dearest Athena and maybe then you'll be able to put together lots of other things about this place as well."

"But if she was there in the real world then is it possible that this place is real as well?"

Marygolde's eyes grew large as she began to respond, but did not continue. Before he could ask her why she wasn't speaking, he knew. Athena had clasped her hand down on his shoulders and glared angrily at Marygolde.

"What have you told the boy?"

"Nothing that he wouldn't have figured out on his own."

"Marygolde you should know better. Of all people, your son would be ashamed that you interfered. It was not your place to tell him anything."

"Athena my dear, what is done is done. It has not hurt your journey in anyway. If anything, it has helped advance your work.

"Again guys I'm sitting right here. I can hear every word you're saying. Not deaf, dumb, nor blind," Ben said very irritated.

"You are right Benjamin. Now grab your things we will be late for today's travel. Let us be gone now."

Chapter 10: Cro-Magnon

Athena walked swiftly from the bar and out the door. Ben had to jog to keep up with her. Outside it was bright and sunny. For the first time, Ben could see Guarroutk in its full beauty. He hadn't even realized he had stopped moving until Athena had pointed it out to him by yelling at him to catch up.

She seemed to float down the street. It was a scene from a 1950's Norman Rockwell painting. It was so bright and beautiful, almost perfect. At the edge of town Athena stopped. When he reached her it literally seemed like coming to the edge of the painting. A veil of darkness dropped in through the woods, severing the road and anything else that crossed its border. The painter had forgotten to finish the painting.

"This will be our entry point for today's lesson."

"Into this darkness?"

Athena rolled her eyes at him, still

very angry and disappeared into the blackness before them. Ben took a deep breath and followed her. Again, Ben could not feel anything below his feet. Though this time it was not total darkness, he could see speckles of light here and there. Eventually, he felt the ground below him pushing his feet into a standing position.

"Athena are you really that mad at me that you haven't spoken to me since we got here."

"I am not mad at *you* Benjamin in the least. You should not let silly matters distract you from the importance of why we are here."

"And why are we here today?"

"You haven't figured it out yet?"

"No not exactly. We are visiting another civilization and the time around us is speeding until we come to the present day."

"Well for one thing, you are not a complete moron. This would be the second civilization in creation. It was started only twenty years after the first."

Ben noticed the ground and the grass. Then he started to notice the lights buzzing around his feet, then his knees and then his chest. He saw what appeared to be mud huts go up before him and then crumble, be rebuilt and then crumble again. This task went on and on until time slowed to a stop. There stood before him, were mud huts all around with a forest to one side, plains to the other and mountains behind the village. Behind him was a lake. In the lake were several hunched over beings playing in the water.

"For today, I have chosen that you not interact with the species of this planet. It is for your own safety."

"What do you mean by that?"

Just as the words left his mouth he realized why. A creature ran past his legs and a spear shot directly through him, wounding the animal. As it yelped, Ben could only imagine what the people of this planet looked like. Slowly he turned to find a caveman standing before him.

"Wait a second. I thought you said this species was brought into existence only twenty years after Brandon's race?"

"It is true. They have been nomads for over a million years."

"Are you kidding me?"

"They have been given nothing. Not even an inkling of help. They were never even shown fire. They know it exists because of lightening strikes and harsh heat fires, but they have no way of creating it on their own. Any major storm or fire and these huts are knocked to the ground and put back up afterwards. It is truly amazing that they are still alive."

"Ok, so let me get this straight then. What you are saying is that the first civilization knew everything. They were brought into creation knowing it all and successfully built a thriving world for millions of years with a life expectancy of well over 200 years old. This group of idiots was brought into their world not given an ounce of knowledge, nor were they ever given help along the way and have remained this way since the beginning of their time."

"That is right Benjamin. They do not even have an understanding of a creator."

"What's their life expectancy on this planet?"

"They may live to see thirty, if they are lucky."

"So, they are a lot like our cavemen then. They hunt, they fuck and they wonder. What a life."

"That obviously is not the greatest thing ever. Look how well they have *not* done."

"They hunt, fuck and wonder around, how could that be so bad?"

"Look at that boar-like creature that just got killed. Look what it did to their village before it was stopped. Do you hear that mother crying over there?"

Ben noticed that a single hut had been knocked down and from what he could see there was more damage, but from his distance he could not make out the extent of the damage. He could hear a woman yelling and screaming while villagers ran from their homes to see what was going on.

"Yes, but what does it have to do with this boar?"

"It just killed her daughter. That is why it was being hunted. It was not killed for the sport or the food. It was killed out of protection. These *great* creatures do not eat meat. They have no way of cooking it. They eat from the trees over there. Once the trees are barren, they will pack up and move to another location and will return here in a few years when the trees have had a chance to become fruitful again."

"Get out of here! It is impossible that they have not learned how to even cook. In a million years? How could a *creator* not allow his children to know how to cook?"

"Look around though, what do you notice?"

On a rock to his right he noticed a younger couple holding hands and gazing into one another's eyes at the edge of the water. A little way down the water's edge was a couple that looked much older than thirty feeding each other berries from the bush that sat beside them. He turned toward Athena and noticed the mother holding her child that had just been mutilated by the boar creature.

It wasn't long before the couples were disrupted by the commotion of the killing in the small village. The only truth that remained was that these people were happy with their situation, even through the loss they had just experienced.

Ben noticed how quickly they moved the body to the plains, dug a hole and placed the small child's body into it. He noticed that the plains were made into a large cemetery, each tiny grave marked with a stone. He tried to pay attention to what they were saying, but they weren't speaking English. It was only a series of grunts.

"It really is beautiful what they are saying," said a small child standing at Ben's side.

"What are they saying?"

"We bury this child before us. She was

the daughter of Simaria and King Jimali. She
was only four years old and was taken from us
so swiftly like so many of us are. May the
ground beneath her swallow her whole,"
whispered the little girl.

"You speak their language?"

"I am one of them. I think that's me
they are putting into the ground."

"Athena?"

"Benjamin she will be your guide in this
place. She is too young to realize that you
are not one of her people and that you do not
speak the same language. Even if it had been
an elder that died, I am not so sure they
would understand that either. In fact, you
may actually have a second unexpected guide
coming to you."

"What do you mean by that?"

"Goodbye Benjamin, I will be back in an
hour."

"Athena! Wait! You can't just leave me
here like this."

"Mommy!" screamed the little girl as she
ran to the woman at her graveside.

"Little girl wait," Ben ran after her.

The woman at the girl's graveside was
holding her chest and crying. The others left
the woman there and walked back toward the
village. The little girl sat down next to her
mother trying to hug her, but could not. She
just fell through her each time. Simaria was
going into convulsions and appeared to stop
breathing. The little girl started screaming;
no one could hear her, but Ben. Ben tried to
do his best to help the woman, he too just
kept moving right through her. Minutes later,

several of the men moved to her but just stood there watching her.

The woman's body stopped moving all together. Ben slammed the ground beside her body.

"It's all right I do feel much better now."

"Mommy?"

Ben turned to see Simaria standing behind him. The little girl ran and hugged her mother. Ben turned and looked at her lifeless body on the ground and back to her living body behind him.

"How is this possible?" he asked.

"I do not know, but it is nice to see my daughter."

"So, why are you here?"

"I don't know. I don't understand what is going on. I'm not even sure I understand what I'm actually saying to you," said Simaria.

"What do you mean by that?"

"This language we are speaking, what is it?"

"English. It's an Earth language."

"What is that feeling?"

"What feeling?"

"It is a strange feeling. There is this feeling in my head. I cannot explain it. There is this knowledge breathing into me. So much my people did not know. A shame. The *creator*, he is calling to me."

"The *creator*?"

"It's weird because my people don't believe in a creator. They don't even understand how they came to be here.

Actually, I don't think it was ever really thought about."

"What do you mean?"

"We just lived. We spoke very few words. Let's see how would a sentence sound like in your language?"

"How do you know all of this information now?"

"I'm honestly not sure. I can't even begin to tell you how my people have lived this long the way they do."

As they walked through the village they discussed more about Simaria's people and what she knew of their existence. She took him to some caves where she showed him some drawings of how to kill a beast, which berries were found to be poisonous, and which were edible. She explained to him that these drawings were drawn and redrawn for many years.

She told him several oral folklore stories of men and woman of her village. None of them included Gods, Goddesses, or deities at all. Every story was about an actual person, especially a king or queen. They talked about her daughter Pathinia who was next in line to be Queen. King Jimali had mated with almost every woman in the tribe, but Simaria was the only one to ever produce a child.

They actually didn't know how a child was conceived. They believed that intercourse drew a new life out of a person. Simaria was the only one that had already been pregnant and was in labor when he was having sex with her. The women of the tribe never gained much weight during pregnancy; probably due to the diet they ate.

Ben was appalled by what he was hearing. He couldn't believe the words coming out of her mouth. Simaria's people lived in the most simplistic way. Barely communicating with one another. They had lived this way since the beginning of their time. There had never been any sort of influence on them from an outside source.

"It is time for us to go Ben. It was nice to meet you. It was nice to understand my people and where we really come from."

"Where do you really come from?"

Simaria did not respond she had turned and walked into a bright light. Pathinia broke away from her mother's hand and ran back to Ben. She gave him a hug.

"You'll understand it all soon. I'm sure you will," she said as she too disappeared.

A tear started to fall down Ben's face. He looked out over the village, at the simple people going about their peaceful lives in complete ignorance. They had love and pain. That had remained consistent.

"Are you ready to go now?" Athena had appeared out of nowhere, as Ben had come accustomed to her doing.

"I'm ready," Ben wiped the tears from his face and pulled himself to his feet. "Are you going to explain this to me?"

"I do not know if it needs explaining."

"Athena don't play games with me right now. I just witnessed two deaths and way too much understanding for me to think about right now."

"Maybe then perhaps you need to go back
to Marygolde's and relax. We can pick this
conversation up in the morning."

Before Ben could speak, they were back
at Marygolde's with a refreshing drink
sitting before them.

"Today was, I am sure, a difficult one
for you. We will discuss it I promise you."

"And Brandon? His people?"

"Will be discussed as well. For now,
drink your drink and go off to bed."

"Can..."

"Yes, you may say goodnight to Marygolde
before going upstairs."

"Why do I feel like a child in this
place? Why do you always know what's on my
mind?"

"In due time, it will all be explained."

Ben finished his drink and made his way
to the bar. The images of Marygolde began to
change so rapidly that she looked like an out
of tune television set. The image began to
clear and before him stood a woman in her
late fifties. She was a very attractive woman
with black hair with spouts of silver here
and there, deep brown eyes, and dressed in
the finest robes.

"You finally see my true form," said
Marygolde.

"This is what you really look like?"

"Yes, my child it is. And I see you are
coming along wonderfully then."

"It's just been a tragic day."

"Sometimes it takes a few tragedies in
our lives to understand the outside world."

"Well I am exhausted and wanted to say

goodnight and thank you for everything."

Ben turned and took off toward the room upstairs. Once there, Ben got ready for bed and jumped into it waiting for the next thing to come down upon him.

This time instead of something pulling him up, a rope fell down upon his stomach. Quickly, he pulled himself to the corner of the bed against the wall. He then saw two tiny legs appear out of the darkness. Then he noticed the face of Pathinia looking into his eyes.

"What are you doing here?"

"Don't know how I got here. I was just walking around and saw this rope and decided to venture down it."

"Well, where were you before?"

"Not sure. I was walking into the light with my mommy and then ended up in this bright place filled with people. I couldn't find my mommy so I started walking around."

"So, you're telling me there is a whole other place above my bedroom ceiling?"

Pathinia didn't answer him. She just sat there staring at him utterly confused.

"Damn it. I forget that you just learned all this language stuff today. I'm so confused on how that's still possible. You speak it so well."

"That woman you were with said its cause we are naïve and open to understanding. The creator takes care of us when we die."

"The first civilization was given everything. All the knowledge they would ever need to know and they basically despise the creator. The next civilization has no help from the creator, but is taken care of by him in the end."

"Benji you've lost me. I am only four. Yesterday it was ee, oo, baa, boo, hee, loo, gah, blah and today its crazy words I think I'm too young to understand."

"Pathinia, you are doing amazing for someone who has never spoken English before."

"I just don't understand it all."

"Well little one, that makes two of us."

Pathinia laid her head down into Ben's lap as they both began to fall asleep. As they drifted into sleep the same red hand lowered down into the room grabbing Pathinia by the back of the shirt and hoisting her up into the darkness.

"Ben…" screeched Pathinia.

Ben jumped up in the bed and tried to grab her arms as they filtered into the darkness. He turned to grab the rope, but it was gone. He jumped up into the darkness trying to feel for anything to grab onto, but there was nothing but a smooth flat surface.

Ben ran to the door and flung it open. The hallway was gone. There was nothing but a black abyss before him. It was too late, he couldn't stop himself. He fell through the blackness and into his bed. The next thing he knew he was awoken by an alarm clock. For the first time, the blackness above his bed was gone. There was now a solid ceiling above him.

Even though he had always wanted to not look into the darkness, it was the first time he wished it had been there. There was no other way to find Pathinia. The red-armed creature had taken her. She was gone. Or had he just dreamt the whole thing like the previous night?

The best way, Ben thought, to find out was to go ask Marygolde. So as usual he showered, dressed and went downstairs. He walked up to the bar and looked for Marygolde. She was nowhere in sight. In fact, when he turned to look at the tearoom there was but one lonely table in the tiny room. There was someone sitting at the table, but he couldn't make out the person.

He walked closer and tried his hardest to see and then he noticed that the person sitting before him looked very familiar. He couldn't believe his eyes. Joy filled his heart. He almost completely forgot about Pathinia, Marygolde, Athena and the rest of Guarroutk.

There, sat before him was a blonde Goldilocks come to save him from the big bad wolves.

"Samantha what are you doing here?"

Chapter 11: Samantha

Ghosts, ghouls, goblins, vampires and a wizard or two scattered the streets of Zion for it was All-Hallows-Eve. The square in the middle of town was the spot where the annual Halloween Ball was held since Zion came into existence. This year, Benjamin and his friends went as the founding fathers of Zion who were rumored of being wizards of a high council. Benjamin was dressed in yellow robes signifying the leader of the clan and each of his three best friends dressed in the colors of each of the other three houses; one each in green, red and orange.

"Dude, your brother should have gone as my son Ollie Jr.," said Oscar the boy dressed in orange robes.

"Why do you say that?" asked Ben.

"Cause you know, Ollie Jr. was suspected of being a huge homo, just like your brother," said John the boy in green robes.

"Guys he's only fourteen. I doubt

seriously that he is gay. Anyway, he has been a vampire for the last five years," answered Ben. "Speaking of which, where did he disappear to?"

"Look he's over there talking to that *guy* that happens to be dressed as a vampire too. Wow, that's a damn good vampire costume too," said Sean the boy in red robes.

"Too bad he's totally flamboyant and trying to seduce your brother. That's actually kind of creepy cause that guy has got to be in his late twenty's," said Oscar.

Ben stormed off toward his brother and the older vampire guy that he was talking to, leaving his friends behind. He was angry with them for making fun of his brother, but he didn't know if he was angrier that they might be right or that this guy appeared to be hitting on Alex. By the time Ben reached them, the rage within him had overtaken him.

"What the fuck do you think you are doing with this guy?" Ben said screaming at Alex.

"What do you think you are doing interrupting us?" replied the vampire in a tone that raised the hairs on Ben's neck.

"I'm sorry, I don't think I was speaking to you and since you feel you are due a response, that is my brother and if I want to know why he is speaking to someone more than ten years older than him, I will ask. Last time I checked he's a minor and my responsibility."

"Benjamin!" Alex yelled, "His vampire costume is cool and I wanted to talk to him about it. If you had been paying any attention to me, you would have noticed that I wasn't the only one here with the same questions. This is Samantha we ran into each other as we were both drawn to the *Count* here and both of us were fascinated with his costume."

"Samantha? Sorry, I'm Ben, Alex's brother," he said to Samantha and then turned to the *Count*, "and do you have a name other than the *Count*?"

"For this evening and this evening only, I do not."

The coal-black eyes and unnaturally pale skin of the guy staring coldly and unshifting into his own grey eyes seemed to almost pierce his soul.

"So, Samantha you don't know this guy either?" asked Ben.

"No, and I don't see how that is any of your business anyway," replied Sam.

"It isn't, but I think you and my brother should make your way back into the crowd and enjoy the party."

"Ben, do not start your bullshit. We will talk to whomever we want and whenever we want to. You just need to make sure I am home and safe in my bed."

"Exactly and that's what I'm doing right now when I say get the hell back down to the party. As for you Samantha, you can do whatever you want."

"Boys, does there seem to be a problem up here?" interrupted Sheriff Scott.

"There is no problem here at all officer," said the *Count*. "Should there be a problem?"

"Look here, 'Count', leave these kids be," Sheriff Scott said, as he never broke eye contact with the Count. "Boys, I think your parents would rather you be down at the party and as for you Samantha, I'm sure your father would much rather you be down there as well. I mean it, go now. I'd like a few words with the great Count alone."

The three kids departed the Count and the Sheriff and returned to the festivities below. Ben kept looking over his shoulder at the two who clearly seemed to be arguing, but from this distance he could not make out what they were saying. He could only hear their voices the party ahead of them drowned out the actual words.

Samantha took Alex's hand and before Ben could say anything to either of them, they quickly disappeared into the crowd. Ben tried to look for them and instead found his friends, lost without their leader.

"So, how did things go amongst the queers?" asked Oscar.

"Ya know you need to stop calling my brother that," said Ben. "As a matter of fact, he was talking to that guy with a girl. Yes, a girl. Her name's Samantha."

"And you really think that makes much of a difference?" replied Oscar. "All right you don't need to give me that look. So, what happened up there anyway?"

"Nothing really, but funny enough Sheriff Scott showed up and interrupted."

"Ben, why is that funny?" asked John.

"Well, the guy only introduced himself as the 'Count'…"

"The 'Count'?" asked Sean trying to hold his laughter in until the others started laughing.

"Shut up guys. I thought it was odd too, but then Sheriff Scott came up to us and he too called the guy 'Count'. That and the way the guy spoke sent eerie chills down my spine."

"You're right, that's so creepy," said Oscar sarcastically. "It just doesn't make sense why the Sheriff would walk up to the guy and make reference to him dressed as the Count Fucking Dracula or anything."

"Guys really, make jokes all you want, but the Sheriff stayed behind to talk to the guy and it sounded as though they were arguing about something."

"Ben I think you're just putting things into your own head," said Sean, "but we need to get going if we are going to enter the contest; it's starting in a few minutes."

The annual costume contest started at 8 PM for the tots, again at 9 PM for the teens, and then at 10 PM for the adults. The crowd cheered for their best costumes, but it was down to the judges to decide the winners. Ben and his friends were of the age that they could enter in either the teens contest or the adults. They had missed the teen sign-in and were forced to compete with the adults.

Ben and his friends sat as close to the front watching the teen costumes. All of them were surprised to see that Alex had entered and that he entered with a partner. Alex and Samantha were dressed so alike that it was as though they had planned their costumes together. Oscar cheered for them the loudest and Ben knew there was a sort of ridicule behind it.

After seeing all the costumes, Ben felt his brother's was probably not the best; however he wouldn't be shocked if he won. Alone Alex wouldn't have stood a chance, but for some reason to see him and Sam together on stage they radiated something that overtook the other contestants.

"And the winner for most Comedic Costume goes to…" the announcer said as he took a long pause to draw anticipation from the crowd, "is Hannah Olsen for her great rendition of the circus clown."

Hannah stepped forward and as she reached for her trophy she released her balloons. Showing shock at her departing balloons, she fell to the ground in a childhood fit only to jump to her feet and accept her trophy. Deservingly so, her performance had the audience in tears from laughter.

"And the winner for the best Horror Costume goes to…" again the announcer took a long pause, "oh now this is shocking. The winner is Shelby Olsen for her take on a psychopathic serial killer clown which is the greatest reason why people are afraid of clowns by the way Shelby."

Shelby Olsen was the twin sister of Hannah and every year the two had played opposites of each other's costume. Like this year playing the two sides of the clown. Last year they were court jesters, one playing a comical one and the other playing an evil one.

Unlike Hannah's stance on taking her trophy as the announcer turned toward her, she wasn't standing in her place. The announcer looked up and down the row of contestants and then toward the crowd.

"Shelby?" he said into the microphone, "Shelby, has anyone seen Shelby? She was just here a second ago."

At that moment she popped up from underneath the stage and crawled up on top of it. Her entrance caused the announcer to take several steps back, falling to the ground. The trophy hit the ground. Shelby picked it up, turned and took a bow and then stepped back into her place in the line of contestants.

"Damnit Shelby and now we know why you deserve that trophy," said the announcer pulling himself back to his feet.

Several other trophies were handed out; most original, best duo also going to the Olsen twins, best single and classic.

"And without further ado your winner for this evening is…" he paused to open the envelope. "The winner is…" again he paused just staring at the card "really," he said to himself and then continued. "Sorry, the winner is or should I say the winners are Alexander Casey and Samantha O'Leary for their costumes of vampires."

The two circled out of the line of contestants and toward the announcer one accepting the trophy, while the other stole the microphone.

"Thank you all and may this be the last

night of breathing, for tonight we feast," Samantha screamed into the microphone.

"Give me that back," said the announcer grabbing the microphone out of her hand, "and if you would all make your way off the stage. We'll be taking a fifteen minute break and we will see you all back here for the adults."

Alex was shocked by the compliments he received from Ben and his friends when he and Samantha caught up with them, before they headed to the stage. They proceeded to take the same seats that Ben and his friends had occupied. The costumes for the adults were much more vivid and realistic than the teens, making it much more difficult for the judges to decide.

Ben and his friends did not win best overall dressed, but they did win most original with compliments for their interpretation of Zion's founding fathers. Had it not been for the *Count* with his eerie looks from the black slitted eyes, jet-black shoulder length hair, pointed teeth, devilish chiseled forehead, undead toned skin, and bloodstained mouth and chin; it all looked extremely realistic.

Ben and his entourage were impressed yet pissed that the guy who had been, in their opinion, seducing Alex, had just beaten them. During the ride home all they could do was make fun of the *Count*. Alex and Samantha, who they agreed to take home, ignored them chalking it up to jealousy.

# # #

"Ben you have known about Alex even before that night I met him, so why would you

abandon him after all those years?" asked
Samantha.

"Sam it's not that simple. You don't
understand."

"I understand that that night you would
have kicked your friends' asses for calling
him gay."

"That's when I thought he was straight."

"You didn't think he was straight, you
just didn't want them calling him gay, and
you didn't think he was in the slightest bit
straight until he introduced me to you and
your parents as his girlfriend a week after
that Halloween Party."

"It's weird isn't it? To think that we
were all pretty close friends for two years
after that. Two years Sam. Then… and then…"

"Ben I'm sorry. I'm so sorry. If I had
it to do over again, I would take it all
back. I didn't mean for you to find out that
way and I surely didn't mean for you or your
parents to disown Alex like that."

"Sam I have been so pissed at you since
then. I can't believe you did that to me. I
can't believe Alex kept it from me. She was
my girlfriend Sam. She was my girlfriend."

"You don't know how sorry I am Ben. If
it means anything to you at all, Alex didn't
even know I had started seeing Tracy. We
never meant to hurt you Ben."

"Alex didn't know?"

"No, Alex didn't know. Are you telling
me you have been punishing him and even
blocked him out of your life because you
thought he betrayed you? For something that
is completely my fault?"

"No, it's cause he was gay."

"That's bullshit Ben and you know it…"

"All right Samantha it may not have been the reason at first, but it became the reason. How deceptive could you guys be? All the deception, the lies, the hiding, of course it was about being gay."

"The deception? Your father was a General for Christ's sake and he still insisted everyone call him that. The lies and hiding go right along with that. Alex deservedly so had all the rights of doing what he did, as soon as you guys found out you destroyed him. I took care of him for the longest time and then he met Maria and then Jimmy and finally started getting his life together again."

"You guys seemed to be doing fine on your own living your secretive life. It takes a lot of strength and determination to live a double life."

"He only lived that way around you guys. Outside of the house we were ourselves. It wasn't…"

"That's just it Samantha, you guys did exactly that. You were in your own lives. Why did he need us? He was doing fine."

"Are you going to actually be that naïve Benjamin? You are almost thirty, you should know better by now. Family is always needed. Think about it Ben, your parents have been dead a short time and you still aren't over it. Now think of how he must have felt. You at least know that they aren't around the corner for you; they are never coming back. With Alex he always had hope. Can you somehow realize how hard it was for him to live that double life? Besides, he wanted to tell you many times, if only it wasn't for that stupid ass, Oscar, who made life a living hell for Alex."

"What are you talking about? He never told me anything of his personal life, other than you."

"Because you always had Oscar around. And besides that, the things Oscar would do or ask of your brother when you weren't around."

"What do you mean by that? Are you saying he made sexual advances at Alex? Cause that's silly, Oscar is married and has kids."

"Yeah well in his childhood he wasn't always what you think he may have been. He used to ask Alex to do things you would have never expected him to have done."

"So, he did make sexual passes at Alex?"

"Well you're a quick one now, aren't you Benjamin."

"Why didn't Alex ever tell me?"

"He was your best friend…"

"And Alex was my brother."

"You're right he was till you disowned him. Then can you blame him for never telling you about Oscar? He would have not only lost you as a brother, but you would have lost Oscar as a friend."

"Do I really want a friend like that? I was his best man at his wedding. And now it pisses me off. Had I known, I would have never have been."

"Benjamin, Benjamin, do you not see what Alex did for you? Oscar may have been a major

- 168 -

asshole, but he was a friend of yours nonetheless and even though he may have made Alex's life hell, somehow it wasn't his place to ruin your friendship. If Alex had known that you would have stopped being his friend for the uninvited advances and not the gay aspect I'm sure he would have told you. For that reason though, he wouldn't tell you."

"How did Alex know that we would have reacted the way we did? Especially when I would defend him against my friends?"

"It was never you or your mother he was worried about. It was your father, however it was the reaction that you and your mother had that completely shocked and hurt him."

"I never meant to hurt him. I was extremely hurt and I'm sure my mother was too."

"It wasn't your lives to decide. It wasn't for you to live. It is because of you that he lost five years of his family and it's time he will never be able to get back, now that they are dead."

"He and my mother had been spending a night a week at dinner together for the last year."

"True he had been, but it's still not family Ben. It's not Sunday night dinners with all of you. The saddest thing about it though… it's exactly that. That's what he chose to remember of you people. The Sunday night dinners, the Christmas mornings, the love you guys had. He always forgot about the negatives. He defended you guys against all of us. We tried to make the best substitute family he could have and while we did the best job we could, you guys were still what he thought about. He blocked the day you guys threw him out of the house out of his head. It truly is amazing what he thought about you guys. Even through it all, he still had the love for you and your parents."

"Honestly Samantha, is that the truth?" Tears started to form in the corners of Ben's eyes.

"It's the truth Ben. You guys destroyed him and were still his saints. His relationship with Jimmy almost ended several times because of you guys. He always thought that he could try to make a relationship with Maria and then you guys would accept him back into your lives. And if he remained with Jimmy, there would be no way."

"He tried to have a relationship with Maria?"

"Yes Ben, he did. Maria was always too smart for him though; she knew him too well. Then again, Alex was always her support as well. Her family life wasn't always the best either. Those two became almost inseparable. I even became jealous of their relationship."

"Is that why you ran off to the big Ivy League college for your law degree?"

"There were many factors, but it's one of them. Probably the biggest one."

"So, whatever happened with Tracy?"

"Oh please, that ended shortly after you caught us making out almost five years ago."

"So, you guys destroyed me and didn't even bother to try and make it work?"

"It's not always about you Benjamin. OK, that time it was about you. Tracy realized that she loved you or wasn't over you and felt horrible for hurting you. She and I tried to work on things for several months after that, but eventually she couldn't deal with it anymore."

"I'm sorry Sam. I never realized how horrible things had got between you and Alex after that."

"You, like your ignorant parents, never thought outside your own lives. I guess that's why you all got along so well and why Alex never fit in..."

"That's harsh Sam. My parents are dead; have some respect and honestly you could stop speaking about me that way while you're at it."

"I apologize for speaking of your parents that way, but as for you, you are a big boy and can deal with the truth. You are going to have to own up to some responsibility for what had happened. After all, it almost ruined Alex's relationship and mine. Then again, it did make us that much stronger in the end, so, in a way I should be thanking you."

"Again, Sam I'm sorry. I don't know how to make it up to you or if I even should. But for Alex's sake, I will make it up to you. I promise that much. That is if I ever get out of this place. I only wish I could make it up to Alex."

"Benjamin whom are you speaking with?" Athena asked, "This is not my table and you should not be sitting here."

Ben turned to find Athena standing behind him. He was shocked to see her standing there and the tearoom full of people. The noise filled the room and he could see Marygolde busy at the bar behind Athena.

"I was talking to Samantha. Samantha this is Athena." When Ben turned to where Sam had been sitting she was no longer there. The seat across from him was vacant.

"Athena, she was just sitting here I swear she was. It was the only table in the tearoom and we were the only two here. Marygolde wasn't even here."

"Benjamin you know that is hard to believe since Marygolde is always here. Now gather yourself, we need to get a move on we are running late as it is."

Ben slowly got from his chair apologizing to Athena for being at someone else's table. He followed her past the bar; occasionally looking back to try and catch a glimpse of Samantha hoping she would be there. As he slowly glanced around the tables that filled the tearoom, he noticed how clear all the people were. The conversations were clear enough that he could make out words as he passed through. As he got near Marygolde at the end of the bar he stopped.

"Sheriff Scott, are you really here?"

"Benjamin Casey, I'm… Athena…?" As soon as he said her name he and Athena shifted out of view from Ben, "Why is he here and why can he see me?" asked Sheriff Scott.

"Doing my job, Scott. I am doing my job and from the looks of it I am doing a good job at it. For Ben realized you are standing here and not just an image of the outside world."

"Still he can't know I'm actually here. He just needs to believe I'm a figment from some reality outside of this place."

"Well you helped that by shifting us out of his view now did you not? Although taking me with you was probably not the best thing to do." And she shifted back to Ben, "Now shall we go?"

"Where did Sheriff Scott go?"

"He was somewhere else. You need to be careful speaking to people here. You do not belong there. You could mess a lot of things up that way. Time lines must be kept in the correct order."

"Athena you may be wiser than me, but I'm not that stupid either, he was here. It wasn't like when I saw my father that was different. Sheriff Scott, he was just physically standing here talking to Marygolde."

"Well then I am sure you are doing a wonderful job and should be ready to go soon then, should you not?"

"Really? I can get back to my life?"

"Soon Benjamin, soon. You still have a few more things to learn. However, you are coming along very well and much faster than expected."

"I don't know if I should take that as a compliment or if I should be offended."

"A little of both would probably be suitable."

Chapter 12: Final Journey

Athena and Ben walked out of Marygolde's Tearoom and into the bright sunshine of the outdoors. Ben was amazed that he could still see the building around him and not fog. Instead of turning up the road to the right, they turned left this time. They came to the edge of town; once again sliced by the darkness, the unfinished painting. Ben could barely make out that there was, what appeared to be a river beneath the blackness on this side of town.

"Are you ready for your final journey Benjamin?" Athena asked with a slight crooked smile that Ben could only assume was a smile of accomplishment or approval.

"I guess I'm as ready as I'll ever be," he responded forcing a smile between his blushing cheeks out of sheer embarrassment. "Where are we going today?"

"Today we will be seeing several separate worlds. I hope you will find them most fascinating. However, all will be remotely similar to Earth with a few alterations. Are you ready?" Athena asked extending her hand out.

Without responding, Ben grabbed her hand and they stepped into the darkness. Immediately Ben fell into the water. Looking up, he noticed that Athena was hovering above him unscathed by the water.

"I guess I should have forewarned you about the water," Athena said snickering to herself.

"That's not funny. Will you please get me out of here? It feels like there is something swimming around my legs and it's about to freak me out," Ben said doing his best to remain afloat, while trying his hardest not to move in fear that whatever was circling his legs wouldn't attack.

"Oh Ben, those creatures are harmless. You may actually enjoy playing with them. They are a lot like dolphins, but as you wish."

As she spoke the words, he slid out of the water and into the air next to her. He looked down at his clothes and to his surprise; they were dry as was his skin and hair. Ben looked around and for as far as the eye could see there was no land.

"You do realize Ben that you will not see anything from up here. For everything you need to see is beneath you."

"Am I going to grow gills and look like a fish in order to see what's down there?"

And with that comment, Ben fell deep into the water. By the time he resurfaced

Athena was gone. He bobbed in the water looking around for any clue as to where he was supposed to go. Occasionally he stuck his head beneath the water to see if he could see anything. The creatures were gone as well.

After fifteen minutes of waiting, he decided to dive as deep as he could. He didn't get very far when he noticed a dark figure swimming directly at him. As the image came closer he could make out that it was a female figure or what he thought would be a female. She hit him square in the chest and pushed him back to the surface.

"Sorry about that, but you are not ready to go under and sorry I'm really late."

"And you would be?"

"Yeah sorry about that too, Benjamin, my name is Melite and I'll be guiding you through the water world. We haven't much time, but we'll make it quick. From my understanding, you're doing very well. Here eat this," said Melite.

Melite was a creature that looked much like a human with a lot of fishlike characteristics. Her body was covered in scales, her hair reminded him of angel hair as fine as glass strands and almost iridescent. Small fins protruded from her forehead, down her back and the backs of her arms and legs. Around her neck were gills and her hands and feet were slightly webbed.

He took the pruned chunk of whatever she had in her hand and swallowed it without questioning her. As soon as it hit his stomach, he felt slightly ill. He pulled his hands out of the water and noticed tiny webs growing between his fingers. He could feel the same thing between his toes. His clothes dissolved from his body and skin grew over his genitals. Melite giggled at his expressions as he discovered each new change to his body.

"Don't worry about it. Here your genitals are only exposed when you are excited. Much like the sea life on your planet. Everything will be back to your human form when the effects wear off in about an hour. So we must hurry, we have a long way to travel before then."

She dipped into the water and swam off. Ben quickly swam after her. He had already covered twice as much distance as he had when he first plummeted beneath the water, in half the amount of time. As he caught up to her he was relieved to find that his voice worked as well underwater as it did topside.

"How did you know who I was and where I'd be? It looks vastly wide up there."

"Prearranged with Athena, of course. I'm not from this world either. The people of this world aren't so forthcoming with guests as the other places you have been. Thus you look like one of them. They aren't as smart as the first planet you were on, but they will figure it out and that's why we will not be staying long enough for you to be found out. They also aren't incredibly stupid that you can go invisible as in the last planet you were on. Oops, sorry I shouldn't call them stupid. It isn't their fault they are the way they are, they have no guidance whatsoever."

Before Ben knew it, right in front of him was a large underwater city. What resembled skyscrapers covered the ocean floor and at their bases were actual streets. The skyscrapers were formed from coral and the vehicles out of large shells. There were public transports that were large centipede-like creatures. At one end was a large gated doorway with several guards swimming around it. The gate seemed pretty artificial to Ben. After all, what would stop people from just swimming through the city at any point other than the gate?

He followed Melite toward some caves on the outskirts of the underwater town.

"Through here is where we will enter the city."

"Why don't we just swim to the city right there?" Ben asked pointing to a building several hundred feet from where they were now standing.

"The city may look like it's in open water, but there is no water in that city."

"What do you mean? There is no barrier up or is there?"

Ben started walking toward the city with his hands extended looking for some sort of barrier keeping the city from being flooded.

"Um psycho boy if you walk any further I'll have to send you home in a body bag. What doesn't look like a barrier actually is, well basically like a gigantic, invisible electric eel."

"Shit really?"

"Yes really. Can you get into the cave so we can see the city?"

Ben followed her through the cave. When he surfaced he was inside one of the buildings. They crawled out of the hole in the floor into a tiny cellar.

"This is my house here. I built that cave to smuggle people in and out of the city."

"Smuggle people out?"

"There are several different types of 'people' living on this planet. Not all of them are accepting of others living outside their cities, especially since they are not all run by the same types of governments. Although this is one of the most, what you would call, liberal cities down here some people still need to escape."

"Where do they live if this is the easiest city to live in and they can't live here?"

"In random caves for several years or they start new colonies. The oceanic floor down here is huge. There is even one settlement top side on a small island."

"There is dry land on this planet?"

"Think I just told you that!"

As soon as Ben stepped outside, he could smell the salt in the air. It reminded him of being at the beach as a child, but yet walking down the streets of London. The city was huge and full of people. He noticed quickly why they would not be spending much time here. The place was much like Earth, just underwater.

They interacted with several people along the walk through the city, but mostly they conversed amongst themselves.

"The people down here are very friendly," Ben said.

"They are for the most part. The people in each colony live harmoniously with one another. The biggest thing that they fight about here is government styles. Though wars on Earth are sometimes fought on the way governments should be run, they are mostly over religion. This planet has but only one religion and has been that way since the beginning of its time."

"Seriously? They fight over government and that's it?"

"I know it's almost too ridiculous to think about, but then again it seems more ridiculous to fight over religion."

"I guess you're right on that, but... never mind, I guess it's really too stupid to fight over anything."

"Yes, it is, but none the same wars are fought, lives are lost, and territories are destroyed."

"Well now it wouldn't be war if there weren't harmless causalities."

"It's shocking, but the thing I wanted to show you is about to happen."

"And that would..."

Before he could finish, the ground rumbled a little bit and the city began to flood with water. The power of the water knocked Ben and Melite to the ground and they started rising quickly with the water.

"What the hell is going on Melite?"

"City cleaning. Since everyone can breathe both above and below the water, the cities can be cleaned by flooding them."

"Um... what about the invisible electric barriers surrounding the city?"

"The barriers are there, the electricity isn't. Every now and again the pressure comes in so hard it knocks someone to the barrier walls. Sadly, sometimes it's before the electricity is turned off. Fish stick anyone?"

As sick and twisted the idea was, Ben couldn't help but laugh. He followed her as she started to swim toward the vacant streets below. Once under the current it was easy to freely move and walk on the flooded streets below.

"So, how long does this last?"

"It will last till it fills in. Which shouldn't be much longer actually."

"Does the barrier extend all the way to the surface?"

"Yes, but not in a cylinder like you think. It looks more like an upside down funnel. With only a tiny tube that extends to the surface and the electricity is only in the immediate dome."

"Where did all the people go? Why are the streets completely empty right now?"

"It's nearing the end of filling. No-one wants to be shot out of the city, so they take cover inside."

"What? Shot out of the city? What..."

Ben was cut off as he was sucked toward the top of the city. He swirled through the upside down drain like a giant toilet being flushed. He noticed a few others circling toward the top with him. They were much younger though, in their teen's maybe. Once in the tube he felt he was on an amusement park water slide hurling toward the bottom. He had forgotten he was headed up. At the top he shot high into the sky. He could hear cheering and laughter coming from all around him.

"It's a right of passage for them," Melite said as she made her way over to Ben in the water.

"Cool, it was a lot of fun. Brought me back to my childhood, but it was a little disorienting remembering that I was going the opposite way that I am used to."

"It does take some getting used to, but it only happens once a month. It's their most vulnerable time with the cities' biggest security system down and their youngest chasing thrills. If the city had been under any kind of an attack, these kids you see here would have been killed as they flew from the top."

"That's horrible."

"When under an attack, another tribe will take razor netting and place it over the top of the tubing. Most of the time if lucky enough, it is blown off by the first amount of water pressure, but if it succeeds then it's like putting each person through a garbage disposal. They are sliced to tiny bits as they exit."

"Disgusting…"

"It's a massacre for sure. Depending on the amount of people coming through the tube, it's usually only the first ten or so, but enough to cause the city great pain and loss. It will only be a matter time before they have perfected one that will stay on permanently."

"You do realize we just went through that piping right? We could have been shark food."

"No, no sharks on this planet and I knew the city wasn't under an attack. I would never have risked your life. If you had died I would have been killed on my return to Guarroutk or just banished to live here."

"That was still risky. Where are we headed anyway?"

"You aren't paying attention to your surroundings much are you? Just hanging on to every word I'm saying, huh?"

Ben kept swimming along by her side, but took a few moments to look around. He noticed a glittering green mound ahead of them.

"Is that dry land ahead of us?"

"Yes, and we need to get a move on because you're about to lose your ability to swim fast and then we'll really be late."

Before they hit dry land, the webbing started to disappear and the gills started to grow over. Other parts started to shed.

"Um... Melite. I'm gonna be naked on dry land or are my clothes going to rematerialize onto my body?"

Melite just laughed at him and told him that he needed to swim fast.

They approached the sandy beaches and Ben was hesitant to come out of the water. He hadn't felt this exposed in years, or at least not by his own free will. As he slowly pulled himself out of the water he saw that Melite was holding what appeared to be a towel.

"Quickly dry off and then put these on."

Melite was holding clothing for him. He dried off quickly and put the clothes on. When he turned around he noticed that Melite had also changed. She now looked much like her human self.

"This is the second stop on your tour."

"I thought I was going to several planets?"

"You might as well be. The people that live here are very different to those under the water. It is shocking how different they are when they are the same people."

As they approached the city, Ben's mouth dropped. The city was beautiful. There were buildings as well as mud huts both on the ground and suspended in the air attached to the surrounding trees. On the mountainside, there were homes chiseled into it and built out on the ledges. There were bridges and ladders all over the place. One could easily get lost in this city.

"Do you like this place Benjamin?"

Ben just shook his head yes as he continued to stare in awe. In front of him he noticed a native. In physical make-up they looked just like humans. As they got closer, he noticed that their skin was the same color as the fish people in the waters below, a light bluish-gray color. Their eyes were a beautiful coral color.

"Greetings," said the man Ben had been staring at, "welcome to our city home."

"Thank you," Ben replied and followed Melite into the city, "Melite don't you think we stand out?"

"Oh Benjamin, look at your hands!"

Ben looked down and noticed that although the fish parts were gone, the color still remained.

"So Melite, why are they so different here? Other than their appearances?"

"Well for starters, their appearances are only different through evolution…"

"Evolution?"

"Yes silly, they have been out of the water for so long that their fish parts have disappeared and they have adapted to being on dry land. Every now and again a child is born with fins or gills. It's an honor for them really to be born as their true ancestors, but a lot of kids look at it like they are freaks of nature. It's only their skin that remains the same."

"Do they not ever communicate with the tribes underwater?"

"Rarely ever. The ground walkers have been exiled and rightfully so, for their appearances alone, but more so because they abandoned their heritage. Some were exiled for being criminals."

"You're saying this place is England's destitute of Australia then?" Ben said chuckling.

"Yeah I suppose so. The other differences would be their government. They have but only one ruling here and it is very peaceful. On this island there are seven different tribes and all seven rule in the same manor. Each tribe has a spokesperson; a lot like a governor that represents them at a council. And then to top it off, they all have the same religion as well. Their religion is the same as it is in the cities underwater."

"Really? Even after being exiled, they all still have the same religion."

"And believe it or not, the government style they have is the exact same style as the city we just came from."

They came to the edge of the city and the base of a mountain. A path continued into the jungle area along the mountain base. The path was wide enough for two people to walk down comfortably, but extremely dark several feet beyond the edge.

"Well you have two options since we actually have a few extra minutes. We can venture into the forest and you can see a third set of people living on this planet, or we can go to the pub down the road and drink the blue out of you?"

"Lead the way. It's not like I get this opportunity everyday ya know."

The two walked onto the path. As soon as it started to get dark, Ben felt an automatic reflex in his eyes and a set of eyelids slid over them. The darkness lifted as if the sun had peeked through the thick jungle.

"Cool isn't it?"

"Wow, that's friggen' amazing. Do all the land people have these special eyelids?"

"Most of them do, but it seems evolution is taking another step forward and now some of the newborns are coming without'em equipped."

"That's sad, but don't you think this is

something they would need for hunting?"

"If they spend enough time in the dark their bodies would keep them, but they just don't anymore. It's like the sun is burning that gene out of their DNA. Think of the mole people on Earth for a minute. They weren't born with the ability to see in the pitch-blackness, but as they spend more and more time in the total darkness their eyes adjust to that. It would be the same thing here."

"You're saying if someone was born without these extra set of eyelids and were to spend enough time in the jungle, they would grow them?"

"No, I'm saying their regular eyes would adjust to it and then they would be able to see. The danger in that is that they cannot easily return to the sunlight. Ah, here we go."

"We're standing in a swamp Melite."

"I know we are and now just shhh and pay attention."

Ben took a seat on a rock and watched the swamp as if it were going to come to life or just start talking to him. Several minutes later, he thought he saw something move. Then he saw it again and then a third time. Finally, something walked right up to him. The creature before him was completely covered in moss. Its eyes were a dark shade of green. Under the moss he could see that it still had gills and fins and its lips were much fuller, much like a gold fish.

"Ah, the beautiful Melite you bring a visitor. He smells neither of the Melisions of land, nor of the Salterians of the water.

What is he of?" asked the moss man before them.

"Let us just say he is not from here," replied Melite.

"Well, not from here, my name is Fen and I am a Quagarian. We live under the swamp, but spend most of our days lying around the base of the trees and in the branches. We are of peaceful people. Or most of the time of peaceful people."

"Well my name isn't 'not from here,' its Ben and it's extremely a pleasure to meet you."

"It is a pleasure. I must be returning. I need to finish collecting food I'm famished. Melite it was a pleasure to see you as always. Tell your father things are going wonderful here and we are looking forward to his next visit."

Fen turned and left the two sitting on the side of the swamp, as he descended into its depths. Ben watched puzzled looking from Fen to Melite. The two had a past together and there had never been a mention of Melite's father. Who was her father Ben couldn't help but wonder, but did not have the nerve to ask her.

"Ben we need to be getting you back to the pub. It's almost time. What's wrong?" she asked looking at his puzzled facial expression.

"Me? Nothing. He was just the only person to really speak to us. Seemed like a really nice guy."

"He is the leader of the Quagarians. He represents them on the committee for all the land dwellers."

"I'm glad I got to meet him then. And he knows your father?"

"Everyone on this planet knows my father. Fen is the only one brave enough to speak to me, if they know who I am. The reason I like the Quagarians so much is that, I guess, living out here they have lost their inhibitions or it's the thick skin they have grown. They're just not as timid as all the others."

They walked in silence the rest of the way back to the village, entered the village pub, grabbed a couple of drinks and then sat down.

"It was nice getting to meet you Ben. The people that Athena gets to work with are always so nice and very different. I get stuck with some doozies sometimes though."

"I've enjoyed my time with you as awkward as it may have been at times, but still I have enjoyed it."

As in the other two places he had been, Ben noticed the same connections between the people. There were a few couples eating their meals or drinking. This time he noticed another human quality about the race he was visiting. There was a nervous guy trying to get up enough courage to speak to a girl. With a little help from the bartender, he sat a drink down in front of the girl and told her it was from the nervous guy. The bartender winked at Ben and he realized it was Marygolde for only a split second.

He then took a drink from his own mug and sat it back on the table. When he looked

up Athena was sitting across from him and
Melite was nowhere in sight. In fact he
wasn't in the pub either. He was back at
Marygolde's.

Chapter 13: Through the Rabbit Hole

Ben didn't bother looking around. The things that happened in Guarroutk ceased to surprise him. He sat there staring at Athena as he picked up his glass and took another drink. Neither of them wanting to start a conversation, the glass was nearly empty before the two spoke. The silence wasn't even broken by either of them, but by a third party whispering into Athena's ear.

"It is true. He may very well be going home soon," Athena said and the figure before Ben whispering to Athena disappeared.

"Are you referring to me?" Ben asked.

"Still a little selfish are we, Benjamin? With reasonable doubt this time though I will say, because this time the conversation was indeed about you."

"It has nothing to do with selfishness and more to do with the fact things here are pretty much exactly as they appear."

"Are they Benja…"

"They are…"

"Then I believe you should take a nights rest and we will convene tomorrow to talk."

"What if I believe I'm ready to talk now? I'm ready to go home now."

"I do not believe that to be the truth. I believe you need another night's sleep before jumping to conclusions of being ready and allow me to decide that for you. If you were sent back now, then I believe it would be too soon and you would not be able to make it through recovery."

"All right, maybe you are right. There is something I would like to take a closer look at before I leave anyway."

Ben stood from the table, leaned down and kissed Athena on the cheek and departed. She was shocked at his departure; a smile consumed her face anyway. He approached an overjoyed Marygolde, stopping only to say goodnight. He didn't bother asking her why she had been so happy for he was too anxious to get upstairs to bed.

He prepared his normal evening routine and sat down on the bed in the corner of the wall staring into the darkness. It didn't take long before the red arm reached down from the darkness toward his neck. This time, Ben welcomed the arm and took its hand. The red fingers gripped his hand and helped him to climb the wall. He could feel the smooth walls of the tearoom disappear and the dirty ones form.

Eventually he could see a light in the nearing distance. The light grew brighter and larger until he was able to grab the edges of the hole. The hand seemed to have vanished and he was left to pull himself out. With only his head out of the hole he noticed a tiny rabbit looking him in the eyes, twitching his nose. Ben had the feeling that he had just climbed through the rabbit's home and the rabbit was pissed.

Once he fully had himself pulled from the rabbit hole, he found himself on the edge of the river. He sat on the bank looking around for the creature with the red arm, which was nowhere in site. He did notice the tearoom off in the distance, which meant he was still in Guarroutk. He felt confused to find that the dark hole above his upstairs bedroom had led to the ground level riverside, to be a rabbit's home, and daylight to top it off. It couldn't have been the rabbit that led him through the hole. Could it? Ben wondered.

He walked over looking into the river at his reflection, but it wasn't his own. Instead, it was Melite's face he saw staring back at him. Without a second thought he reached into the water took her hand, helping her to the surface.

"I can't believe you are actually here. I didn't get to say goodbye."

"Oh Benjamin, you should know that in this place nothing's ever final," Melite said as they sat back onto the bank next to the rabbit hole.

"Of course it's never over Benjamin," said a voice coming from inside the darkened hole.

"What?" Ben asked and then noticed the

tiny head of Pathinia peeking through.

Quickly, Ben reached over and lifted her out of the hole. He could not help but to smile; especially knowing that she was OK. Had she been in the hole ever since that evening he watched her being taken from his room? It didn't matter to him; she was safe now sitting with them.

"And you don't think this little reunion would go anywhere without me?" said another gruff voice from the woods off to the side, "I still always find this greenery a weird sensation of pointlessness."

Ben couldn't help but laugh as he saw Brandon walking from out of the surrounding trees.

"What are you guys doing here?" asked Ben.

"You tell us!" the three said almost completely in sync.

The four took seats in almost a circular formation on the bank of the water, with the hole almost directly behind Ben. Ben knew exactly why they were here. He knew at that moment this was what Athena had been talking about when she said he had needed another night. It was a matter of putting the pieces of the puzzle together. He just didn't understand what he was supposed to put them together.

"I guess it's a matter of me understanding everything I need to understand here and who better than the three of you to help?" said Ben as he looked at each of them grinning with joy.

"That's great Ben. I'm happy to be here.

It's always great to come here, and feel the sun, and watch the water and to just see everything and to see you," said Pathinia.

"You are absolutely adorable Pathie, but where is your mommy?" asked Ben.

"Oh she is safe in the great white light. I was told I was needed here for a while and could go see her when I was done here. But I was happy to, especially when they said it was you I would be seeing."

"But I could use seeing your mommy too. After all she helped me out while I was on your planet as well."

"No, Benjamin she was your guide; not her mother. I don't think you were even supposed to see her mom. That, I'm sure, shocked many people," said Melite. "I take it you believe in ghosts?"

"I do, but I don't understand…" Ben paused thinking about what he was about to say, "…I do understand I think, but I guess I'm puzzled about why Pathie can speak so well. She is only four and her people could barely speak their own language, let alone English. Or why any of you can speak English when it's not even a language on any of your planets."

"It's all right Melite I'll take this one," said Brandon. "Two things, one remember closely when you first ran into me when you were with… ugh… *Athena*, and two, what do you know of death?"

"You didn't like Athena for starters…"

"Think harder," interrupted Brandon.

"You weren't speaking English," responded Ben.

"That's right and honestly I'm not speaking English now. You see now why I don't like those creatures. You are speaking my language and I despise it, but it's not you I can blame. You didn't do it to yourself. *She…*" he shuttered, "did it to you. *She* did it to all of us."

"You are telling me that none of us are speaking the same language?"

"No," the others said together.

"All right, well I guess you guys have been on the same page and I feel the stupid one. So, I'll move forward. The second thing…" Ben stopped and thought. "In death comes knowledge? I guess that is the only thing that would make sense here."

"Very good Benji," said Pathinia. "I learned so much when I was killed. Don't look sad Benji. I didn't feel any pain. I actually enjoy it this way. My people don't know anything. They don't know of a creator, they don't know of an afterlife, they are afraid of everything. It is weird though to know all that I know now, but my people were… are happy. They are still living, after all."

For the first time Ben noticed the hurt in Pathinia. He had always thought of her as a naïve child. He had never thought about how he had felt about death. '*All your questions will be answered in death,*' rang in his head. '*All your questions will be answered in death*', over and over again, first his father, then his mother and then the church. It had been engraved into his memory, but they had never mentioned the pain that must come with knowledge.

He couldn't help but to feel sorry for Pathinia. Her people did not have a *God* to worship nor did they have knowledge to advance themselves beyond a prehistoric, primitive state. He thought about his trip to Laviria and Brandon's people.

"Brandon let me take a guess. You know of *God*, or the creator, but you were instilled with all of the knowledge you ever needed. Is that why your people haven't evolved since the beginning of your existence?"

"The smoke coming from your ears is of great knowledge or good guessing," said Brandon half laughing. "We are better than this so-called creator…"

Melite cringed and snarled at his comment, but she did not say a word and allowed him to continue.

"…Understand it is what my people have always thought. Melite, you have to understand it is our belief. We have been better than the creator since the beginning. He created us with all the knowledge we needed and then some. We sought out to destroy the creator. Whose right was *it* to create others and to play with their lives? Once *it* realized how smart we were, *it* attempted to vanquish us and start over. Why would we, why should we want to worship the thing that created us and then attempted to destroy us? We did nothing wrong."

"Maybe, the creator was trying to create the best beings. Maybe, he tried to create beings because he was lonely and your people rejected him. How would you feel if you were

lonely and the things you created rejected
you?" asked Melite.

"Start over maybe, but not destroy what
I had already created," replied Brandon. "Is
that not the opposite of what he was
attempting to do?"

"Yes, but if you had already rejected
him, then what would stop you from seeking
out and destroying the next thing he created
or giving them the knowledge you held? Thus,
his new work would be destroyed because of
your distaste or disapproval of him and his
creations," Melite said.

"That is what ended the war between my
people and the creator. We agreed to stay
where we were and he could stay where he was.
We never agreed to allow beings to visit our
planet, but yet he sent them to study us. We
were not allowed to give them knowledge; just
let them observe. He built an army against us
Melite, what were we supposed to do? You, of
all people, should know that. I can feel him
in you. You are a part of him, are you not?"

"Wait, what? Would you two quit arguing?
I'm about lost here. Melite what is he
talking about?" asked Ben.

"It's OK Ben. Brandon, he never built an
army against your people. You guys aren't as
smart as you think you are…"

"Watch your tongue," Brandon interrupted
her.

"No, I won't! You need to understand.
The creator was lonely; he wanted companions.
What he didn't realize was that his ultimate
companions would come from his own being."

"Um, now I'm totally confused," said

Brandon.

"That makes two of us!" added Ben.

"Shall I, Melite?" asked Pathinia.

They all looked at her in shock. The youngest of them all from the least knowledgeable planet had the answers. Pathinia sat smirking with her cheeks flushed red with embarrassment.

"Of course you can," Ben answered her before Melite could muster the words herself.

"All right. It was beings like you, Ben that created the others that Brandon calls *it…*"

"What do you mean by that?" asked Ben and Brandon together.

"As the creator tried his hardest to find some companions in his lonely existence, he found himself weakened by those he created," Pathinia continued. "You see, he created Lavirians with knowledge hoping they would accept him and he would truly have equals to converse with, but they rejected him. Upsetting him. Then he created us; this time with no knowledge at all of him or anything. He found that to be just as lonely waiting for us to discover him on our own.

"He continued to create planets with life forms with varying knowledge and beliefs, trying to find the ones that would suit him as companions. For example, he created Earth and slowly he gave them knowledge hoping it would lead to him, but instead it separated him."

"It separated him?" asked Ben.

"Yes, Ben it separated him," answered Melite. "Think about it. Take the ancient

Greeks; for every new thing they learned they attributed it to *another god*. When they did this, it separated them from the creator. It physically pained him to be dissected. It was never his intention to be separated, he never thought it was possible, but the separation gave him the companionship he was seeking."

"However, all the separations weakened him," Ben said.

"Exactly," Melite continued, "for every *new god* that was created, the weaker he became. He then presented himself to the people in the form of a human, in an attempt to reunite his creations and to attempt to rebuild his strength. It worked for the most part, but as long as people remember these *gods,* even in a myth, they continue to exist. They just don't have the power that was once given to them by the people.

"The power returned to the creator. He just couldn't come to terms with destroying the one thing he didn't actually create. After all, he would be destroying a part of himself."

"If what you are saying is true; then we are angrier at him than we should be. And the creator didn't create everything," said Brandon. "Is that possible?"

"You've been fighting a war that was never needed to be fought," Melite said. "And it is possible. It happened."

"And so you are just a descendent of one of the separations from the creator?" asked Brandon.

"That I am. And I serve as a liaison for the ruler of my world directly to the other creations. You see he took direction from, say the Earthlings, and separated himself when he created my home world. He gave the planet its own *god*, a separation from himself, a true companion. That *god* was able to stay with the planet and kept the religion unified throughout. Thus came the creation of me."

"You are not being serious. That is crazy," said Ben. "If that's right, then we as humans have created the mess we are in through our own stupidity."

"That's just it Ben, it isn't stupidity," answered Pathinia. "It's the circle of life. Your planet was a creation, an experiment for the perfect world. The creator would not punish you or any of your people for their beliefs as long as there was not pure evil entangled into their actions."

"She's got a point," Melite continued. "Evil was never something the creator intended, but he realized it was somewhat needed for the existence of life."

"The only evil my people know is for the creator," said Brandon. "I guess you never realize it until you see the big picture. For there to be good, there must be evil."

"I still do not completely understand," Ben said.

"I'm not totally sure you're supposed to. You have your own demons to fight. You're supposed to understand whatever it is in order to destroy those demons, and return to where you belong," said Pathinia.

"What if this place isn't real? In fact I'm not sure if I believe any of this," said

Ben. "You're all sounding a bit crazy if you ask me. What happens if I refuse to believe in this crazy comatic dream state I'm in?"

As soon as the words crossed his lips, Melite started to fade into static until she disappeared. The words she tried to speak to Ben he couldn't understand.

"MELITE," he screamed.

Brandon and Pathinia just shook their heads at him in disappointment.

"Why is she gone?" he asked Pathinia.

"Your disbelief," she answered.

"Then why are you two still here? Why haven't you gone away too?" he asked.

"Because she was the only one that was a part of the creator. Your disbelief in the possibility of anything other than yours, caused her to vanish," said Brandon.

"He's right Ben. We are real or as real as we can be seeing how I'm technically dead," Pathinia joked making light of the situation.

"So you're saying, if I decided to cease believing in ghosts then you too would disappear Pathie?" asked Ben.

"That is exactly what it means Ben," interjected Brandon. "As I'm sure if you stopped believing in aliens I'd cease to exist before you."

"I'd listen to him Ben," added Pathinia, "he's actually got a point. Notice the things you stopped believing-in here, they no longer exist here. As long as you leave your mind open to the possibility, the more things you can see. It doesn't mean that what you believe is wrong. It just means there are more ways to believe what you believe."

"Are you attempting to explain different religions to me?" asked Ben.

"I don't think that's exactly what she is trying to explain to you," Brandon said. "I think there's more to it; it's not quite that simple."

"Is anything that simple?" asked Pathinia.

"I guess not," answered Ben. "It's really hard to grow up being taught one thing only to find out that everything you learned is wrong."

"That's the thing Ben. Is it wrong?" asked Brandon.

"I guess not," answered Ben, "but if it's not, how do you explain all of this?"

"A different interpretation of what you already know and believe," answered Pathinia. "Does every question have a definitive and correct answer?"

"No, I guess it doesn't, but that still doesn't quite explain everything that is going on here. If I believe in what you are telling me, which I'm starting to, then Melite should be sitting here with us," said Ben.

"I'm not sure it works that way Benji. You don't always get to see things in black and white. You don't get to change your mind simply because you want to see someone again. It just doesn't work that way, I'm sorry," said Pathinia.

"I never said I didn't believe. I said 'what if'. It's not fair that she's gone. I didn't mean for her to go. It was just a question damn it," said Ben.

"It may have been, but this place doesn't change based on questioning something. It changes based on your own personal beliefs and no one else's. Even I understand that," said Brandon.

"But you have all the knowledge there could ever be Brandon. Of course you understand that."

"Is that completely the truth? I too learned something here today. Don't forget, I thought the creator built an army against us. I never realized that he was dissected by creatures like yourself. We too have things to learn."

"You're right and I'm sorry, but this whole thing is crazy. It's so hard to believe the things that are being told to me. You're sitting here before me and my belief in aliens is confirmed. Little Pathie here, not only an alien, but a ghost at that. Melite a religion within herself, it's overwhelming; so forgive me."

"Benji, you are the one that must forgive yourself. You can't keep beating yourself up over the things that are hard for you to understand," said Pathinia.

"Benjamin, she's right. You should be proud of the things that you have learned thus far. You have been shown a lot and you have digested many things. You have made friends here. All I, and I'm sure Pathinia and Melite would agree, ask is that you don't forget us when you get to your final destination. You take what you have learned here and apply it to your life on Earth. You

are a very powerful person, very impressive.
I've learned from you, as you have hopefully
learned from me, from us."

"Why are you talking as if you are
leaving? I'm not exactly done talking to you
guys."

"Because Benji, it's time for you to go
now. Morning approaches," said Pathinia.

"It's never been night," said Ben.

"It's a matter of perception Ben. Don't
forget that, it's a matter of perception,"
said Brandon.

As Brandon was finishing what he had to
say Ben noticed the red hands' fingers
wrapped around his waist. The hand could not
have been Brandon's because he was sitting
before him, but whose? He clutched at the arm
to free himself, but the arm was tightly
clinched around him. He couldn't speak. His
eyes shifted from Brandon to Pathinia. With
one hefty tug he was falling. He didn't fight
it; he just drifted down the rabbit hole.

It wasn't totally dark this time. Images
of every planet he had been to and the people
he had met filled the walls as he fell.
Feeling the pillow beneath his head he knew
he was back in the tearoom. Looking up, the
dark hole was gone. A solid ceiling appeared
before him. The light in the room finally
attached to something. He closed his eyes
satisfied.

Chapter 14: Departing

Waking up seemed most difficult this morning, more than it had any other morning in the tearoom. Excitedly, he jumped up and got dressed. He didn't even take a shower. All he wanted to do was talk to Athena. Then making his way down to see Marygolde for one of her famous breakfasts.

"Well, good morning Benjamin. I see you didn't need my help last night. Sleeping in peace was finally your own doing," said Marygolde setting a plate in front of him before he could even order.

"Nope not at all. This whole place looks different with ceilings."

The black abyss that had filled the tearoom had disappeared, as had the one in his room. Each light above the tables affixed firmly to the ceiling. The crisscrossing beams vaulted high above impressed him. It had finally started to look like the cottage he had originally seen from the outside.

"It is a most wonderful morning
Marygolde. Do you think Athena would be upset
if I ventured outside before talking to her?
I'd like some fresh air before leaving. Well
not to get ahead of myself, if I get to
leave."

"I don't think you'll have a problem
with leaving today. And I know Athena well
enough to know that she most likely would not
be upset if you took one last walk around
here."

Ben finished his breakfast as quickly as
he could in hopes of getting outside before
Athena appeared to stop him. He made his way
outside almost in a sprint. Before reaching
the door, he imagined Guarroutk as it was in
the middle of the night. As he opened the
giant door of Marygolde's it wasn't light
that filtered in, but total darkness.

The stars above him were shining bright.
There was no moon, but he didn't expect to
see one. In fact he wasn't expecting to see
stars. He made his way to the water. There,
he closed his eyes tight and imagined it to
be the middle of the day. When he opened his
eyes the sun was shining brightly.

He looked into the water in hope of
seeing Melite's face staring back at him.
There was nothing. He closed his eyes and
imagined her there, but when he opened them
there was nothing. He wondered if his
questioning of her belief had actually killed
her.

Upset, he sat down. A pair of hands
covered his eyes from behind him, "Guess
who?" the soft voice whispered into his ears.

"Melite," Ben said, "Is it really you?"

The hands uncovered his eyes. He slowly turned to find not Melite before him, but Samantha.

"What are you doing here?" asked Ben.

"Wow, what a way to make a girl feel wanted. I…"

"I'm sorry, it's not that. It's just that I came out here to find someone. OK, that didn't sound great either."

"No, it didn't but I know what you mean. And it's OK. I have a surprise for you."

She took his hand and led him to the water. He glanced down at their reflections. He noticed his, but next to him wasn't Samantha. It was the beautiful iridescent-haired Melite.

"Samantha how can that…" but when he looked up Samantha was no longer standing there. "Melite, what the…"

"Never forget that this place is nothing like you will ever imagine. It's a mixture of everything that exists out there."

"Were you Samantha last time I spoke with her? Are you the same person?"

"Don't be silly Ben. I wasn't her this time. For some reason you wanted to see me and that's who was sent to you," Melite replied.

"And I'm sure deep down somewhere you wanted to see me too," said Samantha now standing to his other side.

"What? I may never want to leave this place. But now that you are both here, I do have a question. Why am I able to see Sam, but I can't see my brother? Not that I'm not happy to see you, cause I am; but I would have liked to have seen Alex that's all."

"That is a question that can't be answered Ben," replied Melite. "Not everything can be answered here. Only what needs to be answered to help you fight your demons."

"But my demons, or at least I think what may be my demons, is that I can't deal with my brother's sexuality."

"While I'm sure that is one of your demons Ben, I'm sure you'll find that there are a lot more than just that. There was our past together that you weren't able to deal with and maybe that's why I'm here and not Alex," answered Sam.

"OK, but you're not dead. How is that possible?"

"Again, Ben, all questions can't be answered here..."

"I know, I know, only those that can help me defeat my own personal demons," he interrupted Melite. "And before it is too late and you disappear like everything seems to do here, I want to say a proper goodbye."

He took hold of Melite giving her a hug and a kiss on the cheek. With their goodbyes said, she turned and walked into the river. Her fins appeared on her arms and legs as the water got deeper and deeper. Eventually she swam deep out of sight. Ben forced a smile on his face even though his chest was hurting from her goodbye.

"I take it you aren't done with your goodbyes, are you Ben?" Sam asked.

"Of course I'm not. Can you help me find

the rabbit hole around here?"

Together they searched until he found a tiny hole in the ground. It seemed much smaller than he remembered. In fact, he didn't think it was the right hole, but he stuck his hand into the hole hoping he would find the hand of Pathinia. Instead of finding her, a rabbit sunk his teeth deep into Ben's hand.

He pulled his hand from the hole to find that there was no blood nor were there teeth marks.

"As crazy as this place is, I'm going to miss it."

"Benji I'm sure you will," a tiny voice answered from behind him.

"Pathie, I'm so excited to see you. I didn't get to say goodbye. How could I not say goodbye to you?"

"The light appeared after last night, but I didn't want to go without saying goodbye to you too."

Pathinia ran to Ben, he knelt down and hugged her. The two gave their goodbyes.

"Look Ben, can you see it?" she asked, "It's the light."

Ben looked everywhere and couldn't see it. "I'm sorry Pathie I don't see anything."

"Coming from the rabbit hole. It's so bright," she said as she walked to the edge of the hole. "Look my mommies in there. She's calling to me Ben."

"Then what are you waiting for, get going."

She ran back to give him another hug. He held her tight and a tear fell from his face.

She told him not to be sad. He assured her they were tears of happiness, although he knew differently. Smiling at him as if she knew he was lying to her, she turned and jumped into the hole.

Sam helped him to his feet and hugged him.

"If that's it Ben, I think we should say our goodbyes now and you should probably be getting back to Athena. I'm sure she is wondering where you are."

"You know Athena? You know what, never mind. There is one more goodbye I need to make or two."

She followed him as he walked over to the woods. He walked into them calling out for Brandon.

"And how did you know to find me here?" Brandon asked.

"Actually, I assumed I could have looked for you under that rock if I wanted to and you would have been there. I figured you would rather have appeared from the woods instead of from under a rock."

"Funny boy you are. I'm sure you're right and if so, then yes I would have rather come out of the intriguing trees than from under a muddy rock."

"Then how did you know I was looking for you?"

"I heard your thoughts and I came to you, of course. Besides, I'm sure as you believe we didn't say a proper goodbye."

"As creepy as it is, that you knew that, it's nice to see you again. Even though it will probably be the last time."

The two said their goodbyes and to Ben's surprise, instead of just a firm handshake Brandon hugged him. Before the venture could get too sentimental, Brandon turned and disappeared into the trees. Ben turned to Sam; taking her by the hand he led them out of the woods. They talked as they walked back to the tearoom.

"Well here we are. My final destination, I hope."

"Ben I'm sure your life will be full of adventures to come and this will not be your last."

"Sam if it means anything to you here, I thank you for everything. It's great that you have your dad working on things."

"What do you mean?"

"I remember some things from the hospital before coming here. I remember you coming into the room telling the cops to do their jobs, using your father's pull. Even after everything we've been through, and of course after everything that has happened, I forgive you. We will work on things when and if I ever get back. I promise you that much. I at least owe that much to Alex."

"Oh Benjamin, it means everything that you even feel that way. I'm sure things will turn out great on the other side."

The two said their goodbyes. As Ben grabbed the door handle he turned to tell her one last thing, but she was gone. *Well for what it's worth now. I love you Sam. I'll see you soon.* He spoke out loud in hopes that somehow she would hear him. He pulled the door open.

Marygolde greeted him at the bar. He tried to conceal his emotions, but it was an impossibility, especially against the woman who knew everything. Marygolde poured him a drink, "It'll help with the pain." She directed him to Athena's table. Athena was already waiting for him. Slowly, he walked looking around at the tables and he could clearly make out the people and their conversations. For the first time being in Guarroutk, he was sad at the thought that he may be leaving. If his talk with Athena went well that is.

"It is all right to be sad you know, Benjamin. It is a fact of life. We live, we learn, we love, we procreate, we die, recycle. You are allowed to mourn even those who have not died. You may mourn all those you have lost and may never see again. Lost friends, loves, family, pets, you name it. However, it is also all right to celebrate the lives they lived and not be sad. They are in a better place now."

"I understand that Athena, but this is difficult. Half of the things I'd be mourning here, I'd have problems believing in out there. It's hard to have your life flipped upside down only to realize you've been living your life upside down. Is it possible to mourn your own life?"

"I think it be wise to mourn the death of an old life, but do not forget to celebrate the birth of a new one."

"Of course not."

Ben could not help the single tear forming in his right eye. Silence filled in

around him. He no longer heard the tables
around him; he allowed the darkness to
consume the objects outside the light that
shone on Athena's table. It was peaceful and
at this moment, a bit of peace was all he
wanted.

"You have met a lot of people here
Benjamin. All of them have touched you in a
way that you thought could never be. Your
life has, and will forever be changed."

Ben did not respond to her. Instead he
thought of each person he had meet while he
had been in Guarroutk. As he thought of each
one, visions of them appeared in the empty
chair to his right. The lessons he had
learned from each one reverberated in his
head. A new tear appeared for each one as
they were replaced by the next. Occasionally,
as the images disappeared, he would look to
Athena who also had tears in her eyes almost
as if she could hear everything that was
going on in his mind.

The sadness in her face only made him
more upset. It did not interrupt his thoughts
though. As the last person vanished from the
chair he began to think of all the things he
had done wrong in his life. Even if at the
time he thought it had been the right thing.
Everything had already happened and there was
no way to change the past; for some things
there would be no way to correct them either.
What had been done could not be undone; they
were dead.

Alex and his parents were gone. He
couldn't find anything to make him smile. He
had wronged them all with his foolishness.

"You cannot beat yourself up Benjamin. You cannot hold yourself responsible for ignorance. You acted on what you knew. Is that a bad thing? No, it is not. The thing is, now that you have learned from your mistakes, take that and move forward."

"I guess you are right. Things are not always that easily explained."

"And what else is it that you have learned by being here Benjamin?"

"That aliens do exist and why they exist. That you are, or once were real. That things are not always as they appear. Our demons can be defeated, especially when they are pointed out to us. Ghosts and an afterworld really do exist. My *god* may not be the exact truth and most importantly, he is or could not be the only truth. Evil is real, but without it there could be no true good. So, is everyone in this *realm good?*"

"Not exactly, Benjamin. Good and evil both have access to this place. Besides, even those who are good still have some evil within them. There is no such thing as pure good and with all due respect, there is no such thing as pure evil either."

"What about heaven then, is there pure happiness there?"

"As I said, there is no such thing as pure good or pure evil."

"Athena a simple no would have sufficed. I'm sure it's against the rules somewhere or do you just take pleasure in making people feel stupid?"

"It is not about making you feel stupid. I am merely a guide. All the questions you have, you have to come to a conclusion on your own. No one can tell you how or what to believe. You should understand that by now. It is what you believe, even more so than what you know, that shapes who you are. Simply knowing something means nothing unless you believe it. Some things are a lot easier to believe in. They are as clear as black and white. Such as the definition of a word or of anything that is definitive, wood is solid and water is liquid.

"It is the gray areas that are harder to explain. Even then we tend to force people to see black and white, right and wrong. Everything is not always that easily explained. On Earth it is the struggle of not only knowledge that they fight, it is religion or their beliefs as well."

"The sad thing to that is, I'm a victim of that. I'm partially to blame for my brother's death. I refused to see gray, as did my father. My mother, I'm not so sure anymore. I thought it was because of her that my parents died and then I learned that it wasn't her fault but it was my father's. That makes you question things. Speaking of which, is it normal for evil to be allowed to live in your presence as Wes does?"

"That Benjamin is where you are mistaken. Wes may be an evil person in your eyes because of your parents. Understandably so, your mother was innocent in the situation, or was she? What we do know is that there was something about your father's actions or lifestyle that put him on Wes's radar. He had a choice you know. Can you actually blame Wes for your father's own doing?"

"But he kills people. Is that not wrong? Since when is he the law? Don't answer that, I realize it's a stupid question and that nothing is ever as it seems here. Yes, though my father may have been doing something wrong, but death Athena, death?"

"Again, Benjamin, I cannot tell you anything about that. Your father was not of my concern. All I can tell you is that he had a choice. He made it for himself. The choice he was given, neither you nor I will ever know. It could have been anything."

"And you said my mother may not have been innocent. Is that because she could have helped my father change and didn't?"

"Benjamin you are asking questions I am unable to answer. As much as I would like to, I just cannot."

"I understand. Do you think I could leave now? I'd really like to get back to Maria. I miss her and can't wait to see her again. I'd even love to see Jimmy. It may be that I can't see Alex again, but at least I can make peace with Jimmy."

"I cannot send you back, Benjamin. You are the only one with the power to go back. Once you have learned what you need to know, you will go."

"No, no, no, it isn't supposed to work that way. I feel as though I have learned everything that I can possibly learn here. I'm ready to go back now. And you said you would decide."

"I am sorry, Benjamin. You will go when

it is time to go. Until that time comes, you will be stuck here. I have said my peace to those who need to know. It is known that I feel you are ready to return. From this point it is not up to me anymore."

They sat in silence once again. Ben's hurt turned to furious anger. His eyes had dried. His arms were crossed in front of him. A book appeared in front of Athena and she began to read. Eventually, Marygolde showed up putting a plate of food in front of both of them.

"You know Benjamin it isn't fair to be angry with Athena, she doesn't have control," Marygolde said, having a seat in the empty chair to his right.

"Seriously, now it's going to be like that. You're both going to tell me it's my fault that I have to stay here. This isn't fair. I want to see Maria."

"Oh Benjamin, please, do not be dramatic," said Athena.

"Seriously, you are going to tell me not to be dramatic. How would you feel if you were told you were stuck somewhere? What would you do?"

"Have you ever thought that maybe there are two people you need to say goodbye to before you can go?" Marygolde asked him.

"Um… who is left to say goodbye to? I've said goodbye and made my peace with Brandon, Pathinia, Melite and Sam."

"Huh-hum…" Marygolde cleared her throat.

"Oh my god, I'm sorry, Marygolde," said Ben, as he realized that the two most important people to him in Guarroutk were sitting before him.

He felt ashamed that he had been so angry with Athena. She had sat there patiently reading a book until he figured it out. It had been dinnertime before he realized and he wouldn't have realized it nor would he have realized it was dinnertime had Marygolde not interjected.

"Marygolde, you make things so easy for people sometimes. You must always meddle," said Athena.

"The boy would never have figured it out if it had been left up to you," responded Marygolde, with a tiny smirk on her face. "And I can't have him taking up anymore space in my place. His room is needed."

Ben understood what he needed to do and it wasn't only a few simple goodbyes. He stood up from the table and gave Athena a hug and a kiss on the cheek. He took the time to thank her for everything and what a pleasure it had been to meet her. When he turned to bid his farewells to Marygolde she was already gone. She was back at the bar.

He left Athena sitting at her table and headed to the bar. Turning one last time to see Athena, he saw her wipe a tear from her eye. He smiled turning back to the bar.

"Marygolde, I have to thank you most of all. Its crazy I know, but I feel that despite everything that has happened here, I wouldn't have been able to learn what I needed to learn unless it had been from you helping me out. You are the one who led me where I needed to go."

"My child it wasn't only due to my

doing, it was your own undoing that allowed you to learn what you needed. I just nudged you along the way. I can get away with things that most people can't get away with. It has been nice meeting you officially."

"I do have one last question for you. Sheriff Scott was here and I mean physically here, wasn't he?"

"Benjamin, what a smart boy you are becoming. One day, maybe Sheriff Scott can explain to you what you saw. I feel it is his place to tell you and not mine."

"Grrr… I somehow figured you would tell me something like that. Then I guess that means it's time for me to say goodbye to you as well."

It was the hardest farewell for Ben. Marygolde had somewhat become a mother to him during his time in Guarroutk. It was also by far his most upsetting farewell. It took him awhile to actually spit the words out, but he eventually said what he needed to say, *goodbye*. He finally parted her and retired to his tiny room one last time. He crawled into his bed and waited.

Chapter 15: Demons

Ben stared at the solid ceiling hoping that the blackness would return. He started drifting in and out of consciousness. Several times he wondered if he had really seen the darkness. The thoughts that he had but one more thing to deal with started to fade. He believed that he would never be able to go back; he was stuck here forever.

Angry, he stood on the bed and punched at the ceiling.

"Where are you? Who are you?"

Ben sat back down on the bed. He didn't know what to do next. He had thought the last thing left to do was to confront the creature with the red arm. Especially now that he knew it hadn't been Brandon the entire time. After he had given up and was worn out, was when it happened. A tiny hole appeared directly above where he was sitting. Just as before a red hand extended down reaching toward his neck. '*Not tonight*', rang through his head. He mustered the energy, grabbed the arm with both hands, and yanked as hard as he could. To the floor fell a red creature barely clothed, slick coal-black eyes and hair, and tiny horns protruded from his devilish forehead.

Ben gazed at the creature realizing that the childlike demon sitting before him was a younger version of himself. He didn't know what to do or what to say to the demon. How could he know; it was himself. It wasn't long before the demon spoke to him through his grizzly teeth.

"You look surprised Benjamin. Did you honestly expect to find someone up there besides yourself? A form of you that you would recognize, oh so familiar, you should have known better."

"But I know everything about myself. What could you have to tell me?"

"You have fragmented beliefs of what you think of yourself. I know the truth. I know the person you really are, for I am the evil that resides inside of you. I know every evil thing you did or think you have done. I know your worst fantasies and desires. I know when you've been naughty or nice. I know when you've masturbated and the thoughts you had during them. I know…"

"I get it, you know."

"But that, see, Benjamin, you don't get it. You have had all this time here to deal with your demons and each time you have chosen to do something else. I have come for you every night and every night you have turned me away. You either don't give a shit

or you are scared to know, both of which I
know are true. Your problem all your life has
been about something else; about blaming
others and never taking responsibility
because you're terrified."

Ben grew angry with the demon in front
of him. He knew he had lived a decent life
and had always lived by what he knew was
right. To hear this thing before him speak
about him in another way was not true. He
felt that the creature was trying to upset
him and it was working.

"Go ahead Benjamin. Do it! Plunge at me.
Attack me. You know you want to. Kill me.
Kill your demons. Your suffering will end.
That's it Benjamin, I can feel the anger
rising inside of you. Kill me and go home.
You can be with Maria."

Ben couldn't resist; he lunged forward
at the demon falling full force onto the
floor. When he pulled himself to his knees,
he was no longer in the tearoom he was in his
childhood tree house. Before him sat his
demon self, his childhood self and Alex. He
remembered this day. It was the day that Alex
fell from the tree house. The demon grinned
and his younger self shoved Alex. Everything
froze.

"That isn't how it happened and you know
that."

"That is what you want to believe. Alex
loved you and looked up to you. He loved you
so much that he believed you did it by
accident and so that you wouldn't get in
trouble, went along with your story of
tripping on the loose floorboard."

"He did trip over the loose floorboard. Look right there," Ben moved to Alex's frozen childhood form and pointed out the floorboard beneath his foot.

"And you think he would have hit that going backward, had you not pushed him?"

"I didn't push him."

"You were jealous of him. You knew then he was different and you despised the attention your parents gave him over you. Face it Benjamin, you were extremely jealous over Alex and you always were."

"I was young; of course I was jealous of him. I was the only kid for five years of my life. What child wouldn't be jealous of a younger sibling?"

"Jealous to the point that you were willing to push him from a tree house over a ravine. Knowing that if he fell, his lifeless body would probably never be found. You knew what you were doing that day."

"I never pushed him. I don't know what it is that you insist on showing me here. I did not push him."

"You can say it over and over as much as you like, but what you see is not by malicious intention. I see only what you refuse to. I am the demon you locked away."

The image frozen in front of Ben rewound and played over and over. Each time with a different outcome. Alex fell piercing his temple on a rusty nail. He fell out the door crushing his skull on the thick tree trunk; Ben could hear his skull snap. He fell swiftly out the door through the fog, screaming the entire way down. The final

time, the young Alex was pushed by his big
brother and then saved by him.

"That is what happened Benjamin. You
pushed him out of pure jealousy. It was his
birthday and you hated it. You hated him
getting the attention. You never felt guilty
for breaking his arm. You only felt bad
because you knew you'd get into trouble.
After you got in trouble, you wished you
hadn't saved him. You wish you had let him
fall to his peril. ."

Ben began to remember that day more
clearly. He remembered pushing Alex. He
remembered feeling ashamed for feeling the
way he had and then he caught Alex. He knew
then what he had done, but he didn't remember
anything about wishing he had completed his
task. He only remembered feeling remorse for
doing what he had done. The demon was right
about shoving him, but wrong about his
feelings.

The younger Ben helped Alex out of the
tree house as he remembered it happening. He
turned to argue with the demon and found it
charging him. The demon's horns hit him
square in the chest thrusting him backward
out the door of the tree house.

He soared through the mist. He could see
his demon self behind him. Ben felt the cold
ground smack hard against the back of his
head. His demon self floated gradually to the
ground. Ben heard the noise around him, 'the
annual_Halloween Party'. He stood up brushing
the dirt from his arms, face and then his
pants. He had landed on the path that led him
to where he had found Alex, Sam and the man

dressed as a vampire.

"Why here? What did I do wrong this evening?"

"It's not what you did wrong. It's what you chose not to see."

"What? We are walking toward Alex, Sam, and the guy that called himself the *Count*."

"That's where you are wrong. There was someone else there that night. You chose not to remember this person."

He followed the demon up the hill only to find his younger self arguing with his friends behind him. They arrived before his younger self to find Alex kissing another guy. Samantha was there as was the *Count*, but Alex was indeed making out with another guy. When the group could hear the younger Ben walking through the trails, Alex quickly released the other guy and turned toward Sam and the *Count*. Ben got a better look at the boy that was kissing Alex; it was Tracy's younger brother Matt.

"What the hell? He wasn't here that night."

"Benjamin, he was there. He was there the entire time."

"Then why didn't Sam say anything about it the other night when we talked? You'd think she would bring that up."

"You never caught them kissing. We came here a little early so that you could see what you really missed. Had you not made so much noise coming up the hill, you would have seen more than you did. A piece of you knew that you didn't want to see what was happening up here so you made lots of noise."

- 226 -

"But we could all see them from the square. There was not another boy up here."

"Oh but there was. He left through that way."

Ben noticed that the direction he was pointing was where Sheriff Scott had come up to the group. He started to remember seeing someone leaving in that direction as he approached, but didn't remember noticing who it was. He did remember how he met Tracy. It had been through Matt and Alex.

"Anger Benjamin. You were so full of anger that night you chose not to see everything you needed to see. Or should have seen. You wanted to blame the *Count* for everything that your mind blocked out."

Indeed as his younger self approached, Matt exited. Matt stopped long enough to see who was coming and the younger Ben looked directly at him. Ben hadn't meet Matt at this point, so it didn't seem anything worth remembering until now. Matt had noticed the fury in Ben's eyes and went to find Sheriff Scott.

"So, that's why Sheriff Scott came that night?"

"It is and can you feel the anger, the wrath that was emanating from us? Oh, the anger you could spout out. It felt so good."

"But it isn't me! I'm not that person anymore."

"No, it isn't you anymore. You finally got what you wanted. You got your parents to yourself."

"That isn't how it went. I never wanted Alex out of our lives. Sam and I already went through this. I'm sorry things happened that way."

"You may be sorry, but you can't be totally sorry unless you remember everything that you did."

Sheriff Scott arrived and broke the group up. Ben's younger self escorted Alex and Sam away. Knowing that in a few seconds he would be able to hear finally what they had been arguing about. Ben walked over to where the two were standing in hope that the images wouldn't fade before he could listen in.

"You will leave those boys alone," said Sheriff Scott.

"And who do you think you are? We go way back Scott and you know you are not powerful enough to take me out," said the *Count*.

"You have your night here in town, but you take your ass back to Calgary by morning. If I find out that one hair on one person in this town is harmed by you or any of your people, I will have no problems hunting you down and driving a stake through that pathetic chest of yours," said Scott.

"I may just take the younger brother. He would be a great addition to my clan," said the *Count*.

"You will do no such thing. Both of them are to be left alone," replied Scott.

"The older one has such anger inside him. Very powerful one, maybe I'll take him instead."

"You will take neither of them. If he doesn't watch that temper of his, he'll be of Wes's concern."

"He's here you know?"

"Yes, *Count* I know he is here."

Ben turned to his demon self to ask if they knew they were there, but found the creature on the ground ready to pounce. It leapt toward Ben and they both fell to the ground. Rolling through the dirt, they were stopped by a wall. Ben jumped quickly to his feet to find himself standing in his parents' house. The demon stood across the room from him, his horns had disappeared and his eyes were no longer yellow. Its eyes were the same color blue as his own, leaving the creature to look more like him.

"They knew we were listening. How is that possible?"

"You knew that when you were younger. You tried so hard to hear them because something in you told you that they were talking about you. It was you they were talking about. It wasn't Alex, but your anger for him allowed you to believe they were talking about Alex."

"I never thought anything about what they were talking about."

"Then why did you listen so hard?"

Ben knew the demon had a point. By now he knew not to argue with it. Everything thus far the demon had been right or mostly right.

Tracy walked past them and up the stairs. This was the night that Ben discovered that Alex was gay. Ben followed her up the stairs. She had just left him in the kitchen. She walked into Ben's room to find that Samantha was already in there.

"Why are you in here? You know Ben is

right downstairs. What would you have done had he been with me?" asked Tracy.

"I don't know. I didn't come in here in hope you'd be alone, but to help shield things from Ben," answered Sam.

"What do you mean?"

Sam did not answer her and instead walked over and kissed her. They made their way to the bed and sat down. Ben could feel the fury rising inside of him. He could see the horns reappearing on the demon's head. He knew his younger self would be walking through the door at any moment. He was right; at that very moment the door opened and his younger self walked into the room.

"What the hell are you two doing?" asked Ben.

Neither of the girls could respond. They both jumped up quickly. Tracy straitened out her shirt.

"Tell me what is going on here?" Ben asked again.

"It isn't exactly what it looks like Ben," said Tracy.

"It's exactly what it looks like," said Sam.

"I don't give a fuck what it is exactly. Does Alex know you have betrayed him like this, Sam? And Tracy, does Matt know about your extra curricular activities with his best friend's girlfriend?" Ben asked furiously.

"I'm sure they both already know everything," Sam responded.

"Really? Well let's go find out shall we?"

"Benjamin, you may not want to do that," said Samantha.

Ben didn't listen to her; instead he flew out of the room toward Alex's.

"Ben wait, stop. You shouldn't," said Tracy.

Ben opened the door to find Alex and Matt lying in bed together kissing.

"You're gay?" exclaimed Ben.

"Yes, big brother I am," replied Alex.

"And of all days, of all days, you pick today to tell me? To tell mom and dad?"

"It's time Ben, IT IS time!! I have lived with this for long enough. Besides, I wouldn't have had to tell anyone had you not just walked into my room."

"You Sam, you did this to him didn't you?" asked Ben.

"I did nothing to him. He was this way when I met him three years ago," replied Sam.

"And all of you. All of you have known about this? Your relationship with my brother was a lie, a cover up so that they could sneak around. Tracy, you knew?"

"I did know. Ben I'm so sorry. I never meant to keep secrets from you," Tracy pleaded.

"At this point it doesn't matter much. You've already done your damage. You need to get out of my house and take your filthy brother with you."

"Ben, that isn't your place."

"Oh, you'll be right behind him as soon as we talk to mom and dad. I can't believe you all are doing this on my parents' anniversary," said Ben angrily.

"Ben I had no intention of doing this today, but since you know, it's time for everyone to know. It's time for all of us to have a clean slate and start over," said Alex.

"That's enough. I already know how the rest of this goes. You can stop showing this to me," said the older Ben.

Everything froze as it had done in the tree house.

"The anger arises in you again. You're right! You know what happens next. You outted your own brother to your parents and then took joy in knowing that you'd finally be in the spot light again. The perfect boy wouldn't be perfect any longer. The truth of him being different was finally out there. You'd no longer have to be jealous."

"That isn't true. I admit that I was jealous when I was younger, but not now. Not at this point. He was gay and that was disgusting. I realize now that I was wrong and that he was normal. He was himself."

"But that's not the point. Your anger was so high. You blamed your anger on him being different and you held it against Samantha. You never took the blame yourself. It was someone else. It was something else. It wasn't you."

Everything unfroze and Ben followed the gang out of the bedroom. At the top of the stairs, Ben looked back at the demon that once again was flying toward him. Ben fell down the stairs submerging him into a foggy smoke. When he pulled himself up this time he was the only person on the dance floor at E^2.

The demon was nowhere to be found. He walked all through the bar, across the main level and the catwalks above. Nothing. He proceeded outside with a decision to go up to Heaven or down to Hell. It wasn't a hard choice for him, where would he find a demon but in hell.

He walked down the stairs toward the bar. He was actually nervous to see what he would find. There was no-one at the bar. What he had remembered was the bar was pretty crowded and they went to Heaven, they never came down to Hell. Sitting at the bar was the demon having a drink. There was a full shot sitting next to him.

"Take it, it's for you after all," said the demon.

"Not thirsty and besides the last thing I want is alcohol and definitely if it's coming from you."

"From me is from you. Don't forget I am you. Why would I want to hurt you? If you die so do I? But if you kill me you're free of all of your sins."

"Why do you keep trying to get me to kill you?"

"So, that you can be free."

"No! That I don't trust. What are we doing here?"

"It's somewhat the last of the puzzle for you."

The bar immediately filled with people. The demon disappeared into the crowd. Ben followed him. They moved their way through the crowd up to Heaven. He could see Alex, Jimmy, and Maria sitting with his present day self talking. How could this be a part of the puzzle was beyond him. He knew that at this point he was trying to work on things with Alex. Maria and Ben left Jimmy and Alex and ventured back into the bar. After they were gone he got to hear what had gone on between Alex and Jimmy.

"You believe he's really had a change of heart?" asked Jimmy.

"No, not really. I think it's only a matter of time before he gets pissed off at something again and leaves. It's taken me a long time to realize it, but with mom and dad gone there's no attention for him to try and win, so maybe he has really changed," said Alex.

"He really didn't feel that way did he?" asked Ben to the demon.

"Of course he did. I told you. He chose to defend you, but he never forgot what kind of person you were. He knew of your jealousy of him and of your wrath," said the demon.

"And he's downstairs lusting over Maria right now and there is nothing I can do about it. I'm so glad she hasn't slept with him. For her sake, I hope he has changed. I hope he isn't the same person," said Alex.

"And he knows of your lusts for women. Especially after being betrayed by Tracy for, not another man, but a woman," said the demon.

"It's a competition with him. First it was my parents and now it's going to be with Maria. He's a greedy son of a bitch sometimes. He'll try to take her from me, as he did with our parents. I'm not going to fight him Jimmy. I'm not. If she is stupid enough to fall for his bullshit then so be it. I'll still have you and I'll have Sam if she ever comes home."

"Your greed for attention," said the demon.

"You honestly think he's still that immature Alex?" asked Jimmy.

"Jimmy I know my brother. I wish differently, but since we were kids he's always wanted me out of his life. He's always envied the relationship I had with my mother."

"Ah, and with envy comes jealousy. We are back at the beginning Ben with everything leading to your anger, to your demons. Is everything he is saying making sense to you now?"

"So, if this is all true, then why haven't I been visited by Wes? Isn't he the deadly sins guy?"

"We all indulge in the seven deadly sins at some point in our lives. But yours always result in the same end, anger. If you keep going down this path I'm sure you will be a target for Wes. Now, let's go find yourself and Maria," said the demon.

"Please lead the way. You're not pushing me down another flight of stairs."

"Oh Benjamin, how quickly you learn. Follow me then."

The two left Alex and Jimmy to sit at the bar. Ben followed the demon. The demon stopped at the top of the stairs and turned to Ben.

"I'm sorry Benjamin. I can't help myself."

The demon jumped onto Ben and sunk its sharp, pointed teeth deep into his shoulder. Ben screamed in pain and fell forward down the stairs. When he landed he pulled the demon and threw him across the floor of the tearoom. They were back where they had started the evening.

"I will not fight you," said Ben.

"You may not fight me, but I'm going to fight you."

Ben pulled himself up sitting on the bed, watching the demon licking the blood from its lips, craving more. The demon jumped again pushing Ben back into the bed. Ben held the demon under the arms. It clawed at him scratching his arms and cheeks.

"I will not fight you. If you are a part of me then I have to live with it. I will not kill you."

The demon's hands slipped down around Ben's neck. He found it harder and harder to breath. He closed his eyes and opened them. The room switched between his room at the tearoom and a hospital room.

Chapter 16: Awakening

      Ben struggled with the demon on top of him, trying to afflict as little damage as possible to it. The hospital room became clearer and clearer. The demon began to fade into his chest; Ben continued to pull at the invisible hands around his throat.

    "Get the fuck off of me. I will not hurt you," Ben screamed.

    "Benjamin you're awake! You're awake. Nurse, Nurse, he's awake. Come in here!" screamed Samantha.

    The nurse came into the room.

    "Calm down Mr. Casey. Calm down. Quit struggling. You are all right now. You are awake," said the nurse.

    Ben stopped struggling as he opened his eyes. The demon had completely vanished within him. He blinked several times to see the nurse. Then he rubbed his eyes to make sure he was seeing clearly. Standing before him in a nurse's uniform was Athena. He couldn't believe his eyes.

"Athena, am I still in Guarroutk?"

"You are in Zion General Hospital, Benjamin. You had a horrible accident and have been in a coma for almost a week now. I am your nurse, Nurse Zorbas, but you may call me Athy."

"Athy, as in Athena right?"

"Yes, my first name is Athena, but I think you may have me confused with someone else."

"Don't play games with me Athena. You look and speak just like, well, just like you."

"I have been in your room almost every day. I am sure you have picked up on my voice. It is not uncommon for someone to hear voices and then incorporate them into their dreams, especially comatic ones."

"That is not what I have done and you know it."

"Benjamin, I do not know what else to tell you."

"Look at her Benjamin and you'll see it. You will," said Samantha.

"You, Samantha, you stay out of this. You should not even be here," said Athena glaring at Samantha with very cold and unfriendly eyes.

Ben looked at the nurse standing before him. He concentrated on her. The nurse's uniform disappeared and the green putty-colored robes showed through.

"It is you!"

Athena stood before him in her goddess robes, shaking her head in disagreement at

Benjamin. She continued to take his blood pressure and temperature. She kept working as if she had not been listening to him at all.

"Athena I can see your robes. I really can see them, damnit, quit playing games!"

"You have done very well my sweet boy, but here you will know me only as Athy, your nurse," said Athena. "Is that understood?" Athena turned toward Samantha with her eyes tightened and eyebrows twisted up, "You will not acknowledge me at all, is that clear to you?"

Samantha just shook her head and didn't dare to open her mouth.

"I think it is clear to both of us, but I'm really back. I'm home, right?"

"You are home, Benjamin."

"Seriously, I am home. I'm not going to wake up back in the tearoom am I? It's not that I'm not going to miss it, but I just want to make sure I'm not still stuck in that crazy dream state."

"No, Benjamin. You seem to have beaten your demons or learned to live with them. Most importantly, you have seen your mistakes. Take it and learn from it. You have a lot to do from here on."

"What is left for me to do?"

"It will all be made clear to you soon enough. Have you not learned to be patient? Everything will be revealed to you in due time. Do not rush life."

"Athena, there is so much I want to take back. There are so many things I want to do."

"But, Benjamin, you cannot…"

"I know I must learn from it and move

forward."

"Everything is not as you think it is. Let me go and find Maria for you. I know you have wanted to see her."

With that, Athena left the room before he could ask any more questions.

"Sam how is everything here?"

"What do you mean Ben?"

"Have they caught the guy who did this to us? Is your father working on the case?"

"My father isn't working on the case. He has had other things to deal with, but your case is being worked on. I think it better that you wait and speak to Sheriff Scott about it though. I don't know much more than you do."

"How do you not know more than me? I've been in a coma for the last week or so and you've been here."

"Oh, Benjamin. I wish I could help you more than I already have, but I can't."

The two sat in silence for a while. Ben lay there enjoying the fact that he was finally back. Although he missed Guarroutk and the tearoom, especially a good breakfast with Marygolde, he was glad to be home. He wondered if everything had actually been a dream since he was here in the hospital. But if it had been completely a dream, then how could Athena have been here. Could the nurse have been playing along with him the entire time or was it really the Goddess of wisdom making sure he awakened all right.

Then again, Sam sat before him. She had been there too. Maybe he did just hear the voices in his room and dream the whole thing up. The nurse played off the dreams well and Samantha acted like he was crazy. Ben came to the conclusion that he had indeed been dreaming. He learned important things about himself in those dreams. After all, dreams are windows into our subconscious. Some part of them had to be real. He never thought he was that creative though.

"Sam, have you been here the entire time?"

"I've been with you Ben. I've been watching over you."

"And I've been laying here in this bed the entire time?"

"What kind of question is that? You've been in a coma. It's not like you've been out shopping."

"OK, I was just wondering."

Ben laid his head back onto the pillow; he picked up the remote turning the television on. He flipped through the stations looking for anything to take his mind off of Guarroutk. He stopped on a program that reminded him of Melite. The show was about the lost city of Atlantis. Ben sat up turning in shock toward Samantha.

"How many times has this show played this week?"

"Benjamin, that is an odd question."

"Sam, please, I'm not in the mood to argue with you about this."

"It's played a few times I'm sure, but I don't ever remember your television being on."

"It must have been playing. It explains a lot."

Ben laid back down staring at the show on the lost city of Atlantis. They talked about Poseidon and the sea nymphs. His eyes began to water. He realized he had been dreaming. It was the program about the underwater city that made him dream of Melite and the Ocean world. 'Melite had been a dream', he thought. One of the 'friends' he had made that helped him understand his life was a dream. She wasn't real. If she wasn't real, that meant the others weren't real either.

The door opened. Athy walked through the door with Maria following behind. Instantly a smile came over Ben's face. He had wanted nothing more than to see Maria. He knew she was real. He had no idea what to tell her or how to tell her the things he had dreamt. He couldn't wait to get out of the hospital and be in her arms again.

"Benjamin, I'm glad you're awake. How are you feeling?" asked Maria.

The love and warmth he was used to hearing was gone. Her voice was cold. The way she spoke to him was a general concern and not that of someone he had fallen in love with. He chose to ignore it, thinking that it was because of Alex's death. He had just expected to hear more excitement now that he was awake and well.

"I'm so happy to see you."

"You are happy to see me?"

"Of course I'm happy to see you. Why wouldn't I be happy to see you?"

"Because she thinks you've lost your marbles that's why," said Sam.

"Why would I have lost my marbles?" asked Ben.

"Ben, what are you talking about? Are you sure you are all right?" asked Maria.

"I'm fine. I've supposedly been having the craziest dreams. I'm extremely glad to get to see you again."

"Again with the crazy talk? Why have you requested to speak to me?" asked Maria.

"A lot has happened to him Miss Logarakis, Maria. I am sure his perception of what has happened has been skewed a bit. You will have to listen and understand what he has to tell you," said Athena.

"She knows what she's talking about. She's pretty smart and understands a lot," said Sam.

"Thank you, but I have not lost perception of anything. Maria, I've been looking forward to seeing you. We have so much to talk about."

"Ben, I think you need to listen to Nurse Zorbas, I mean Athy. You've had a traumatic thing happen to you and you're not thinking correctly," said Maria.

"Maria, damnit. What is it with you people? Can I please speak for myself? I don't need any of your help."

"So then talk," Maria said.

"Why do you seem so angry with me?"

"Because I know that I was just a trophy for you to win. You sought out my attention just to steal me away from Alex. That is something that would never happen."

"I don't know why you guys thought that. I wasn't trying to steal you away from anyone. I genuinely liked you. I do like you. I think I may even love you."

"Benjamin, cool it with that, you may have gone too far with that," said Sam.

"But it's true," said Ben.

Ben could see the anger growing in Maria's face. He was confused. All he could think about was the amount of time they had spent together. The closeness they had developed and the support he had offered her after Alex's death.

"I don't know how you can say that Benjamin. It's crazy to say that. You barely know me," said Maria.

"I told you it was too much. She's not ready for this Ben. You should just stick to telling her about your *dream*," said Sam.

"I'm getting there," said Ben.

"Getting where?" asked Maria.

"To telling you about my dream."

"So, then tell me and leave this crazy love talk out of it because it's nonsense."

Ben went over everything that had happened to him in his dream state. He told her about his past. The things he had done to Alex. How his anger and rage overtook him. How the comatic dreams had changed the way he believed. The people he had met. He even told her about Brandon, Pathinia and Melite as well as the different worlds he visited. He talked about the demon that took him through his past and how he had to beat his demons in order to return. He could not resist telling her that the one thing that had kept him alive and strong throughout was his returning back to her.

"Ben as great as this all sounds, why is it me? Why is it me that kept you going?"

"Because, Maria, of what we had?"

"What do you mean, what we had?"

"Ben, you are opening up something you are not ready for," said Sam.

"Would you let me just tell her what I need to tell her?" said Ben.

"Tell me what?" asked Maria.

"The month we spent together was the most amazing month. I have never felt that way about anyone. You helped me through so much. The way no one has ever been able to do. I would never want to hurt you, nor would I have ever wanted to hurt Alex. I fell in love with you, Maria."

The anger that had started to fade with him telling her about the dream, flooded back as he mentioned his love for her.

"What month, Ben? We had one date. One whole date, Benjamin, one. I admit it was great and I was looking forward to spending more time with you, but then everything happened and you ended up here. I learned a lot about you as well while you were in this coma."

"What do you mean only one night? Maria, we spent almost an entire month together."

Sadness and confusion washed over him. There was so much he didn't understand. Guarroutk and the places he had been to, showed him his wrongdoing. He was ready to change, but there seemed to be more he had to figure out.

"Ben you must have been dreaming something more than you remember. We never spent a month together. We spent the one night out at dinner and the movies. Then we went to the diner where we spent the night talking. It was great. You took me back to Alex's and you stayed there. That night, we went to the club. We had an amazing time there as well. I was shocked that you were really as open to the idea about being there. Then I realized it was about you and an ongoing childish war with Alex and had absolutely nothing to do with me."

"That's bullshit Maria."

Ben could not help the anger. He hadn't even realized he had snapped at her.

"It's not bullshit Benjamin and you shouldn't yell. If you don't want to piss her off, I'd just be quiet and listen to what she has to say. She knows more of what's been going on here than you do. After all, you have been in coma. Right now you don't want to upset her more than she already is," said Samantha.

"It's bullshit? Really Benjamin? What exactly is this bullshit about Ben? You were so quick to rat Alex out to your parents to get him out of your life. You won that one," said Maria. "Then you wanted to take me from him as well didn't you? It would never work. Plus, you just admitted the things you have done to him. You just backed the stories I have heard."

"No, I'm not that shallow. You were his friend. I found you attractive. I am very appreciative for everything you had done for him. I'm so happy he had someone like you in his life. But it's too late for that now. At least I can make up for it with you and Jimmy."

"Oh Benjamin, you really are a stupid git sometimes," said Sam.

"Why do you keep interrupting me?" asked Ben.

"I'm not interrupting you, and what do you mean make it up to me and Jimmy? Jimmy's dead," said Maria.

"Jimmy's dead too? He didn't make it through? I don't get it. You were both fine. I may have been unconscious, but I remember you here in my room together. He was all right."

"Ben, you are crazy. He is dead." Tears fell down Maria's face.

"That's insane. It doesn't make sense at all. Two attacks and two deaths, how are they doing on the investigation?"

Through sobs and tears Maria spoke, "Ben, there was only one attack and only one death." Athena handed her some tissues.

"Maria, I understand I was in a coma, but I remember it clearly. In the first attack, they killed Alex and injured you pretty badly. We then spent some time together and went to the club for Alex's birthday. We were then attacked again where they tortured Jimmy pretty severely and left me to die in the brush behind the car."

"You're mistaken Ben. There was only one attack outside the diner. We were all hurt pretty seriously. I was knocked unconscious, after being thrown into the wall. You had a pipe slammed against the side of your head while you were attempting to save Jimmy. You fell into the guy holding the gun. The gun went off and Jimmy was shot in the head and killed. Please don't look at me like that. No one blames you for Jimmy's death. You attempted to rescue him. It was the pipe striking you in the head that put you into this coma," Maria explained.

"So, then when did Alex die?"

"What are you talking about? Alex isn't dead. He is alive. He is pretty broken up, but he is alive. Both his legs are broken and he has several broken ribs, but mostly a broken heart and spirit."

"Alex is alive?"

Tears began to fall down Ben's face. He had thought all this time that Alex had been dead. It now made sense as to why he never saw Alex in his dreams. He hadn't been dead after all. He would be able to make up all his mistakes to him personally.

"Silly boy, stop your sobbing and be a man, you'll see him soon," said Samantha.

"You really had no, clue did you?" asked Maria.

"Do you think he would be crying if he did?" said Sam.

"Of course I didn't know. I thought I'd never get to see him again. I wanted nothing more than to see him in Guarroutk. Athena, why didn't you tell me he was alive?"

"It was not my place to tell you. I figured you would want to hear it from your friends instead," answered Athena.

"You're a nurse," said Maria. "Why didn't you tell him? Isn't that what you are here for?"

"I had not the time. He was asking for you and besides that, I did not know until just now that he did not know. Between Ben and I, I think he knows now why I did not tell him. That is for him to know. Maybe one day, he will be able to share that with you," said Athena.

"You tell her Athy," said Samantha. Athena did not respond to her. She just stared at her which made Sam sink back into her chair again.

"Why do I feel like there is more going on between you guys than you'd like to tell me?" asked Maria.

"He's told you everything," said Sam. "Haven't you been listening to him?"

"Enough already," exclaimed Ben. "When can I see Alex?"

"I'll go tell him you are awake and try to find a nurse to help him. Athy, do you think they will be able to wheel him over here?" asked Maria.

"My dear, if they are unable to wheel him over we will take Benjamin over there. However, I think they will want to bring Alex here until we know for sure that Ben is stable," said Athena.

"Don't worry Ben if everything you say is true we have time now to work back up to what you remember. Just understand that right now it isn't as easy for me to feel the same way you do. What you remember of the events and what really happened are not the same. I am willing to work on something with you, but it also depends on what Alex has to say about it. You do understand that, right?" explained

Maria.

"I do. I am just ecstatic that things are not as I thought they were. This is such a relief. It makes me extremely happy that Alex is really alive."

"Well, try to keep your happiness under control when Alex comes in here. After all, his boyfriend is dead. You may not want to seem too happy about that," said Sam.

"I'm sure you are happy he's alive, but Ben when he comes in here find another way to say it. He lost Jimmy. You might not want to seem too happy," said Maria.

"Ok guys I get it. I only need to be told once."

Maria just looked at him and continued; "Besides, it may be harder to convince him that you have changed than it was to convince me. For some reason, I feel closer to you than I should. I believe what you have told me. Otherwise I wouldn't be willing to work on things with you. Something about it makes me happy and warm. I'll help you work on Alex, but he is very angry right now. Also, he knows you didn't get Jimmy killed, but part of him still blames you for it."

"You just told him no one blames him," said Sam. "Why are you playing games with him?"

Maria didn't answer Sam. She kissed Ben on the forehead and left the room. Athena followed behind her. Ben turned his attention back to the television. There was now a program on about Mars, the Red Planet. The announcer talked about how life could have existed on the planet at one time and about the famous satellite photo of the face on the surface. The picture reminded him of Brandon.

"Let me guess, this show has played several times too?"

"I'm sure it has," answered Sam.

"You know Sam; it isn't only Alex and Maria that I need to make things up to. I owe you an apology as well."

"Benjamin, you owe me nothing. I know how you feel."

Before Benjamin could speak, the door to the room opened again.

Chapter 17: Closed Case

    To Ben's surprise it was not Alex that came through the door. It was Sheriff Scott and Athena. Ben didn't know if he should be angry or relieved to see Sheriff Scott; but a little bit of both was how he felt. However, not for the reason he had expected to feel them. He wanted to confront Sheriff Scott about being in Guarroutk. How could he though, he had come to the conclusion that it was fantasy; it was a dream and not reality. He figured mentioning Guarroutk to Sheriff Scott would only make him look insane, but he had to know.

    "Benjamin, I came as soon as I heard you were awake. I'm glad to see you came through," said Scott.

    "Yes, I took care of what I needed to take care of and came back to you guys. Is that not right, Athena?"

    Ben knew that if Athena were who she was and Sheriff Scott was truly there, then there would be a way of discussing it to catch them both off guard.

"You did just fine on your own and you came back to your loved ones just as you were supposed to do," said Athena.

"Athena, there are reasons you are my favorite person," said Sheriff Scott.

"You're on to something Benjamin," said Samantha.

"Oh foolish girl. Of course he is and we are not going to play silly games with him like you have done," said Athena.

"Wait, so you guys aren't going to play like I'm crazy? Sheriff Scott, you were there weren't you? I know you were," said Ben.

Behind Sheriff Scott on the television, a commercial was playing that drew Ben's attention away from the conversation.

…discover the lives of the Caveman. How they hunted? How they lived? Did they live in harmony with one another or were they ravaging animals? Next, on 'The Truth of the Caveman'.

"Of course it is, of course the show of Cavemen will follow the 'Mars – A Discovery', and before that was a damn show on Atlantis. You are doing this somehow to make me feel crazy aren't you Athena?" questioned Ben.

"Benjamin, no one is doing anything to make you feel crazy. I told you that people hear things around them while they are in comas and those sounds become part of the dream," said Athena.

"You two are a piece of work aren't you? Trying to make him feel crazy. Why are you doing this? Just tell him," said Sam.

"Look Sam, it isn't that simple. This has been explained to you. They will be explained to him, but right now there are more important things to handle right now," said Sheriff Scott.

"Wait, what are you three hiding? I don't want to talk about anything else until we discuss what you guys are hiding from me," said Ben.

"Too bad Benjamin. There is nothing to explain and I'm here only to discuss the progress of your case and that's it," said Sheriff Scott.

"Whatever, I understand. 'In due time', blah, blah, blah."

"Exactly Benjamin," Athena said and let out a slight chuckle.

"Anyway, your brother told us that as you lunged for the guy holding the gun, you screamed a name…"

"I did?" Ben interrupted Sheriff Scott in amazement, "has it at least helped you with your case?"

"Well, he still hasn't learned patience now has he Athena? Anyway, we have picked the person up for questioning, but we need to hear your side of the story before we can go any further with the investigation."

"Oh great," said Sam. "His version of the story we already know is flawed. He thinks there were two attacks. He's heard a lot of voices that weren't really there. How are we going to know what he says will help him?"

"Sam," said Sheriff Scott, "there are things you don't understand. He could have had fifteen versions of the attack, but all we need is for him to identify the voice in one attack and one only."

"Yes, but Scott if there was only one attack and he remembers fifteen, won't that be enough for…"

"Sam, don't you say the name. We need that to come from Ben without any coercing from us," said Scott. "Is that understood?"

Sam shook her head and sunk back into her chair.

"I heard Richmond or at least I thought I heard Richmond's voice once. But it was in the second attack and that attack, from what I have been told, didn't take place, did it?"

"No, Benjamin it didn't," said Scott. "However, that doesn't mean you didn't hear it the first time just before you were struck on the head. Everything you remember happening after being struck may not have been true, but you needed it to happen that way in order to deal with your own problems. Therefore, you probably heard it and incorporated it into the timeline the way you needed it to fit."

"Had you remembered it after the first attack, in your dream, you would have gone straight to the police. The other attack would not have happened. You would not have dealt with your problems," continued Athena.

"Then you would have woken up here and things would have gone back to the way they had always been. You would not have had the chance to, nor would you have wanted to, apologize to me for everything. You definitely wouldn't have been able to make things up to Alex," concluded Samantha.

"So what you three are trying to tell me, is that I actually heard Richmond during the first and only attack. My mind just didn't allow me to end it there, because I needed to believe the things I remember?"

The three just nodded their heads in agreement.

"So, then you can go pick up Richmond and arrest his ass right?"

"Well what you have told us helps, but Sam is right they can use the thought that you believe there were more than one attack against you in court. They'd be able to say you dreamt hearing him because you guys had been arguing," said Scott.

"Yes, but if everything after the first attack didn't happen, then neither did the fights. They didn't really happen and Richmond would know that."

"He's already gone on record about you staying at your brother's a couple of times after arguing with him," said Scott.

"That's not true. We had a disagreement about my seeing him and that's it."

"Well now it's a case of your word against his."

"All right then, I won't mention the other attacks. The person responsible for Jimmy's death and for all of this should come to justice. He shouldn't be able to get away with it."

"Do you really mean that Benjamin?"

Ben had been so intensely involved in the conversation that he hadn't realized that Alex and Maria had just entered the room.

"After all he was your roommate. You guys shared the same viewpoints," said Alex.

"We shared a lot of the same viewpoints on certain things, but violence was never one of those things. It doesn't matter how much I *used* to believe you were wrong, I still never wished harm upon you or any of your friends. I especially wouldn't want anyone dead for their actions."

"Why do you think that really changes anything? You think that people wake up from comas completely changed? That just doesn't happen," said Alex.

"Alex, you surely can be an ass sometimes," said Sam.

"Alex, there are things that happen in dreams that one cannot exactly explain, but can indeed change a person's life. I am sure if you think hard about things, you will notice that he was attempting to work things out with you prior to the accident," said Athena.

"What would you know?" asked Alex.

"I think I would know more than you think I know," replied Athena.

"Wait a minute, Athy? Really, is that you? You are a nurse here? My brother's nurse at that?"

"Yes, Brick it is I. I know more about things than you think I do. Your brother and I have an understanding. Trust me when I tell you that things can change in a dream. For some dreams are more real than reality itself."

"She's got a point Alex. Just listen to her," said Sam.

"Sheriff, you have heard it from Maria and me and now you have heard it from Ben, can you please go get that asshole off the streets before he does this to someone else?"

"Alex, it will be taken care of, that I can promise you," said Scott.

"Scott, will my testimony really help? Or will he really be able to weasel his way out of this?" asked Ben.

"Well Ben, it's hard to say, but with you waking up and with you hearing him we may be able to get a confession out of him without anyone having to testify. Hopefully now it will be an open and shut case. I will be back, first thing in the morning, with an update. Until then, you should talk to your brother…" he paused looking around at everyone in the room, "alone," he continued looking directly at Sam as he spoke.

Sheriff Scott left the room. Sam followed him out, muttering to him about leaving. *'He's just not ready for it and you need to let them be alone'.* That was the only thing that Ben could hear and understand that Scott had said to Sam. She just continued to follow him down the hall.

"Now as Sheriff Scott and I think, you should leave the two boys alone. Allow them to work things out," said Athena taking Maria by the hand and leading her out of the room.

"Alex, I am sorry for everything. I feel that you think there is more that has gone on in our lives than there really is or was."

"Benjamin, you have always tried to be the center of attention. You haven't been the best one for me in my life and out of everyone, out of everything that has happened you are what I'm left with."

"I know how angry you must be with me, but you have to understand that I'm sorry. I have never meant to hurt you."

"Ben, somewhere in me I do believe you on that, but that doesn't matter much to how I feel. Knowing and feeling are totally different things."

"I understand that, Alex, and I know it will take time to become the brothers we should have always been. I don't care what your sexuality is or how you live your life. All that matters to me now is that you are in my life. I know mom thought that. I know now that dad and I were wrong. We should have reached out to you sooner than we did."

"All this you learned in a dream?"

Ben explained his dream to Alex. Even though he noticed Alex's confusion and disbelief, he continued to tell him everything. With everything that Ben had told Alex there was only one thing that Alex had problems with.

"You want me to believe that mom and dad were killed?"

"I know it's hard to understand. It's hard to believe, but they were and it was because of dad's wrath."

"And you met this guy that killed them?"

"I did, but he isn't exactly a bad guy. It really is hard to understand."

Dreams and how they relate to real life. Tonight at 9:00 PM following Cavemen…

"Are you kidding me?" exclaimed Ben.

"Ben, what are you talking about?"

"Did you just hear that? Everything I have told you has been on TV and has related to something in my dream. Now there is a show about dreams. This is just insane. I feel like someone is trying to make me feel crazy."

"Well big brother, it all sounds a little crazy if you ask me. You should hope they don't send you to the seventh floor for evaluation."

"Somehow I don't think neither Scott nor Athena would allow that."

"Why because they were in your dream as well. Because it was real?"

"Alex, I know it is hard for you to understand what has happened, but even if I'm insane, at least it has helped me realize a lot of things."

"So, this Wes guy. You think he's real?"

"Yes, I think he is real. I think we should hunt him down. I know he has done his job, but I want to talk to him. I want to know what it is that he does. How he picks who he picks."

"If this guy is as powerful as you say he is, do you think that's a wise idea?"

"Probably not, but if I had you with me I think we would be all right."

"I'm not going on any wild goose chases with you."

"It's not a wild goose chase; it's the guy who killed mom and dad. You're going to sit there and tell me you aren't the bit least curious as to who the guy is and what it is that he does?"

"Ben I'm not sure if I even want to let

you back in my life, let alone chase down some fictional characters."

"It isn't fictional. Think about it. Don't you think it's odd that you met Athena at the gym, I met her in my dream and now she is my nurse? I don't think it's completely coincidental."

"All right say I believe you, how do you say we go about this?"

"Sheriff Scott knows something. He knows Athena. He really knows her, the real things about her. I just need you to believe me and play along with me tomorrow when they are both here."

The two discussed their plan for the rest of the evening, until the nurse came to take Alex back to his room. Surprisingly, Maria had come back. She wanted to say her goodbyes for the evening to both of them. She was happy to know that Alex was OK with Ben and that she could stay and talk to Ben. It was a relief to know that he wouldn't stand in the way of her getting to know Ben like he remembered things.

Maria was too afraid to go home. She didn't want to be alone and she didn't want either of them to be alone either. She spent half the night with Alex and then the rest of the night with Ben. She waited until Alex had fallen asleep before she left him. She knew that being alone right now was difficult. It wasn't her boyfriend that had died and she also had problems sleeping at her own house. She had spent every night in his room, so that he didn't have to be alone.

She spent those nights there out of

support, but also out of fear of being at her house. If the attackers had been Richmond and his friends, then they knew where she lived. She didn't want to take the risk of them finding her at the house alone. There had been several times when she had gone to the house to shower and change that she felt as though she was being watched. She figured it was just her nerves and that she was just insecure.

The morning light filtered through the blinds in Benjamin's room directly into Maria's eyes. Slowly she opened her eyes to find Athena in the room. Ben was already awake.

"Well good morning sleepy head."

"Good morning Ben and good morning to you too Athy. How is he this morning?"

"I think he is doing fine. He should be able to be released in the next couple of days. I am shocked to find you here. Here in this room I mean."

"Athy, it's been a difficult journey through all of this, but I'm here for both of them."

"It is a good thing my child. You have a lot at stake here. There is a great future for you."

"Great yesterday it's him talking crazy, today it's you. I'm going to the bathroom."

Maria got up and went to the bathroom. While she was in the restroom she heard the door open and then heard Alex's voice, and then she heard Sheriff Scott. What she heard next was even stranger.

"So, you guys will never believe who

visited me in my room last night. This guy named Wes. He came to make sure that I was all right. He said he was a friend of mom and dad's."

Athena and Sheriff Scott just looked at each other, not knowing what to say.

"Did you say a guy named Wes came to visit you?"

"Wes, really it was Wes. Benjamin, Wes was in Alex's room. Alex you have to believe him now," said Sam.

Maria almost fell off the toilet. She remembered who Wes was from Ben's story the previous day. The racket that came from the restroom startled everyone in the room.

"Is Maria still here?" asked Alex.

"Yes, I'm still here," answered Maria as she washed her hands. Her being there could only help the brothers. She walked out of the restroom. "Wes, he came to visit you? Isn't that the guy from your dream Ben?"

"It is, but it was just a dream."

"I am not so sure about that Ben. This Wes guy knew details of mom and dad's death. He knew me by name, he knew them by name, and he knew things that no one else knew, Ben. He really scared me Ben. He really spooked me out."

"When was this Alex? I was in your room until almost two thirty this morning," said Maria.

Sheriff Scott and Athena still just stared at one another in confusion. Ben tried his hardest to keep from cracking the slightest of a smile.

"I think I have some work in another

room I must attend to, if you would excuse me. Officer Scott, I believe you have updates for the boys," said Athena.

As she attempted to leave the room, Alex wheeled his wheelchair backwards. He noticed the discomfort in both Athena and Scott's faces and he knew that Ben had been telling the truth.

"You aren't going anywhere," said Alex.

The confusion disappeared from Athena's face. She turned toward Ben and then toward Scott.

"Athena, Wes wouldn't do that would he? He wouldn't be so stupid, would he?" asked Scott.

"They are setting this up," said Athena. "They are all in on it. Well except maybe her. She is clueless about what is going on at all. As for you Scott, you fool, and now they know."

"You're kidding me right? You guys really set this up didn't you? Good play," said Scott.

"We should have known. You will have good adversaries here to work with you Scott. These three will make a great team for you. Even the girl will make a great addition as soon as she realizes what power she has."

"I work alone Athena. I don't work with anyone."

"It is better that they work with you than that they work alone. You will need them Scott, you will need them, trust in me Scott," said Athena.

"I guess. You have never failed me before and have never been wrong," said

Scott.

There was a long pause as everyone just stared at one another. Ben looked at Scott and then at Athena. She just shook her head at him and then pointed to Scott. When Ben looked at Scott he noticed that he looked much older. His hair was almost completely white and his skin slightly wrinkled. Ben's eyes grew wide in shock. Again Athena just shook her head and smiled at him. As Ben looked at everyone else's face in the room he could tell that they did not see what he did, until he looked at Samantha, who was gawking at Scott in utter awe. She could not believe his appearance had changed, neither could Ben.

At least there was one person in the room that understood what Ben could see, although he couldn't understand why no one paid any attention to her.

"You are leaving my lord?" said Scott.

"Leaving I am. It is time for me to go. The brothers have been reunited and you have been joined with them. My work here is finally completed," said Athena.

"Alex, go ahead and let her go," said Ben. "We have got what we needed. It was easier than I thought it was going to be. You'd think that a Goddess and a Wizard would be smarter than that. Or did you two think we were too stupid to come up with a plan like that?"

"Goddess! Wizard! What?" asked Sam, Alex and Maria together.

"No, Benjamin, we do not think you are stupid. We are surprised at you Alex. You trusted in your brother. You believed in him. That has made you strong enough and it is what made me realize that you have become what you need to become. Therefore my work here is done. I shall be going now," said Athena.

Alex wheeled out of the way of the door. Athena took the door handle, opened the door, and turned back to Ben.

"Oh, and Benjamin, Marygolde is very proud of you. She is looking forward to seeing you again. You know where to find her if you need her."

Ben just nodded his head as the goddess disappeared through the door and into thin air. He smiled as the rest of the group looked at him in confusion. Ben explained who Athena was and who Marygolde was. It was shocking to Ben to realize he had not been dreaming after all. What he could not explain was how he knew that Scott was a wizard.

"Very impressive Benjamin. I do believe that Athena was right. I'm sure that you will make a great partner for me. As for you two, I'm not exactly sure how you fit into the picture just yet."

Maria and Alex looked at each other puzzled. Samantha felt left out. She wanted to be a part of the gang too. She didn't know why or how she could be excluded.

"You are a descendant of one of the founding fathers aren't you, Scott?"

"Yes, Ben I am. I dropped the last name Zechariah about forty years ago."

"Forty years! You are nuts," said Alex.

"If you dropped the name forty years

ago," said Maria, "how old are you?"

"I'll be almost one hundred this year."

"You're full of shit," said Sam.

"And Ben, you are the first person to ever see me in my true form. You see me for me. Your mother and father knew me as my father. Do you know how hard it is to pretend to be two people?

My wife had a miscarriage and it couldn't have been better timing. I pretended to be both son and father. My wife was happy because she had a child in the house. It was very painful to keep her under a spell like that. She never figured out why the two of us were never in the room together. When I became old enough to assume the Sheriff role, I killed my father off and kept this persona. It is the second time I have had to do it.

However, I feel that this time will be my last. I am feeling the age getting to me and I have yet to marry. It's been very difficult this time. I must do something soon or my generation is over."

"What about the others, Scott? There has to be others from the other families," said Ben.

"There are not. At least there are none that I know of. Maybe that is why Athena connected me to you boys," said Scott.

"You know how to get into Guarroutk don't you?"

"Yes, Benjamin I do. And so does she."

Ben and Alex turned and looked at Maria in Surprise.

"Not her," Scott added.

Alex and Maria looked at Scott for

answers. Ben immediately turned to Samantha.

"He means you, doesn't he?"

Alex and Maria turned their attention to Ben and then to the empty chair to which he was talking. Scott smiled and chuckled. Samantha had no idea what to say. She was shocked to realize that Athena had been talking about her and not about Maria. She indeed had not been left out.

Chapter 18: Release

The silence between them was broken by the television playing in the background. A commercial was playing about a psychic who was able to communicate with the afterlife. By the expressions on Alex and Maria's faces he realized that the entire time that Sam had been there with them neither Alex nor Maria could see or hear her.

"She was talking about me? I wasn't left out after all," said Sam.

"Sam for being a law student you sure act like an idiot sometimes," said Ben.

"Um, Benjamin, there is no one sitting in that chair," said Alex.

"Actually Alex, Sam is sitting here with us now," said Scott.

"How is that possible? Sam is dead," said Alex.

"I am not dead. What is he talking about Ben, Scott?"

"All I know, Sam, is that after the

first attack Alex tried to get hold of you. After the second attack, or at least the second attack that I know of, you were here. Just before I lost consciousness, you walked into the room with your suitcase in hand and announced that your father would be working on the case. That's it Sam, that's all I know and we all know that I'm not the best one to tell the details."

"Surprisingly, Ben you are close. After the attack I did get hold of Sam. She flew in as soon as I told her what had happened. She's doing an internship with some law firm that deals with hate crimes. I figured she would be a great asset to have on this," said Alex.

"Yes, I remember that. I flew into the airport and I was on my way here," Sam said, "Oh my god, Benjamin, I remember! The cab I was in was hit by another car. I was killed on impact. I was on my way to the hospital though. How could you have known that?"

"He knows that because as soon as you had died you became a part of his journey. You entered his dreams as a guide. Why you stuck around after that is the question that needs to be answered? It makes sense now what Athena was talking about. However, that means that if you were the female he was talking about that means, Alex, you are the other one for this group," said Scott.

"Wait, you mean the dead girl, no offense Sam, gets to be a part of some group and I get left out?" exclaimed Maria.

"Not exactly Maria. I think that's why you and I have a connection together," said

Ben. "I could not have become as strong as I did had I not met you. You are my strength."

"Why do I have to be the dead one? The only people I get to talk to are you and the cop? How is that fair?"

"Sam, you sat in that chair and cringed when they spoke of Wes," said Scott. "You know who he is, don't you?"

"I do. He approached me while I was in school. I was told that I needed to stop with my pride. I never understood what the guy was talking about. He told me that I couldn't have things my way all the time. There were things in this life that were out of my control. I refused to listen to him.

"However, I did allow things to fall by the wayside. I started admitting when I was wrong. I tried to control my pride. The job that he promised came to me. Then I heard what happened here. How much more selfless could this have been?"

"That's exactly why you are here. You died before you were supposed to. You had followed what Wes expected of you and he failed to protect you from the car accident. Your work here was not complete. The unfortunate part of the whole thing is that you cannot cross over to where you belong, until after you have completed your work here. And with us I am assuming?" said Scott.

Ben filled Alex and Maria in on what was going on. Maria was still very skeptical about what was happening before her eyes. Alex believed whole-heartedly in the plan. He had always believed in the afterlife. He had also been a firm believer in life on other planets. He believed his brother had been somewhere else while in his dreams more than Ben believed and he hadn't made the journey. It was like a dream come true for him.

"What a team we are going to make," said Scott. "A seer, a believer, a ghost, a wizard, and you, Maria are our glue that will end up holding us all together.

"All right, now that all that is clear could someone please kill my suspense, no pun intended, and tell me if we busted the son-of-a-bitch that killed Jimmy and hospitalized the rest of you?" asked Sam.

"Just so you guys are up to speed, Sam has a good point. Scott, what's the status on Richmond?" Ben added. "I think you should have an update for us?"

"Indeed I do. I am happy to tell all of you that Richmond signed a confession last night. He also gave up the three guys that were with him. Ben, I think you will also be shocked to know that one of the guys was Oscar."

"Oscar! You mean that evil son-of-a-bitch of a friend of yours Benjamin," said Alex. "Oscar was in on it?"

"Yes, he was. He was the one that pulled the trigger. He killed Jimmy. However, the gun belonged to Richmond. They are both going to be locked up for a very long time."

"Anyway we can get the word passed around as to what crime they are being locked up for? So we can make sure their lives in prison are the least enjoyable," said Samantha.

"Well, Sam I think arranging that

everyone knows what they are locked up for is
not going to be a problem. However, you know
once you get the hang of being the way you
are, you'll be able to inflict as much terror
on them as you want. Just because you are
dead doesn't mean you can't have fun."

"What about the other two?"

"They are looking at about eight to ten
years in prison possibly getting out in five
with good behavior, but that's where your
amazing friend comes in handy. She can make
sure that they all never see the daylight
outside of prison for the rest of their lives
if she wanted to."

"Sam is going to have the power to do
that?"

"She definitely will. Once she learns
how to use it."

"Scott, if you are a wizard and all, why
can't you cast a spell on Maria and myself so
that we can see Sam. It's not fair to her
that she only gets to see and speak to you
and Ben," said Alex.

"It's not that easy Alex. Over time you
will be able to sense Sam's presence, but
that will be about it. When she learns things
she will be able to communicate with you in
other ways. Sam, close your ghostly ears. An
interesting way will be through possession,
but more so in other ways. Possession will be
very difficult for her to learn and very
draining on her."

"Sam and possession," said Maria,
"that's all we need! A bisexual chick with
the power to take over whomever she wants,
whenever she wants. What is the world coming

to?"

"The nice thing is, she won't have that power on any of us. That, I can protect you guys from."

"OK, even though half of you can't see me, I am still in this room. I think that I wouldn't do anything like that to any of you."

"Well Sam, like all powers, and this goes for me as well, we get carried away sometimes and lose our heads. You will do some things the more powerful you become that you will regret. It's just impossible not to."

The gang continued to talk well into the evening. After several hours a nurse came to take Alex back to his room. Maria went to his room with him. Scott left shortly after them. Sam stayed with Ben until he fell asleep.

When she left, she went to her father's house to see him. It had been the first time she had seen him since her passing. She spent the next several days with him trying to figure out how to let him know that she was safe.

Back at the hospital, Maria spent the next few nights splitting her time between Ben and Alex's room. During the days they all spent their time together. Everything that had happened seemed too outrageous for them to believe. Even though the comatic dreams had happened to Ben, he was still skeptical. The television seemed to have programs on that reminded him of Guarroutk that only helped solidify his skepticism. He could have been dreaming from the programs that were on the TV.

Maria always had problems believing. It was her love and bond to Alex that assured her that what she was hearing was true. She also had a feeling that the things Ben had told her about their relationship were real. She had several dreams herself about some of the things that Ben had talked about, but that was one secret she would always keep to herself. She felt that if everyone had some sort of supernatural thing happening to them, then she could as well. It was hers and she had no desire to share it.

Meanwhile, back at the Governor's Mansion Samantha was still attempting to find a way to communicate with her father. Governor O'Leary sat in his office with the deep purple drapes closed tight, the room dimly lit by the small desk lamp against the dark mahogany woodwork, almost everyday, depressed and gazing at his daughter's picture. Everyday he would pick it up and ask it why he never spent more time with her. He would ask the photo why he allowed her to go so far away for school. Eventually, a small tear would form in the corner of his sober eyes. At this, he would rise from his desk and move through the ominous mansion.

She would follow him from room to room. Occasionally, she would shout at him. She would attempt to touch his hand. She would do both when he was feeling most responsible staring at her photos hanging on the walls. She would try screaming as loud as she could and try to knock the photo from his hands or off the walls. Neither worked, neither would break his concentration.

The depression started to affect his work. The governor's assistant tried to cheer him up. She attempted to help him with his work. She ended up doing his work for him to keep his depression from reaching the public. Dodging the phone calls for him by creating reasons for him to not attend meetings or return important phone calls started taking tolls on the young assistant. Sam felt bad for her.

After three days of trying her hardest, Sam found herself back in his office yelling at him as he stared at the photo just as he had done everyday.

"If only mom were here. I'm sure she would be able to sense me and tell you everything was all right. Why are you sitting here fat man? Get up and do something for Christ sakes. Your assistant is doing your work and now she looks like hell. Take her. I know you two have had an affair. I'd be glad to have her as a step-mom, even if she is only a few years older than me. Anything to get your stupid ass up from sitting here moping around. I can't wait for Ben to get out of the hospital and I know Sheriff Scott won't do it. You have to hear me."

She looked at the picture on his desk of her mother holding her when she was a baby. A tear came to her eye. She was upset that she was trapped here and couldn't talk to her father and the worst part was she couldn't see her mother. She found this *gift* to be a nightmare.

She concentrated on the picture as the

anger built inside her. She didn't even notice that she had slapped the picture frame out of her father's hand until after he stood up having made a blood-curdling scream for Julie, his assistant. The thin woman with her long blond hair, dark circles under her solemn eyes, clothes wrinkled from the lack of care or stress, came running into the office as if to find the man lying on the floor from a heart attack.

"What the hell is your problem? Look at this fucking mess! You are about to lose the only person keeping you from a world of hurt outside these walls. I don't know what else…"

"Stop Jules, I didn't do this. I was sitting here wishing to only have one more minute with Sam and the picture just flew out of my hands."

"Dammit Michael, I can't do this anymore. I have been covering your ass for over a week. This is the last straw. Look at me Michael, look."

"Jules, you look like hell."

"I've been sleeping here in the manor and you have no clue I was here. You have no clue what I have been doing for you and here you sit throwing photos at the fucking wall and you expect me to believe it was some sort of supernatural bullshit."

"Jules, I'm sorry you have had to cover for me. How can I make it up to you?"

"You could start by cleaning this mess up and taking on some responsibility around here, instead of having me do it. I know you're upset about Sam, but Mike, you have to suck it up and deal with it during work hours. You didn't let you work suffer this much when your wife passed."

"Yeah, look at what happened from that."

"*That's why you started sleeping with her? You were upset about losing mom. I figured you guys had been sleeping together before mom passed away.*" Sam asked her father as if he would answer her. The hatred she had previously had for her father and the reason the last few years between them had been rocky was because she thought he had been cheating on her mother. All this time she had been wrong. Her stupidity fueled her infuriating temper.

"Exactly, and we haven't slept together in months and now I'm doing your job. I can't do this."

Sam noticed that the distressed expression on the assistant's face upset her. She turned and looked around the office; the drape-drawn windows along the east wall, to the history, law, and classic novels that filled the dark wooden bookshelves of the south wall. Then at the hand-painted portrait of the governor to the left, and one of his deceased wife to the right along the wood-paneled wall of the west, and finally stopping at the hand painted portrait of herself on the north wall. *Possession,* she thought, I wonder if it works on objects.

Sam concentrated on the painting of herself as she unnoticing floated toward it. She felt a zap and a blue crack of an electric shock as she came into contact with the canvas. The light was visible to the governor and his assistant. At the sight of

the tiny lightening bolt spurring from the
wall, the assistant ran to the governor who
wrapped his arms around her and sat quickly
into his oversized desk chair.

The painting seemed to come to life. The
ridges of the dried paint seemed to almost
completely smooth out as the portrait became
3-D.

Sam turned her head toward her father
and said, "Dad, I was so wrong to be angry
with you, you were a great father, and I am
OK."

"What the hell is going on?" asked the
Governor.

"It's me dad. Please use this time
quickly. I don't have much time left. I am
starting to get weak."

"But you're dead!" said Julie.

"But you're OK baby girl?"

"Well, I'm still here and no one can
hear me or see me, so it sucks, but I'm OK.
I'm glad that I finally got you to listen to
me. I've been yelling at you for a week."

"That's my girl. Upset that people can't
hear her." The governor let out a barreling
laugh that rumbled the windows.

"Dad, it's not the time for games.
Listen to me now. Stop moping around. Listen
to Julie, you two are right together, pull
the curtains open, and get your ass back to
work. Make sure that the sons-of-bitches that
did this to my friends suffer the maximum
punishment. I l…"

A snapping blue light brightened the
room and Sam fell from the portrait,
returning it to original state. The governor

ran to the wall dropping Julie to the ground. He pounded his fists on both sides of his now lifeless daughter hanging on the wall. The painting had never seemed as dull as it did at that moment. Julie stood to her feet, walked to the curtains ripping them open allowing the morning light to engulf the room. She ran to his side where he turned and hugged her.

Samantha woke up facing a darkened window with rain beating against it, the full moon barely seen behind the clouds. She looked up hoping to see her father sitting at his desk. Instead, she saw Ben packing his bags.

"Well morning sleeping beauty," said Ben.

"What am I doing here?"

"You have been there since yesterday morning, just sleeping. I've tried to wake you a couple of times. Where have you been for the last few days?"

"I've been trying to tell my dad I was OK."

"And were you successful?"

"I managed to possess a painting of myself. It was weird, bone-chilling and completely scary. I could barely breath, could hardly see my father, but I could hear him."

"Let me guess, it was yesterday morning?"

"Yes, is that when I appeared here?"

"Yup, you just materialized in a sleeping slumber in the chair. I tried to wake you several times, but you were not moving."

"Odd… wait… what's up with you? You going home?"

"Yeah, they released Alex two days ago. Today, I get to go home. I'm going to stay with Alex for now and we'll see how things go from there."

"Well that's perfect. You'll be right down the street from Maria, ya know, to work on things and you'll be in the same house with Alex, so you can become the friends you guys were when you were little."

"Well Sam, that's the game plan."

"You ready to go Ben?" asked Alex as he walked through the door. "What's that odd chill in here?"

"Funny ass, get off of me!" squealed Sam.

Ben grabbed his rib cage from the pain of laughter that seemed to consume him.

"You're standing on, or is it in? Sam," said Ben.

Alex shuddered with chills, turning a pale white, as he quickly moved from where he was standing.

"Well on the bright side guys, you can now feel Sam's presence."

"Funny Ben, and I never want to feel that feeling again."

The door to the hospital room burst open slamming hard against the wall behind it, startling the three in the middle of their conversation. Sheriff Scott rushed into the room, soaking wet, water still dripping from the brim of his hat.

"SAM," he bellowed.

"What the hell did I do?"

"I think you know what happened. What do you think you were doing?"

"Uh-oh, I possessed something," she said forcing a smile on her face. As ghostly as she appeared, her blushing cheeks were still visible.

"Good job I guess, but that is not the point. Your father has been bothering me all day."

"Then at least he is back to work or something other than mourning me."

"You are not strong enough to be doing stuff like that though. You cannot be leaving yourself vulnerable like that."

"What do you mean? I was in good hands with Ben."

"What if you had been transported somewhere else?"

"I didn't know what was going to happen. I just knew I had to let my father know that it was OK and that he needed to get back to his life."

"Take things slowly. That's all I'm going to say." Scott took his hat off and shook the water from it. He turned to walk out the room and said, "We'll all get together soon, but for now, Sam stay away from your father. You two get the rest you need and heal and Ben for Christ sakes keep her from doing stupid stuff."

Ben's eyebrows raised, his head lowered, as he looked back and forth between Sheriff Scott and Sam.

"She's connected to you Ben. I don't know why and I don't know how, but she's connected to you. Sam, you should be able to hear Ben call you from pretty much anywhere you are. While you are weak, Ben should also be able to drag you to wherever he is."

Sheriff Scott left without another word leaving the three speechless. Ben gathered his bags up then followed Alex out of the room. He stopped in the doorway and turned in hope to catch a glimpse of Athena or anyone else he had met from Guarroutk, but no one was there.

Chapter 19: House Warming Gifts

Several months had passed since they had
left the hospital, although the wounds were
still tender, the memories ran deeper and
more painful. Ben and Alex had been getting
along well, in fact probably better than they
had when they were kids, if that was
conceivably possible. Maria and Ben had also
grown very close, much more than either had
expected. Then there was Samantha who of
course had her moments of irritation over Ben
being the only one who could see or hear her,
other than Sheriff Scott, who tended to
ignore her presence until needed.

Alex and Sheriff Scott had started
working closely together on Alex's recovery,
through which he healed quickly. They then
proceeded to work on training, when Alex
effortlessly picked up martial arts. Scott
had explained to him that if Ben had a link
to Guarroutk then Alex had an inner strength
that would be essential to the 'team'. The

two trained almost everyday together and the days that Scott couldn't be with him, Alex trained on his own. They did their training in secrecy until they knew the timing was right.

While Maria and Ben's relationship grew the bonds between her and Alex strengthened even more than before, for now they were even more of a family. One night Maria shared with Alex that she had a vision, a dream, but only she was awake, when she had touched Ben's arm. It was the most real dream she had ever had, so real and shocking that her heart actually skipped a few beats taking her breath away. While she was happy with the feeling she felt it was too early, too soon, too much to handle at the moment. After all they had just recovered from a tragic accident and the loss of a friend, a lover.

The next day while Ben cooked dinner, Alex felt the need to discuss Maria's vision with him, even though she had asked him to keep it between them.

"So, you know the big house out on Acropolis Avenue is for sale," asked Alex.

"And? Are you asking me to move out? Besides I think that place is too big for me."

"Not at all. In fact I was thinking it would be perfect for you, me, Maria and of course Sam. And speaking of Sam... if I was asking you to move out without me, you'd still have Sam with you."

"Sam doesn't need a room."

"Hey screw you guys, I am sitting here you know," Sam exclaimed.

"Well Sam if we took this place you'd have several rooms to choose from and of course there'd be room for other stuff and definitely room in the backyard for a wedding," said Alex.

"What? She told you that I asked her to marry her? That was supposed to be a secret until we were all together before telling you. That's why Scott's coming to dinner tonight. I can't believe her."

"Well Benjamin, you just messed up because she didn't tell me about that, but I figured with her condition that there would be a wedding. It just seemed only fitting. Plus, it has a huge basement that I could have as a training room at home and wouldn't have to keep leaving."

"What is all this training anyway… wait her condition? What's wrong with Maria?"

"What do you mean what's wrong with me?" Maria asked as she walked into the room. "Alex, you didn't?"

"I said no such thing. He did," Alex said pointing at Ben.

"What did you tell him Benjamin Casey?" she asked, as her faced turned red with anger.

"Hey, don't pin this on me, he is the one that said something about you having a condition that would need us to move and he wants us all to move into the big old house on Acropolis."

"Well that would be fitting wouldn't it? Maybe Athena can help us get the place. But besides that, he said something about my condition?" She glared at Alex and then back to Ben, "But he didn't tell you what condition? And so you felt the need to tell him our news, huh?"

"No, I didn't. He said the house had a big enough yard for a wedding. I thought you told him, but if he put that together from your… condition… then I'd figure you were pregnant."

"I'm not pregnant."

"At least not yet that is and the house is big enough for a nursery and a play room, plus for each of us to have our own rooms. Even Sam."

"Ya know I'm tired of you guys talking about me like I don't exist," sighed Sam.

"Well, it's nice that you both told on one another without actually telling each other the situation, but Ben I bet you still confirmed what happened the other night after big mouth over there said what he said."

"As confusing as that was to follow, yes, I did confirm it and I'm sorry," said Ben and turned his attention over to Alex, "so you'll have to act surprised when we tell Scott tonight."

"Of course I will," agreed Alex.

"I will never share with you if you are going to run your mouth to everyone, big mouth," Maria said annoyed with both of them. She attempted to face Sam, "Sam, sorry if I'm not facing you, but I really wish I could hear and see you because I could use the girl bonding that these two seem to suck at being."

Ben responded for Sam, "She said that she agrees with you and that… hey I'm not repeating that, it's rude… OWE…" Ben paused for a second after being pinched by Sam. "OK… she says, and getting good at letting her presence noticed for sure, that I'm a moron, that should respect what you tell me even if provoked by my brother. Are you happy now?"

"Yes," said both Maria and Sam in unison.

At dinner that night, they shared their news with Scott who was extremely happy for them. He agreed to the thought of moving into the big house on Acropolis. He also shared the secret that Alex and he had been keeping from the gang and that training at home would be better, especially with the little pitter-patter of tiny feet running about.

"How did you know about that?" asked Maria.

"Well, you saw it didn't you?" asked Scott.

"You saw it? What does he mean you saw it?" asked Ben.

"Right after you proposed to her, she saw it after touching the ring, which I see you aren't wearing," said Scott.

"That's right. I did see it after touching the ring, I thought it was Ben, but it was the ring. That still doesn't explain why you know this."

"Well, Ben has his connection to Guarroutk, Alex has the inner strength both physically and mentally, and well Sam is Sam and we all know she can be important…"

"It's about time you acknowledged me sitting here," interrupted Sam.

"…that only leaves you, Maria," Scott

continued as if Sam had not said a word. "You are the reasonable one to have visions. It only makes sense."

"So, you are telling me that the vision I had was true? That it is going to come true. How is that possible? I mean it felt real, but more importantly how could you know what I saw and when I saw it."

"I've been around for many, many, many years to know. It would take something… something… that heart felt especially after the tragedy you have endured. It was only a matter of time. It only makes sense to come out when Ben finally proposed to you."

"OK, well from now on, just act surprised, because that was just creepy," said Maria.

Scott just chuckled and nodded his head. After dinner while they were cleaning up, Maria took the opportunity to pull Scott to the side.

"I need to ask you a very important question or should I say a favor?"

"What can I do for you Maria? You know I'll do anything for you if I can."

"Find a way for me to see and hear Samantha. The boys have each other and I know you are getting tired of listening to her." She paused long enough to take notice of the shock that had fallen over his face and before he could rebut what she had just said she continued, "don't give me that look. Your expression when she cut you off at dinner…"

"How do you know she cut me off at dinner?"

"Look here old man; you aren't the only

one that has intuitions."

Scott just shook his head and smiled, "If only I could, I would and trust me it would be nice to have someone else to listen to her. I know she means well and I know she is lonely, but sometimes the girl is too much. I don't mean to be rude to her."

"I know, I know, trust me I knew her when she was alive and I could only imagine what she is like as a ghost only having two people to talk to. It's gotta suck."

"I'll see what I can do, but don't get your hopes up."

During the next week the group went to look at the house and decided to put their bid in to buy it. After all, it was perfect for them all to share and enough room to leave each other alone. Even Sam was happy with it and was ecstatic that they took her opinion into consideration. Although it didn't matter much to Maria, in fact none of their opinions mattered much to her since she knew the house was theirs as soon as she touched the doorknob.

She allowed them to have their fun with it and didn't mention the vision to any of them. How could she, it would spoil their fun. It was nice to know what was going to happen, but it removed the suspense and excitement out of everything for her. It was something she would grow to get used to; in fact she did a damn good job at the present moment. Finally it made sense to her as to why she would be the one to have this ability.

Within the month they were moving into

the new house. Everything went smoothly and they got the keys in no time. It was as if the house was theirs all along. The rooms were picked out giving Maria and Ben the largest room on the third floor adjacent to a tinier room for a nursery. On the second floor were Alex and Sam's rooms with another room for a playroom and another for an office. The first floor comprised of a living room, family room, kitchen, and a huge dining room. The basement was large enough for a games room and for Alex to have a training room. Each floor had its own bathroom, but Ben and Maria's room as well as Alex's had a private bath. It was the only thing Sam agreed on easily was that her room did not have a bathroom. It wasn't like she had to use it anyway. She was actually just happy to have her own room.

With boxes everywhere and definitely not in shape for a viewing, there came a knock at the door. Sheriff Scott was standing at the door.

"Make it known this will probably be the last time I actually knock on this door," he said smiling at the four of them looking whipped. "I'd hate to see you guys out in the field if you let a few boxes kick your asses."

"What do you mean by that?" the four asked.

"This team of ours. What did you think we were doing, just joking about that?"

"OK, we gathered that, but what do you mean out in the field?" asked Ben.

"Fighting off… what would you say…

demons or the supernatural."

"That's what we are signed up for?" asked Maria.

"Unfortunately, you didn't sign up for anything you were chosen and trust me, it has taken me a long while to get used to because I'm definitely used to being by myself. I've been working alone for what… like 200yrs."

"WHAT?" All four yelled in shocking surprise.

"Um… that it has taken me so long to get used to?"

"No Scott that you are like 200yrs old. How have you got away with that?" asked Ben.

"That is a long story for another time, but for this evening I have come bearing good news for the ladies. I have figured out a way to help you with your problem Maria."

"Have you now? That would be great," said Maria.

"What are you two talking about? How does this help me and why wasn't I informed of this before hand?" asked Sam.

"Trust me Sam…"

"Now you want to acknowledge me?"

"…you will greatly enjoy this… present."

"Scott, I can't believe you figured something out. This is amazing."

"Would either of you care to share with us what you are talking about?" asked Alex.

"Well, this actually benefits you as well Alex, so I guess yes we can tell you. Sorry Maria, there is no other way to do it without including Alex, but I think in the end it will be better for all of us if he is included. And this will also affect your baby…" Scott paused when seeing the shock on Maria's face, "when you have kids that is."

Maria could not say anything, but just sat there looking very angry with Scott, yet puzzled at the same time.

Scott explained to the gang that they were going to be able to make Samantha visible and audible to everyone in the gang. They gathered into the dining room, the one room that remotely had furniture in place. They sat around the table and lit some candles that Scott had brought with him, placing them in a circle in the center of the table. In the center of the ring of candles Scott placed a pillow asking Sam to have a seat.

As the others sat at the table they could see a tiny indentation curve into the pillow as Sam sat down on it. Scott proceeded to pass a scroll of parchment out to each of them.

"Wooooo… how Harry Potter of you Scott," said Alex.

"Take this serious or it won't work. And anyway, there is nothing Harry Potter about the whole thing. Do you want this or not?"

"Don't mind him. Let's please get on with it," said Maria.

They sat around the table in the candle lit room each taking their turn at reading their scrolls. As each one finished reading, the scroll burst into a tiny flame turning to ash. Sam's image became slightly more visible as the scrolls' ashes hit the table. Samantha grew anxious and almost uncontrollably moving around on the table from one person to the next. She was being reborn in a way. Shockingly in a way it was the most alive she had ever felt; dying was the best thing to ever happen to her.

Sheriff Scott said the last words on his scroll, "Materialize the unseen immortal before thee who set before me, make that for what could not be heard by them now be heard."

Puff… the scroll shot into a tiny burst of light, a tiny firecracker before them. The ghost once not seen nor heard now stood on the table a little transparent, but visible squealing and laughing. Maria could barely control her excitement either. The two shot out of the room like schoolgirls. In all the commotion, none of them noticed another tiny creature leaving the opposite side of the table to Sam.

The guys retired to the living room. Scott shared with them the first adventure was approaching and that they needed to be ready.

"I'm as ready as I can be," said Alex.

"You should be. You've been down in that basement twenty-four / seven lately."

"It's good he has ambitions, but you both realize this isn't playing cops and robbers. The stuff we are up against is nothing like you have ever seen before."

"Would it be, could it be, Wes?"

"We will not go after Wes," said Scott. "I don't know why you are so gun ho about bringing Wes down. You will learn that there are good demons out there and there are bad. Wes is neither and cannot be stopped."

"Who the hell is Wes?" asked Alex.

"There is another time and another place for Wes," responded Scott.

A noise from the kitchen rumbled through to the living room startling the guys in their conversation. Scott jumped to his feet. The girls ran down the stairs asking if everyone was all right for they had heard the noise all the way upstairs. They stopped suddenly, shocked to see the guys all standing staring into the kitchen.

Scott led the way down the hallway and through the kitchen door. Broken glass sprayed across the floor; the backdoor stood wide open while several boxes had been flipped on their sides.

"Um... did someone break in or out? The glass is going the wrong direction for someone to be leaving, but yet the path of boxes looks as though someone was in a rush to get out?" asked Sam.

"Damn it Maria! This is exactly why I didn't want to make Sam visible to you. We brought something through while we were trying to materialize Sam," said Scott.

"So, how does this make it Maria's fault?" asked Ben.

"It doesn't..." Scott paused.

A darkened figure appeared at the back doorway. Even with all the lights on his face could not be seen. He wore all black with a black hat. Even as he spoke the whites of his teeth were shaded.

"Nice one Scott, nice," came a gruff voice from the figure before them.

"I know that voice," whispered Ben to

Maria.

"I don't know why you are here, but…"

"Don't be foolish Scott. Do not try to faze me with your nonsense. I will go where I want, when I want and you know there is nothing you can do to stop me. I am here out of sheer concern for what you let out. Do you really think your band of misfits here is going to be able to take control of it?"

"WES!" screamed Ben, "it's you. Why don't you honestly tell us what you think of us? Such an asshole, this is the man that killed mom and dad."

"What?" said Alex.

"Don't kid yourself boy. There is a lot you have to learn about life."

"Well I, we, may not be strong enough to take you down now, but one of these days you will eat those words you bastard."

"Control your toys Scott or you'll lose them. That is no way to send them into battle. And just to show you some good faith little ones, you can rest easy for now. I'll deal with the mess you've caused temporarily until you think you are ready to face it."

"Thank you Wes, now please leave us be," requested Scott.

On that notion, Wes vanished from sight. Scott shut the door and ushered the gang back to the living room. It took Scott almost an hour to calm the group down. Ben tried to explain to Alex that Wes may have been involved in the death of his parents, that he was entirely to blame.

Maria attempted several times to change the topic from Wes to the creature that they let loose. Eventually Scott was able to get the boys to turn their attention to the serious problem they had on their hands.

"How are we going to track that thing down?" asked Maria.

"Well we have a couple of days to prepare, but don't get used to that. We won't always have someone's help with these things. We will have to be more proactive in dealing with situations like this one. Wes probably feels guilty, in his own pathetic way, and that's why he is helping us. You kids need to take a break for the evening and we'll deal with this problem starting fresh tomorrow."

"How are we supposed to sleep and relax knowing that there is some creature out on the street? Knowing that it could be causing damage?" asked Ben.

"Well, I have a housewarming present for you that I think will take your minds off of it for the evening. The spell that we cast earlier for you all to see Sam, well, it will work for you in double Maria," said Scott.

Scott then stood without saying another word, kissed Maria on the forehead, and left them staring at one another puzzled by his words. The door gently shut behind him without a sound. Ben was the first to speak:

"What does he mean Maria?"

"Well, I was going to wait, but I figure now is as good a time as any. I'm pregnant."

THE END